Darling

Darling

Rachel Edwards

4th ESTATE • *London*

4th Estate
An imprint of HarperCollins*Publishers*
1 London Bridge Street
London SE1 9GF
www.4thEstate.co.uk

First published in Great Britain in 2018 by 4th Estate

1

A catalogue record for this book is
available from the British Library

ISBN 978-0-00-828111-3 (hardback)
ISBN 978-0-00-828112-0 (trade paperback)

Printed and bound in Great Britain by
CPI Group (UK) Ltd, Croydon, CR0 4YY

MIX
Paper from
responsible sources
FSC® C007454

This book is produced from independently certified FSC paper
to ensure responsible forest management.

For more information visit: www.harpercollins.co.uk/green

To Peter
and
Patricia, darling Mum

'If you prick us, do we not bleed?'

William Shakespeare, *The Merchant of Venice*

What's Done is Done

It took less than six months for everything to fall apart. Six months of fighting, competing, whispering, each of us trying to be better, to love him better.

I knew she was trouble from the moment I saw her. I felt it as she stood in our doorway that day: disaster. Not just because she was so different – that skin and that hair, as opposite to me as it's possible to be. More than the way she always looked through me, right past me, straight at him. There was something wrong about her. Wrong for us. We would never fit. It was never going to work.

I did try. I tried more than anyone will ever know, in my own way. I tried to welcome her. Tried to meet her halfway, like he said. Didn't get stressy when he locked himself away with her for hours on end, even though I needed him too. Even when I started to get suspicious, when her lies built up around her, I tried to give her the benefit of the doubt. But before the Christmas storms – over the top, like the crappy clichéd ones they teach you about at school – before the rain and the branches and the roof could fall on the four of us, she was dead.

She is dead.

Now only I am left to love him and it's all my fault.

PART I

Darling

I ran. Ribcage, feet and thoughts pounding, I ran and ran and kept on running.

What had we done? *Why* had we?

Blue, blue, blue, blue, yellow, yellow, a whole buggeration of blue: on and on the results had flashed up, all the live-long night, and now we were *out*.

Fuck it. Brexit.

Now I needed a fag, I needed my dead mum and I needed a new passport, in that order. The latter two were out of the question, so I had bolted to the supermarket for cigarettes.

When I reached the doors, I eyed myself in the glass. My lips were mud red. I was puffy, my eyes salt-stained and dry; worst of all I was panting in public. Over-exercised, out-voted, thwarted and screwed, but alive and still here, wherever *here* was now.

On the bright side, nothing made you appreciate a fag like a good sprint.

Two people had arrived before me. There was an old lady wrapped in thick, well-cut mustard – years of knowing that summer mornings could be chilly in this corner of the European Union – tying up her spicy little terrier. And him.

The woman blanked our smiles but he and I met each other's eye. I was ready:

'Not long now …'

He was too:

'Here's hoping …' His first words.

A pause; we were taking our time. I could see up close those cuffs that commanded a second look, the sun-starved wrists, the moon rising from each cuticle. The hair, organised, showed more salt than pepper in that still-shocked light. But these were unimportant details. All I could *feel* was the pressure, building in the nothing between us. With pressure like that you just knew that the universe, or the Almighty, or whatever the hell, was getting ready to give one mother of a push.

6.58 a.m. Friday 24 June 2016.

'I'm here for my daughter,' he began at last. 'She's turning sixteen and wants me to get "a tonne of good stuff", whatever that might mean …'

'It's her party?'

'Only the sleepover tonight, the main party next week, but I have no—'

'Oi-oi!'

Just as he was about to tell me what he did not have, we heard it: the unmistakable cadence of trouble. A heap of a man was arriving, belly first; lumping his way down from the high street, prickled scalp tilted high. From where we stood you could see he was a meeting of both triumph and disaster.

'Out! Out!'

The red face, the glittering glare: joy gone bad. He was coming closer.

'Enger-lurrnd!' he sang, as three more prickleheads straggled around the corner behind him. 'En! Ga! Lund!'

More fat than muscle but still, he was *big*.

Then he was nearly upon me, blue marble eyes swivelling, ready to bash at this other *thing*, this *other* thing, this dark blot on his brand-new swept street, his clean sheet. A black woman wearing rushed make-up and a look of contempt for his playground punch-up politics.

He spoke:

'We voted Leave, love. Outcha go!'

I gaped, eye-level with the chest of this sweaty fiasco. Tattoos all over his thick neck.

'I don't think there's any call for that.'

A voice as dark as my skin, it flowed with a current to it. It was him. This man beside me, feet fight-distance apart but fists at his sides, a heat in that count-to-ten stare.

All I could think of was the blood spurting on to that pretty suit.

Then the big man inflated his cheeks and chest, became whale-big. Big of body was a thing for him, you could bet on it, but he liked his ideas small and hard.

'Wotchoo, er fackin' 'usband?'

'Yes,' said the suited man, moving closer to my side.

The eyes swivelled wilder, the disgust too great. A torrent of blood was surely coming – and then the stragglers caught up.

'Trev!' They swept him along, shambled away, a colourous bobbling of orange and dark red-pink T-shirts. As they rumbled on, with the man-mound clasped in their loving headlock, one mate rubbed his knuckles into the headstubble, and the smallest man pressed a lager can up to Trev's lips. The meaty fist punched out, now into only air, into no one.

'Whoa,' I said.

'Indeed,' he said. The laughter lines, the rivulets of skin that danced at each idea that rose behind the eyes, eyes that shone. Yes, he was appalled to the core and embarrassed, but above all relieved he was not them. To make sure I knew it, he offered his smile; one warm poultice for our wound.

'That was scary.' I stopped short of patting my chest. 'I have never, ever had that said to me. I was born here—'

'Idiot,' he said.

'Big mad angry violent idiot.'

'So *dumb*.'

'As in "referendumb".'

'Ha, precisely. Don't worry, though. He's just one nutter.'

'But he's clearly swallowed at least two others.'

He laughed, shook his head. 'They feel emboldened, they were always going to. It'll pass.'

'Or get worse.'

'It'll be fine. We're all better than that.'

'Well … Thank you.'

'Pleasure.'

'No, seriously.' It had to be now. 'How can I ever thank you?'

'Actually …' he said.

'I always buy them and she pretends not to mind, but she does. I'd be so grateful—'

'I'm not *actually* going to bake you one, you know!'

We walked on through the aisles and, laughing, stopped.

'Here we are,' I said. 'Look.'

'Great.' He reached for the nearest factory sponge.

'No, listen.' I surprised myself with that flirty-bossy tone, me trying to take over his senses so soon. *Look … listen …* 'You don't want a big-brand one with loads of E numbers. Think cricket wife. Wonky, homemade.'

'Oh, but I—'

'Hang on.' There I went again. 'This one, with apricot jam. Ah, organic. Perfect.'

'Hold your horses,' he said. 'It's a bit … you know.'

'What?' I scanned it for flaws.

'A bit …' He smiled. 'Naked.'

'Forward,' I said, walking on.

We put the nuddy-cake in his trolley and continued, weighing each step.

'Look,' I said, a few steps later. 'Icing sugar. You—'

'I ice it myself, slap "Happy Birthday" on it.'

'You catch on quick.'

'Insanely good teacher.'

'Damn right,' I said.

'Best home-made money can buy.'

'Our secret.'

'Our naked secret.' He shook his hair out of place. 'Sorry, way too forward, crass of me …'

'No problem.' Then, new in this territory, in this changed world, I dared:

'We're married, remember?'

His eyes sparked, looked away:

'Whatever happened to our honeymoon?'

Cloud to ground flashes, electric potential under the strip lighting. An atmosphere. After such a bad night I must have looked jaundiced, a proper fright, but his eyes were saying no such thing. I lowered my gaze, too.

'You don't even know my name.'

'Care to rectify that?'

'Darling.'

Delight, disbelief, then that dink of dropping copper. Every time.

'You're called *Darling*?'

Genuine pleasure, as if I'd chosen my ostrich feather of a name just to tickle him under the chin.

'That's me.'

'I'm Thomas,' he said and I knew, before he had even unlocked his phone, that my digits would soon be safe inside, if …

I ran the test.

'Go ahead, you can laugh, my Stevie's friends find my name hilarious too. He's five; my little terror.'

'Bet he is,' he looked down for a moment. Two.

I counted in my head. Six, and then he said:

'We could meet up sometime. Do you know Andante? The café on Stewart Street?'

I did. 'I'll find it.'

'Could I take your number please, Darling?'

We met at Andante on the Tuesday; a safe get-together over coffee. We knocked around a little conversation like beginners playing pool. I did not smoke. Small sips, no clattering spoons. Then, someone else's boldness breaking through: honeyed nibbles, unasked-for *struffoli* doughnuts which the owner brought to our table, flushed and apologising for the interruption, telling us that they meant all our Christmases had come that very morning. It was impossible not to give sweeter, more rounded smiles after that. Fortified, we ventured opening gambits, a brisk mapping out of our positions. I told him I was a trained nurse, and lived alone with Stevie; he was an architect, father to sixteen-year-old Lola and the widower of one Tess. The next time, Friday cinema, brought kisses that were warm if prosaic. I believe we wondered if it could be enough. Did we still carry the seeds for so much *possibility*? We were hardly teens, after all.

We went back to Andante twice the next week. He dropped in on the way back from the office; the first time I left Stevie with Ange, and then the next time with Demarcus, his father. Thomas revealed that this café had become his preferred thinking space in recent years, somewhere to be when Lola was out and he did not want to sit at home alone. In the battered leather and wood landscape we pitched our hopes on common ground. We drip-dropped our thoughts, tongue-felt the body of the house blend. Short, untroubled dates, tuned and timed so I could leave with a little regret, not too much, go home to breathe in secret smoke and marvel.

The second evening at Andante, a confession:

'I never loved my wife enough.'

After that, a kiss that mattered. A little too much. Slow and familiar, rude and strong, not so dull as to be perfect; a real headfuck of a sensation, a first. It lifted us. We opened ourselves up to the times that might come after that moment; to possibility.

We stayed up.

Later, in the smallest hours, I dropped the DMD bomb.

'Stevie has this … He's been diagnosed with Duchenne muscular dystrophy.'

'God, what?'

Guilt. Always that pressed-down guilt at tagging the disease on to my son's little life like some fucked-up medical degree: Stevie White, DMD. But that's just how it was: one day you were considering the diagnosis and – pow! – your Wonderboy's future was punched into the ether.

'Yes. Sorry, this is hard.'

'Take your time.'

I hesitated. I would indeed take time to explain everything to Thomas: DMD takes time.

'DMD is a muscle-wasting disorder, a serious one, that mostly affects boys. It's progressive. The weakness in the thighs starts at around age five. It makes walking more difficult and climbing the stairs, balancing … and obviously running …'

'Poor kid.'

'His callipers, or KAFOs – knee-ankle-foot orthoses – make life easier, although Stevie has better balance than most. Terrible rhythm though …'

(*Badaboom!* Nerve-soothing black joke for new boo.) I raised my sights, determined not to falter before I had picked off the devastating facts.

'It is not curable—'

'Really? God, but—'

13

'No. It takes and takes until you have to think about things like sitting, ventilation, fractures and swallowing.'

'No.'

'It is rare. Affects 1 in 3,500 males and … the average life expectancy of DMD boys is twenty-seven years.'

'Shit.'

Yes, Duchenne takes time; all of it, in the end. But that was why Stevie would hear over and over that he was my boy, my lovely little one. As long as he stayed my baby, he would be safe.

'So you see, Thomas,' I said. 'Every moment counts.'

'I *do* see. Oh. Darling.'

And just like that, I was not alone.

Entangling my limbs with his, I brightened the tone:

'It's fine. Stevie and I talk about it, you know? We even laugh, get silly about it. He doesn't need to know it all. I tell him, "I will look after you always, sweetness. No need to worry, ever."'

'That's good. And his splints, his callipers, does he have to …'

'His "superlegs", you mean? Yes, he wears his KAFOS all day long to help him, but none of that is a problem, I take care of it all.'

'You're a great mum.'

'We've had some fantastic support, too. These girls, they call themselves Stevie's Wonders and they're a miracle, really. About eight months ago, I told this new nurse, Paula, about Stevie's diagnosis and next thing all her young student mates started fundraising for him. They've raised over £12,000 so far. Amazing, isn't it?'

I went on to tell him how my son had tried a 'Wonderburger' at the launch barbecue – cheese and double bacon! – how I had a framed photo of him with smears of it all over his smiley chin. How the girls had got serious about that smiley chin and next thing done a sponsored bike ride; how boyfriends had joined in with some extreme ironing stunt up a big hill; how a newsletter had emerged. Soon to come was a marathon walk, maybe something in the *High Desford Gazette*. It was without a doubt the most wonderful miracle.

'They sound ace,' said Thomas.

'Yes, they are, totally. But' – I eased up on an elbow – 'I have never wanted Stevie's needs to be anyone else's problem. Do you get me? He's my responsibility.'

Thomas raised himself up to meet my eye. 'I get you. But help – support – is always better. Right?'

I kissed him in place of a reply. Stevie had always been my responsibility. I was still the one who needed to make everything all right for him. Our generous, warm, bacon-fat days together were destined to be short. Moreover, Duchenne's was carried in a female carrier but overwhelmingly it affected the male offspring. Passed on, from the mother to the son. I was responsible, in the eyes of those who judged such things. All my fault. I was his cherisher,

I had to be, whatever might happen, whatever had happened.

'He's a good boy, my baby. You'll like him.'

'Of course,' said Thomas. 'He does sound wonderful. You're ... Come here.'

After that night, I slapped on nicotine patches and chewed punitive mints after meals. By our third Friday we were doing dinner at the proper-bonkers Lunar (my next test for him: they name tapas-sized Portuguese dishes after dwarf planets and the décor is holiday-misadventures-on-acid, but the guy can *cook*). He saw past all the crazy-name *petiscos*, straight to me. And me? I could barely see past the mental fug of non-smoking and the heat-haze from Pluto's *pataniscas de bacalhau*, or think past our awed mouths, or get past this interior tightening, this fresh hot-blooded ache ...

My phone rang during pudding.

I saw the caller's name. It took everything not to turn it off altogether – my fingers strained but I simply passed the water jug. Had to let it ring: Stevie was with Ange and my mobile was our mum-hotline. The ringing stopped.

'What's wrong?' Thomas reached for my restless hand.

'Nothing,' I said. 'Thought stupid PPI was dead already.'

I turned the ringtone down as low as it would go and raised a *pastel de nata* to his lips.

*

On our next date, I would take care of dinner.

The first time you cook for a man is important. It doesn't just tell him about your tastes, it tells him what you think his tastes are. I had weighed and measured Thomas, more than he would ever know. And so I would cook for him, but not nursery food, no shepherd's pie cuisine; I was nobody's bloody nanny. It was summer, but I would not do him the usual platter of cracked shell and bivalve and sea juice. Despite the ordered hair, any fool could see that he was a man who might be persuaded to crunch, suck and snap a bone, when no one else was looking. Meat then, the best, rare sirloin. A bastardised tagliata. A well-hung porterhouse – charred, smeared in garlic, olive oil, lemon and Parmesan, on a bed of rosemary and rocket. Europe slain, seared and bloody on its greenery, there all for him on a plate.

'I'm going to cook you something,' I said. 'Something simple, but a bit different.'

'Oh good! I've always wanted to try real home-cooked Caribbean food.'

'But, actually I—'

'I mean, I've had a bit of jerk chicken once or twice at a barbecue, but that was just … they were from Devon.'

'Uh-huh,' I said.

Mean. It would have been mean, self-defeating and, as the kids had it, 'awkward', to say anything more than:

'Uh-huh, I'm going to cook you up a real Jamaican treat.'

'Great. What, might I ask?'

So, of course, I had to say:

'Well, wait and see. But it will be wonky and homemade. It may be naked. Or saucy.'

My mother had fed us well; we ate it all up, with thankful mouths and hands ready to do the dishes. She had grown up in the hills near Negril, where food had winked and dangled from every last tree and nigh on every day had ended in satiety, but for us she worked hard at all those meals that aspired to Englishness, the cabbage-and-potato dinners you could make from ingredients bought from up the road, boiled hard. Just like her cousin, Ionie, who had come over a few years before; just like any other 1970s housewife round their way. One generation on, I stirred up flavours from our blended world in a reduced-to-clear cast aluminium pot from a department store off the M40; a Dutchie by any other name.

She had never sat me down and told me a recipe from back Home – I doubted she even thought of such recipes as formalised processes, never mind written-down documents – and I am sure I never asked. Although a certain amount of osmosis had let the right knowledge flow from her generation to my own, I did not wear the wisdoms of 'our' food around me in the way she did, easy as a shawl on a cool Home Counties evening.

And so, two nights before I first cooked for Thomas, I ordered a small cookbook, *Jamaican Home Cooking Secrets*, for next-day delivery. When the driver, a young West African guy, rocked up with my parcel, my eyes dropped to his trainers, though he had no obvious ability to see my shame through cardboard. I don't know why I felt so bad; I was born in Basingstoke.

I read, and chilled. Nothing tricky or unfamiliar here; not a single 'Secret' worth the name. Just enough prompts to turn the pages of memory: my mother's island childhood at the kitchen 'fire', written down and bound. A right result.

The simplicity itself made me a touch cocky. For my dearest English Thomas, I might start *slow*: Brown Stew Chicken. I would perform the optional washing of the supermarket chicken with lime even though there was no need: no germs, no heat, and competent fridges. But some traditions existed for good reason; the lime also sharpened the dish. Still, only two-thirds of the Scotch bonnet, without seeds, for my man. The stew would get hotter each time until he became accustomed to 'our' levels. I was sure he would like all the teasing, the special treatment.

I tasted the stew.

As sauce hit tongue my mind was shaken by something more surprising than savoury, a memory so strong that it might have come from behind me, or just beyond the door.

I lifted the spoon and turned it in my hand, a dripping totem.

Wah yuh ah duh? Mo salt, yuh si mi?

I turned to face the empty kitchen, then back to my chopping board. I choked on a laugh, silent but fierce, almost a shudder. The black tear fell into the stew.

Dat better, gyal.

The chilli caught the back of my throat.

'OK,' I coughed. 'I hear you.'

A quarter-pinch of allspice and the flavours dropped, settled. This was the right stuff for Thomas. This food sang of bright afternoons to be devoured before they darkened, of passion plated high, of a belief that hungers had to be sated. These dishes stirred you right back.

Not enough though, yet.

I had never once bought callaloo; spinach or kale were more readily available in High Desford. However, I had tracked down a supplier in Brockton – forty-minute drive, plus a full five minutes of speed bumps, mind you – where I bought an astonished boxful of the leafy veg, common to even the most spit-poor yards in Jamaica. Including the petrol, it cost more than Stevie's shoes. But that green haul of social climbers deserved a Thomas to appreciate them. At the same time, I did wonder whether preparing this authentic Jamaican meal for him was in itself inauthentic, from a woman mostly reared on plain grey mince and plastic butterscotch desserts, just like him. Still, I knew it was a dinner that told more truth about me than lies. Each mouthful would seduce. A sweet smack of plantain and it was done: our hot lovers' spread.

Thomas, as it happened, would never forget it. Nor would I.

Halfway through, the door went *bamm-bam-bam*. I knew it was Demarcus, still too much man for doorbells. Thomas shot up, rice falling to the table from his brandished fork.

I opened the door to Demmie, coiled tight as ever and dressed sharp, holding my sleeping son.

'Y'alright?' he nodded darkly at Thomas, who sank back down and started piling up my killer crisp-soft plantain on to his plate. 'Got to go, Darling. I'm going out.'

I kissed Stevie, took him. 'Where though?'

'Just out, innit, change of plan. One-off, promise.'

'Is it a woman?' I did not smile but I felt no anger either. The spices and simmering had soothed me, and I had missed my baby.

'What women? Don't know no women.'

I smiled then, an easy reflex; this was our usual banter, our stock exchange. We were cool with each other, Demarcus and I. He was always a good dad, at least for a dad who couldn't keep it anything like in his pants. His pants flew off weekly and landed in a different time zone without ever fulfilling their cotton destiny of keeping anything in them. However, when I got pregnant he stuck around, unlike some – unlike many – and we had talked about a flat-pack future, living together, even a wedding at the town hall where his brother could DJ, crack out the old-school ragga. I had been serious and so had he; we were not tripping off down any bumpy babyfather route, I did not want some cartoon of a bruvva cliché. I wanted a real husband, to be a father and son and mum, an all-together family like the one I grew up in.

Our truest story, to be fair: he was no stereotype spat out by potty-mouthed politicians – those whom Mum had christened *battymouts* – and nor was I. We were just not ready for each other. He liked having a boy but did not rate the stink of nappies. He had liked my milk-heavy breasts but had not wanted to miss Amsterdam to watch me push our son out of that same swollen body. He liked to stroke his son's cheek goodnight but never woke for him. Or he would already be out. Then my Stevie was diagnosed and Dem, still my anti-husband, would stay out longer, later and longer, until I noticed that I had not seen him for three days and he hadn't left his best jeans for me to wash and soon he wasn't even calling me any more to tell me, 'Don't know no women.'

Game over, then. But only because I had been ready anyway.

So that night Dem stood there breathing in the peppery tang of another man's dinner for two and I closed him out with a calm click, and brought Stevie in to meet my new friend, Thomas, and my boy was too drowsy to ask questions, and Thomas was fantastically uncool and kind – with a proper sleep-tight voice, that very first night – and it was enough.

Dem deh two gwan be like bench an' batty.

As I turned to take Stevie to his bed, my phone went. I stooped to answer it, arms full of son.

'Oh, I really can't be arsed to—'

'Easy, turn it off,' said Thomas, rising to make us coffee.

I turned it off.

My man, his back to me, waved a silver pouch high. He had sought out some Jamaica Blue Mountain to make for us in my home, perhaps his way of telling me something about how he *got* me even though he didn't know me.

Later, in that same kitchen, I was taken aback by just how much he knew me. We went together. He got me.

Stevie was pulling at my hand so hard I nearly sloshed coffee on to the floor.

'Don't go out, Mum.'

'I won't, poppet, not until much later.'

'Cuddles!'

'I've told you, darling.' I bent to hug him. 'The big lorry was far away, not here.'

He had been clingy ever since that morning, when a new terrorist atrocity had driven a hole through his innocence. He had sensed my alarm at the rolling news. Unable to find the controls I had stared too long, wearing the fear for both of us. My Stevie knew, despite my efforts, and now he did not want me to go out tonight.

'Are you crying, Mummy?'

'No, sweetness.'

'I can stay here, with you. I won't go to Ange.'

I could not stay. We had awoken to brutality, and to more wrong to come, to every shade of evil directed to extremes. And to change.

But you had to run. *Run* towards what they hoped you would hate.

'Ange would miss you too much, my precious. You need to go see her. First though, cornflakes.'

We left the TV off all day and before I could think twice, I was there.

Littleton Lodge, in High Desford Old Town. From my house, it was across the main park and along a bit, on the corner of a lane so green it felt like the gateway to another country. I had walked past it often, this house: set right back, three storeys high and wide, really bloody wide, and *white*, with wisteria swagged across it. A great fat wodge of Tinkerbell's wedding cake, it even had the nerve to stand at the end of a muesli-crunch driveway.

Walking up to the house I had noticed a scuff on my black court shoes – bloody gravel – but the door opened before I knocked and – *blouse an skirts! Mi neva si huh dere* – there she stood, the happy fairy or nymph or sprite, shifting her weight from foot to foot in a pink playsuit. The girl, his girl, with her father coming close up behind her. As I neared them I could see they shared the same welcoming gaze but hers shone from grey, almost metallic eyes, eyes that you knew would not look away first. Her face was warm cream, her shoulders bare, no wings. Lola.

'Pleased to meet you,' we said.

I stepped in, Thomas stepped back, there was a hefty *ker-chunk* of the door and before I had stepped off the doormat Lola had moved forward to wrap me in a surprise: a free and fluid hug. Then she stepped back and smiled up at her father. The dance of greeting, done.

Father and daughter were both barefoot. Burnished floorboards stretched back into hard acres behind them.

The air was so harmonious I was afraid to disturb it:

'Should I take my shoes off?'

Thomas parted his lips.

'If you don't mind, thanks,' said Lola.

I felt their eyes on me and my marked heels. I should have worn tights: my surprised toenails were unpolished. My toes were silly, stubby and two were considering corns; I had always hated my feet. I was wondering how to work gravel damage and hours spent standing on wards into the conversation as she took my hand and said:

'Come, I'll show you around.'

Another easy glance; and yet such ripening wisdom in those silver disc eyes. I put down my handbag. I was dazzled. Truly, I could not take her in.

'Good girl.' Thomas was nervous too. 'I'll potter off and get on with our dinner. You're in for a treat! We're having my special pasta sauce. A real family fave, is it not, Lollapalooza?'

Lola took me from room to room, looking back at me now and then with a certain intensity as if to check that I was missing nothing, noticing it all. How could I not? This was Thomas himself in brick: a home that challenged you not to find it charming and well appointed. It was the generous but cosy, life's-goshdarn-rosy nest of an architect who had been born with that true American optimism in his blood and still felt he was coming into his greatest powers. As I walked his hallways I believed in him more than ever. Later on he might provoke, or dissemble, or build sustainable grass-roofed mansions, or fool around with the conventions of loft apartment chic, or offer answers to clients' most difficult prayers in cathedrals of black brick and zinc cladding; later, there was time. For now he lived somewhere that suited him. Clever, with a heart. I was inside what he called his 'three-dimensional canvas', in which walls would have been moved, spaces taken up and down and outwards. Lola was formal and proud, but I understood that. I followed her and paused to admire, followed and paused as she padded with unsettling poise – ballet? – around her home. I shuffled through the full tour on my ugly bare feet. We stood caught in our unblinking double glare, the light sting of her scrutinising my back as I wheeled, toes resting to hide for a moment in the pile of a rug, in slow humiliation through the study and the snug, through the whole of her too-lovely world.

Lola beckoned me to the next stop on the tour with a steel-tipped wave. (*Her* nails and toes were both painted, a shade lighter than her stare.) She was set on showing me all five bedrooms. These would not have been tidied, armfuls stuffed into cupboards, for my eyes only. It was a well-ordered house, grown-up and yet designed to fulfil the grandest hide-and-seek fantasies. By the time we went from her room to the attic (up the secondary doll's house stairs behind a Narnia door, I kid you not), which they had thought about converting – not her dad, *they* – I almost wanted to say, 'OK, I get it and yes, I'm impressed not accustomed, and yes, I'm just the guest ...'

But then I thought *sixteen* and bit my tongue – actually gave myself a salty little nip – and I beamed and nodded, every inch the spellbound stranger, when she asked:

'So, Darling, would you like to see Dad's favourite place?'

We traipsed back down the main attic stairs along the landing, and carried on down to the hallway without speaking. A shout from the kitchen over the effortful jazz:

'All OK, girls?'

'Fine, Dad!'

Lola and I kept going, to the right, to the left, to the side, through a door hewn out of the fucking Faraway Tree and into the dust of a red-brick landing. Another smaller door. I hesitated:

'Basement?'

'Cellar.'

She flicked on a sickly light and I squinted, unsure. Before I could think of three good reasons why not, we were going down. I descended into the B-movie, my mind's camera shaking, her he's-behind-you blonde hair swishing in too much shadow to be funny. But something about her steady pace told me she was not acting. Lola led me down into the dark must.

'Watch these steps,' she said.

'Will do, thanks.'

I tried not to mind her. Of course she was showing off the house as if it were double-glazed with diamonds. Anyone would be proud with a dad like Thomas Waite.

At the bottom, another switch; more powerful illumination. Racks stood in rows, housing aristocratic boozers asleep under thin blankets of dust. The stone-carved ceiling curved in places and the ends from wine boxes tiled the walls.

'Ta-da!'

I nodded and smiled, as required.

'Go ahead and take a look, it goes right back.'

I had never been a huge wine drinker – a vodka, gin or rum girl, me – and could not spot a good year, coo with urbane delight. However, even I could work out, without looking too hard at the labels, that if wine had been left alone for a few decades you had to be confident that some poor grape-trampling sod would have made it worth the wait.

'Yes, Dad? Coming!' A yelled reply to a call I could not hear. 'Back in a sec.'

She skipped upstairs and left me gazing, with the same eyes I had turned on the 'original' fireplaces and the 'spacious' study, at a bottle of 2012 Côtes du Roussillon Villages Le Clos des Fées. Ah, *fée*: French for fairy.

Thud-click.

'Lola?'

Nothing. Nothing except a muffle-thump of bass, some new and energetic tempo. Was that *Queen*?

'Lola?'

I moved, with laboured nonchalance, to the foot of the stairs. Slow, slow, feet chilling on dank stone. I stared up: *please, not this.* Where the oblong of daylight had shown there was now only black.

'Lola!'

Nothing but the *dun-dun-dun* high above, through dense, deaf floors – 'Under Pressure'? Within seconds the room was pressing against my skin. I sank into a crouch. Walls locking down on me, dead air growing sweet in my nostrils, a sharp whiff of red flowers; the lights dimmed and in my ears *dun-dun-dun* a drum beating, a dangerous vibration, my lungs tight and full because I must have stopped breathing and then I was pounding upwards, upstairs *dun-dun-dun-dun* pounding hard into hard blackness:

'Lola!'

I hit at the door *dun-dun-dun*. Not goddamn 'I Want to Break Free', no way. She couldn't have.

'Lola! Lola, let me out. Get me out now!'

Too loud, too far. My mobile; it was still in my handbag by the front door, next to my shamed shoes.

'Lola! Lola!'

I could feel tears bleeding into the sweat at my temples.

Then a blinding of light and air and noise rushed in and she was there, a bending shadow. Oxygen, music washed me down (my hysterical ears now heard 'Killer Queen') and Lola swept me up.

'Oh, you poor thing, I'm so sorry!'

'I thought—'

'This stupid beeping door. God, Darling, so sorry. It must have locked behind me, it's been sticking lately.'

She took my hand and led me through the first door back to safety. Thomas danced out, a seafood cocktail in each hand. Seeing me he stopped dead:

'What's wrong, what—?'

'The cellar door, Dad. Knew it would do that sooner or later.'

'I'm fine.' The veil of sweat said more, the tacky film noir on my face. I dropped her hand.

We ate. The prawns were perky, the pasta porky; *paccheri* topped with a fat chop, rubbed with salt and fresh oregano, in a more than passable passata. But I was done in. I laughed too loud, complimented everything Thomas had created: the dinner, all things Lola. I tried, but the pulsing music was all *dun-dun-dun* and I could not follow the chatter, my flesh had been rubbed with salt sweat and fear, and my wine tasted sharp, all wrong. We ate on as my toes curled up on themselves, defeated. My smiles lied broad and long, as did the yawns at around 9.30 p.m. Enough. Our night had been left behind, locked in the cellar, and I pleaded an early start with Stevie: physio. I would gather up my boy, he could sleep in my bed after all.

I pecked Thomas and hugged Lola, realising as I backed away that I knew little more about her than when she had first landed those eyes on me. As the door closed, those eyes put me in mind of magnesium, with the potential to flare bright. Or perhaps the casings of incendiary devices, of dormant bombs. Yes, that was it. In a certain light, Lola looked like she could go off at any moment.

Lola

So, getting right down to it – we good girls always do our homework.

If you are my future child, going through all my old crap as I dribble Happy Oats down my knitted front in a nursing home you can't afford, please ignore anything that you read here – I already have.

Introduction

Welcome, Ms Waite, to the inside of your brain!

This pointless but scenic ride through your psyche is your buy-one-get-one-free, no refunds, pain-in-the-ass complimentary gift, for which you are eligible thanks to the £110 per hour (I googled her) your dad has spent on 'talking therapies' every fortnight since you hit puberty and cried all night because you wanted to try on your mum's bra (totally logical, how the fuck else would I know how it worked?).

So, no one even thought to get me as much as a training bra before thirteen (if I get saggy tits I will sue EVERYONE) but hey, two thumbs up for Alison Thoroughgood!

BTW innocent dinky future kids: that's true, but it's not actually a reason anyone ever got a shrink, not any girl anyway, let alone a fine specimen such as your drooling mother, but I really can't be arsed to go into it all right now. Also, I'd just be happy with a bit more tittage generally – there's always lifting tape for when you hit thirty.

Never mind that though, it's basically:

£110 x 26 fortnights x 5 years since my nipples first weirdly popped out (still joking) = £14,300 minus holidays. About £14k spent paying someone he hardly knows (we love our letters after names, Dad and I) to get into my head. No wonder AT wants me to deliver some serious goods, aka 'exploratory homework' #cantbearsedwithfuckedupgirls #fundingmytibetanyogaretreat.

Still, £14,000 says something. It tells me two major things about Dad.

First thing: he has a lot more money than you might think to look at his car. Even I, who deleted all his lame old-guys-in-flying-jackets-speeding shows, know a Volvo's too safe a choice. Alfa, Dad? Audi? Merc?

Second thing: he is an optimist.

He wants to cure you. Aka me. But none of us – especially not Alison Thoroughgood BSc, PG Dip whatever – is sure of What Underlies The Problem. All my mouthing off may be suppressed sadness, ask AT. So what's my issue? My Dead Mum blues, no doubt. My stinking attitude. That 'horrible' obsession with hotness (is this really a fault? If you have to live your shitty life, you might as well look good). Bra fetish?

I probably am crazy, but point me to a teenage girl who isn't. 'Talking therapies?' Chemo = therapy. Talking = fuck off, I'm watching YouTube, right? Just saying.

Make yourself comfortable, Lola, and I hope you have plenty of biros.

This is a piss-poor introduction to my head, but then who likes saying what they're supposed to say? It's tragic. Long story short: I will make the Notes every week or day or month or whatever and make my long list of five Achievements, as instructed, because as I have mentioned, I am a good girl. Not four Achievements (four's for losers), not six (arsewipe show-offs) but five, as in 'high five, AT, woop-woop!' But basically these will be no more than DONE LISTS. I told her straight 'No thanks, I'm more of a Nike kind of girl: just do it' but that Alison, she needs to see where I've been – she's always looking backwards. Isn't that a bit lazy, or nostalgic, or even romantic for a therapist? Obviously I don't think AT is actually in love with me though, thank Christ. Scary old geezerbird when I first met her. Now I think she's more straight and tough than butch. Whatever. She won't be reading any of these lists either, she just wants me to keep telling her whatever the hell I want in our sessions – an important part of the process she says –

but at least she will get me to spend my whole time looking backwards too #timewasters101. I think the idea is that I am to feel I have got somewhere, DONE something just by making it to the end of the week without pausing to blow my brains out. Or something. Still, better than the sad-sack page-a-day diary with spaces to note your mood and that weird teddy on the front she tried to shove on to me a couple of months back. I didn't mind giving her what she wanted to hear for a while: 'Dear diary, I'm so fat and why can't I get anyone to screw me blahblahblah ... Mood: So Very Sad ...' I aimed for devastatingly sincere with a tiny hint of piss-taking, but I guess she didn't buy it which is why we're now doing this. 'I won't read these lists, Lola. You decide how much and when, Lola,' in her ever-hopeful voice. Touching. I suppose I do owe her a brief go at this thing, although the diary fail was definitely not my fault – don't give me some fat teddy holding carnations and expect me to spill my guts like you're doing me a huge favour.

Notes

First off, I don't get it. I just don't. So three even four times I offered to give him Viv Halston-Jones's mobile. Pretty, freshly divorced, perfect. Lizzie HJ's a laugh too so if the parents hooked up it would be exactly like some cheesy old sitcom, brilliant. Him – 'I'll think about it.' That usually means 'yes'. Next thing, he comes back with her?

I don't fucking think so.

I strongly suspect I have failed all my GCSEs. Why not? Screw A*s – nothing you really expect to happen happens. Things you don't want: <u>boom</u>. Who needs it?

OK, massive dilemma – how best to slut-shame Caro Francis?

a) FB? Might actually be that much of a loser, but everyone would think I was joking. Who takes those posts seriously any more?
b) SnapChat? Yaas! Snap of me with my tongue poking way into my cheek, nice. Will try not to send it to Eli C instead of Ellie this time. #bloodydisaster
c) Old school … Yes! Scream with laughter around the Dovington boys then shout to Anna about what is so piss-yourself funny. Bingo. (Hey, Dad, you were right! Sometimes life <u>is</u> better without a digital trail.)

Seriously – who the hell gives someone a blow job in a hot tub? At a party? When it's Will Benton? Caro Francis is <u>rancid</u>. Caro bloody Francid. She must secretly have been a total <u>ho</u> this whole time when we thought she was just a bit of a dick whose mum massively over-Bodens. It was probably because everyone reckoned they had holed themselves up in the parents' en suite doing all that blow first. Anna was too drunk to freak. Lucky her mum was on another cruise with Tobias (*the* dilf to end all dilfs) and not just out. Someone's hot tub – since when is that OK? Other people went in there afterwards as well. Ewwww (add ws. Ad infinitum. Rocking that Latin revision a little too late, Lola Waite). No wonder Anna was so pissed off in the morning that she cried, what a way to start the summer. I think she is planning to drain it just in case (sperm swims, right, but does it float? Maybe the filter got it all. Caro certainly did lol). How does that even work: why didn't she drown?

I want to know all of these things, now. Sooner.

You've got to be fucking kidding me.

He saw her again. Until after 1.30 a.m. last night, 'dinner round hers', and apparently she's 'quite a bit more than just a date'. I mean … what?

For a start, let's get the obvious thing out of the way. Since when was he into black women? I mean, Mum was it for him – the bomb – natural blonde, like me; she was your genuine Alpha^2, your total headfuck dreamgirl. I've got the photos to prove it. Dad's always said: they simply *went* together. Tall, slim; him dark, her fair. All that genetic pay dirt I would get on my knees and thank God for every day if I believed in all that crap. Then Mum dead, nothing and no one for years, a few pointless dates, and now Darling. Is she his change that is as good as a rest? I doubt it. She must have been some kind of sexual accident. But then AT always says there are no such things as accidents. This does not make any <u>sense</u>.

Listen up, Roxie McFoxy. Stop torturing us with yet another tragic end-of-year routine … Rrrrring! The Eighties called, they want their Electric Slide back (told you – YouTube never lies). And why is Jane Forte in the front row? Her arse alone will eclipse us all.

Darling. She's kidding, right? She tried, I'll give her that. Obviously right out of her depth, nice enough, just <u>wrong</u>. Wrong for us, anyway. Nothing intelligent over dinner – except how lovely the pasta was, how lovely the daughter was, and had she mentioned she loved the pasta? Just rolled her eyes at Dad and laughed the whole bloody time. Some sucking up to The Lovely Daughter (that's me, kids), all a bit obvious. Pretty sure Dad was finding her painful too because he wasn't bothered when she sloped off early. That's old people for you: need to get their rest.

Did she really think I'd find <u>her</u> lovely, what with her rolling her eyes and dragging her minging feet all over our poor house (hello, tights? Pedi?). Plus, she kept sniffing and coughing all over the wine, all like 'Why do you people drink this dusty old crap?' It's true, they don't like wine. Ellie went to Antigua and all her parents could drink was rum and beer, so her mum spent ten days with a massive air-conditioned migraine. True story.

Darling White is rude and I was angry. So – a little chill-out time for her in our cellar. Only for a few seconds and I was right there outside the door the whole time, but she screamed the goddamn place down. Lola! Lola! You'd have thought she was being murdered.

Now or never: a big shout-out for Caro Francis tomorrow, outside Maccy Ds, ably assisted by Anna #slutshaming101. The boys should be needing a Quarter Cheese, a fag and yet another pathetically unsubtle stare at our tits by about 5 p.m. No Will, I hope, or it's obviously a non-starter.

Now she's even getting into my head, into my warm-down space. This is literally the only time my head ever clears into whiteness and silence. That's why I do it, the dancing – it all ends in the white and silence in my head. Now Darling White's stolen even that.

I did mess with <u>her</u> head, though. Thinking about it, she nice-freaked all over me at dinner the other night, after the cellar thing. Trying way too hard. I watched her: super-nervy. She cut the pasta using her knife for a few bites, then remembered and picked up the spoon. I pretended not to see, but Dad saw and he saw me not noticing and told me later that I have great manners. I really do.

If she turns up again she'll get 100 per cent The Lovely Daughter and fuck-all of me.

I can't wait. I <u>literally</u> can't wait for things to get back to how they should be again.

Dad reckons I'm impatient, but in some great way. I know the truth: it's not that I'm actually patient, I'm not, I'm impatient, but it isn't all so uncomplicated and great, it's more of a juicy flaw, a fat complicated spot that I enjoy squeezing. As soon as I see a dress online I want it not only delivered now, I want to be wearing it while I look for the next one I want. I actually do! I might eat a GoGo bar all nice and slow when my friends are around, but on my own it's all over before the wrapper's hit the bin. What? Just the way it is. If by any miracle I ace my GCSEs then I want the results today, I can't wait weeks, I've earned <u>now</u>. Tiring, but

I've come to appreciate it – patience is the most over-rated virtue, as Mum used to say, apparently. That must be why Dad likes me not having it.

It's like with Will. Why should I wait for him to come to his senses and realise that his decision to let Caro Francis anywhere near him was just *horrible*? I mean, she's all lumpy hips and boobage and no brains and she doesn't even get his jokes so it's not as if they can have a proper laugh together. And why would he be interested in someone who – let's face it – he's much better looking than? Like putting a 10 with a 5 ½ (the half is because boys seem to like obese chests, the five is basically for showing up and breathing); it won't work. Seriously, she's got these weird eyes, all puffy and glassy, clueless. Dead walrus eyes, I swear. He must have been <u>so</u> wasted. I'll be doing him a massive favour by exposing their whole stupid human hubbly bubbly scenario. <u>How</u> tacky? He'll thank me one day. Even if he won't, I don't think I can stop myself.

No, I don't like waiting, not for anything. But I have waited for Will Benton for over nine months.

And for the record, I've always thought my own impatience started out as a rebellion against my stupid surname (any thoughts, AT?). Whenever someone says my name in full, I just think 'Why the fuck should I?'

Mission accomplished! I yelled to Anna about the whole ridiculous hot-tub thing, she shrieked back and there you go – if Will goes near that sket again he will be torn to pieces by all his piss-taking mates (btw I'd never heard of a 'nob-gobbler' until Martin Howe shouted it mega-loud, then the staff asked us to please move away from all the Happy Meal eaters). Now I feel <u>calm</u> again. So that's where the hell my white and silence went after the Year 11 (Group A) Modern Dance Prizegiving rehearsals yesterday – all sucked up by Caro Francis, never mind that bloody Darling.

When I'm furious in the morning and sunny at night, Dad tries to hug me into submission and says I'm a funny old mix, and don't I just know it?

Sure do, Pops, sure do.

Can't sleep again.

Was going to bin this crappy book as I can't, to be honest, be arsed with yet more writing after weeks – literally gazillions of seconds I will never get back – spent in exam hell #smothermenow. But making this sad sacrifice to the great god AT is better than trying to lie still until I have another one of those dreams where I run and run and get nowhere.

Maybe it is good to keep track of what I've done. Especially during the summer – I need structure, apparently. AT might say that's linked to my impatience issues but I can't hang around to find out (ha!). Gotta get the DONEs done.

So. End of term tomorrow. End of Harbrooke House too, forever – one final dull-as-fuck Prizegiving but Dad's not bringing her, so that's good. Time for the mums to get all teared up again (not mine, lol) and the dads to snort a term's fees' worth of champagne and canapés. Our parent-pleasing (rated U, no twerking) dance, then a trillion+ hours of the annual Year 13 tears and snot festival, bring wellies – ohlike-myGodIcantbelieveIllneverseeyouagaaain. Then I'll dance my lil white mighty-fine booty off! Sorry, must stop doing that. I'm really not a racist.

All this to come, tomorrow. Will might even get dragged along to the evening – Georgie Benton wins everything in her year, always. That would keep me awake at least. After that it will finally be the start of my actual, proper life. No more Harbrooke House, no more rules to do my head in, just a crazy-long summer, then college and my time at last. End of.

Achievements

1. Started a FB group (no Caro Francis) for everyone going to the Mungojaxx festival which is actually going to be on Josh's cousin's farm, some fields near Henley. Have kept the Caro/Will cumfest offline for now (the screaming plan worked big time).

2. Added ten extra squats and twists to my morning workout. Roxie will cream her pants when she sees my insane leaps tomorrow. Get the fuck into the back row, Jane Forte!

3. Bought my first ever packet of Golden Kings using my fake ID. Sweated it, but Delhi Deli don't give a toss. They're not even a proper deli (no salami, no pastrami, no scotch eggs #grossguiltypleasure). No meat at all, people, bad for you or religiously impure or whatever … but go ahead, smoke yourself silly! (Don't do it, kids, ever.)

4. Lost Thursday's lunch. Mistake.

5. Practised in my head being nice to Dad's date. Did not tell her she was totally not his type. Did tell him, of course. Did not ask her, 'And who in Mcfuck's name is even called "Darling"?'

Darling

It was time. My baby had been brought along to meet everybody, but he decided to show the world his tonsils at high volume when I tried to get him out of the car.

'Come on, Stevie, sweetheart, they want to see you!'

'No, Mum!'

'Please, baby, come on, I'll help you. My little Wonder-boy ...'

Just like that: the cheekster smile. My son took an inordinate, lips-pulled-wide pride in his name, especially when we played 'Fingertips', turned right up. He would not have to sing or perform, ever. But from the moment my future mathematician or philosopher or astronaut had first been flopped on to my chest, I knew he was Stevie (never Steven) Marcus White. My little star, my baby emperor.

'Please, my love, for Mummy.'

In the distance a train shrieked its passage through the town into the fast-rolling fields.

'Choo-choo!' said Stevie.

'Yes, sweetness, that's right,' I said. 'Now … please?'

With a damp frown up at the strangers, Stevie swung his legs sideways, exactly the way I had shown him, and eased on to my arm, on to his sticks and out of the car.

Once again the door was already open, but this time Thomas stood on the doorstep, a controlled explosion of blonde hair behind his shoulder. She'd washed it and let it dry curly and natural, and I knew there was a reason for that but could not think what it might be. Was she unwinding follicle by follicle or simply trying to make us feel more at home? Both?

'Hello, Darling! And here's super-Stevie …' said Thomas.

This for his daughter's benefit. *Stevie the Wonderboy*, I wanted to correct him but I didn't. Let them get to know him in their own time.

Then I saw her face.

Her father's shoulder and shadow could not hide her. There it was, the spark of disgust, swiftly snuffed out, when she looked down at my boy. This is why I needed to protect him, right there, in that look.

'Stevie, Thomas, remember? And this is Lola.'

When I turned the spotlight on her she sprang into action:

'Ah, OK, would … you … like … to …'

I had to jump in: 'It's fine, it's only in his body. He's a smart boy, aren't you, Stevie?'

A squirming, wide-eyed nod.

'That's good,' said Lola, looking at her feet.

Young. She would learn.

Morning unfolded into afternoon with an unhurried Saturday vibe; we were all to hang out together and enjoy the blueberry bran muffins that Lola, Thomas swore, had insisted on baking all by herself in Stevie's honour.

Stevie winced at the murky sponge and the berries that bit back, but I caught his eye in time; good boy. Lola sat with him for over an hour after lunch and left Thomas and me to chat, mostly about surviving the summer and binning off the school run.

Lola had finished now, but Stevie had another week to go until he got his end-of-year medal. I was so proud of him. Once, home-schooling had appeared to be the only way, but he had been a true lion as ever:

'I want to play with my friends, Mummy!'

I could not hold him back, I would never do that. So off he went to High Desford's best primary, no trouble at all. Lola had gone to that nicety-nice girls' place up the road, of course. Lovely blue uniforms, but – *la!* – they all wore them so short. My mum would have slapped me upside my head if I'd tried that on.

From the kitchen we could hear them discussing favourite cartoons. That was kind of her, helpful; good to see.

Meanwhile, I twitched. I had vowed not to smoke, in honour of us all. I would end those dashes into the en suite to brush my teeth before kisses, before talking, before breathing; the dashes out of the door to top up on nicotine; the miserable yellow-toothed excuses to the one person who wanted to see me happy. Straight-up cold turkey quitting. No fags, no patches, no nicotine chewing gum, no sugar-free mint chewing gum, nothing but the taste of Thomas. Who needed cigarettes when we had us? Lips were for lovers; from now on I would practise full oral fidelity.

More than the urge to smoke, the blueberry muffins had set off in me a strange urge to bake. It was Stevie's birthday in a few weeks and I figured I could whip up a dozen or so soppy little chocolate frosted cupcakes with those silver balls.

I am not a natural baker. I like preparing things with skin and bone, skimming fat and salting sauces. But this afternoon something made me want to try. Maybe it was a faint hope that Lola might sniff out a mother figure. We needed a crumb of that sticky stuff. She was embarrassed: we both knew, from as soon as the actual dust settled, that we both *knew* she had locked me in the cellar. But I was an adult; I had moved on. Just a little kick-out at the nasty ole lady who was kissing her daddy, all pretty textbook. More than that I was a nurse: caring was my life and so was understanding. I got it. And I never planned to try to be 'Mum'; that would have been wrong, insensitive, futile, crazy. I would simply, as people liked to say, *be there* for her.

It took me a moment to realise that Stevie had walked in, holding something.

'Put that down, Stevie! That's not yours ...'

I could not hide the panic in my voice. Dark red-pink and orange in his hands: he had walked in holding a Bright New Britain flyer, snatched up from the hallway. What words – incomprehensible to us both – might he try to read?

'Come and see our garden, Stevie,' said Lola, taking the leaflet from him and placing it on the side. 'Can he …?'

'He'll be fine, he can get around with his sticks, just watch him a little.'

'OK.'

Thomas pulled me to him as we watched them disappear up the garden.

'We can go and see the pond!' The small voice drifting over the lavender.

'Sure,' said Lola.

The girl didn't go outside much. A gorgeous garden, but she preferred Facetiming her friends all day. So many friends too; Ellie seemed to be the closest at that time, but it changed from week to week. Girls were strange, these days; I had either had someone for good, or not at all.

I lifted the leaflet from the work surface:

BRITAIN FOR THE BRITISH
We are taking back:
Our borders
Our jobs
Our NHS
Our streets and our kid's futures … today!

'What the hell is this?'

'We never used to get them but they come every few days now. They must be targeting the area …'

'Oh God, we—'

'No, sorry, ignore me. We get all sorts of crap through, every day.'

'And what about my kid's future? Are we no longer British?'

'Just ignore it, Darling, please.'

'I was British, apparently, when I was cleaning up their wasted kids' fluids and saving their bleeding lives in A&E. Or when I spoon-fed their grandmas. Or when I—'

He pulled me into a hug, into that compelling, hard-won privacy that only parents could know. 'Time is short,' he said. 'Too short,' I said. 'I love you,' he said. 'Me you,' I said. The urgency of our kisses became uncomfortable.

Hands on cheeks, hands on shoulders, at my waist, his hands …

'Dad!'

Lola running up, nearly at the door, no Stevie. No Stevie. Blood? A forever loss, a fall, a drowning – I sprinted, seeing it all already. My boy. I raced past the flowerbeds and bench and vegetable garden, far to the back, by the chestnut tree where the pond hid, dank and gorge deep, skulking away from our eyes. So wide and *deep*: with those things strapped around his legs he would sink to the bottom. Stevie was nowhere, no Stevie.

'Darling! What's wrong?'

A bewildered bass; Thomas running behind me.

'Stevie,' my voice snagged. 'Where's Stevie?'

Thomas held up his arms, shrugging his whole body. I wanted to punch him in the chest.

'Stevie! Where?'

'He's—'

'Dad!'

We both spun. Lola was ambling up towards us. I could have flown at her, tugged answers out of that tousled hair. She could see it.

'He's fine, Darling, he's just on the swing.'

'What?'

'Look.'

She ran-skipped back up the garden and parted branchlets of willow tree. There was Stevie, sitting immobile on a wooden swing, no longer hidden by the weeping canopy. I ran to him.

'Push me, Mum!'

It was then that I realised my feet were cold, dirty and bare once again.

'I was only calling for Dad,' said Lola, 'to ask if he would be allowed to swing—'

There, that. Was that *triumph* in her voice?

'Of course he can't fuh—' I said; Thomas was walking closer. 'He can't go on swings, Lola, sorry.'

'Push me!'

'*No*, Stevie!' The look I gave her was as direct as I could make it. 'If he breaks a leg he'll be … it could set him right back. Permanently.'

Thomas took in a rapid breath. Lola lowered her chin.

'Yes, of course. Sorry. It's OK, you meant well, Lollapalooza,' her father said.

'Of course you did,' I agreed. 'No harm done.'

I never wanted him to feel he had to defend her from me. We both knew how well she had meant.

We binned the leaflet and tied up the swing.

Later, Lola disappeared off with a group of friends to something that gloried in the name of 'Mungojaxx', a 'festival for faux-boho future bankers', as Thomas described it, which drew a tight snort from me. The girl seemed keyed up as she walked out of the door and as she went a certain tension in the breeze whistled right out with her.

The next time we came over, I arrived with two small overnight bags.

Lola had let us in; Thomas hurried into the kitchen ten minutes later, fresh from work.

'We were just saying yesterday,' said Thomas, 'it'll be lovely to have him stay over. Weren't we, Lollapalooza?'

'Were we?' she asked.

My back to them both, I pressed down on banana flesh with my masher.

'Come on, Lo …' he said.

'What?' She walked out of the kitchen.

'Lola!'

'It's fine,' I said, breaking eggs into a bowl. 'It's all still so new to her. Go get changed, relax, I'll bring you something.'

That won his smile back. We were still so new to ourselves that every hackneyed and cosy gesture felt daring, sexy; mixing him a drink in his own home, baking in his Aga. I was now spending so much time at Littleton Lodge that we had decided: time for our first sleepover with Stevie.

'OK. I'll just go see to Lola first.'

I nodded and started whupping the eggs, quite hard. After he left I googled on my phone. As I had thought:

Lollapalooza

/ˌlɒləpəˈluːzə/

Noun, North American, informal – A person or object that is more than usually impressive or attractive.

I had heard the word out of that soft mouth a few too many times already. Time after time. I found it irritating, but I needed to stay calm. To relax. Vodka. I would make vodka tonics to ease us into our weekend. First, I scrolled down:

Lollapalooza; also, a gambling term for a made-up hand of cards.

In other words, tricky. I never claimed to be an intellectual, far from it, but I did indeed read into things. Meaning lurked everywhere, even though we could only look back or around us, never see what was to come.

And what *was* to come?

It had been over a month since the referendum. A lucky seven days since I had last smoked. Things in this country – as with things in my lungs – might have been calming down, or they might not. For a few days after the referendum I had raged. *Raged.* Then, Thomas had called and I had started to hope we would all just get on with it; rise in the heat, as we always had done. We got on with it. High Desford – not famous, not distinguished, beautiful to few – excelled in that it had become a truly blended town. White English people, Sikhs, Poles, Hindus, Afro-Caribbeans, Chinese, other Europeans and yes, Muslims; genders and sexualities every colour of that proud rainbow; all generations, everyone; even one local character who liked to drape a Partick Thistle scarf across his chilled wares in the market square. Surely, unless you mixed it all up, gave it some heat and bit in brave and hard, you never could know. And maybe a Swedish-born oven, raised in Shropshire, was always destined to bake some bloody lovely Jamaican banana bread.

As it rose in the oven, I went to the drinks fridge. But the bottle of vodka had gone, and the tonic too. I did not stress: that sunshine aroma was already billowing out from the cast-iron conundrum, filling such cracks in our day. Wine would do.

'Mum?' Stevie wandered into view. 'The cartoon finished.'

'OK, sweetie, I'm coming through.'

'Can I have some 'nana cake, please?'

'Not right now, after supper.'

No, the youth was not in charge, today; the grown-ups had already plotted. As our reward, the evening had passed off quietly – Stevie, having seen the size of his new room, lit up the longer silences – and everyone had gone to bed early and eager. None more so than Thomas and I.

Lights left on, always. Our pampered mouths – brushed clear of crumbs and newly minted – were now more than stunned by their discoveries, they were over-sexed and delighted for it. Our bodies were ahead of even our lips. Thomas had seized a no-messing handful of right thigh. With my toes pointing past his shoulder, he eased my thigh higher as we sat, naked, facing each other on the bed; higher he stretched me, back and higher …

'Mum!'

'Oh God!' A hamstring twanged, good as snapped. 'Stevie darling, hi—'

Thomas had already yanked up the duvet.

'What are you doing, Mum?'

'Exercises, poppet. Physio.' I gave Thomas my first cross look. 'Door?'

'It was locked, I swear!'

'What did you want, baby? You can't sleep?'

'I dreamed of Lolly and she came.'

'What?' we said.

'Lolly was here, she told me you wanted me.'

Neither of us spoke for a moment. Then:

'Of course,' I said. 'We always want you, my lovely one.'

Stevie, free of his callipers but broken by bad dreams, clambered on to the bed so he could throw his insubstantial arms around me. I sat back on my haunches, the right one aching like hell, and I pressed my lips to his crown. He wormed into the bed, nestled down under the duvet.

Behind me, a swallowed sigh.

In the morning, Thomas was all smiles and 'more coffee?'. As the first sure-bring-Stevie sleepover it had not been an unqualified success. Not knowing which child to blame, we yawned, gulped the breakfast blend faster than normal, and blamed neither. But I knew.

I watched as Lola, triumphant, made a show of cutting soldiers for Stevie's dippy egg.

'... and this is the soldier that guards the queen!'

She caught my eye; we smiled. Yet my faking lips fell when she said:

'Next time, Stevie, you'll have to top-to-toe with me!'

Thomas laughed, grateful. I said:

'His legs, though, you see ...' and the laughter died.

Maybe I was being too harsh on her, on all of us. Thomas doted on Lola, and Lola might have been coming to dote on Stevie.

I never meant to panic, to make a big deal, to give the impression that he was totally helpless. But that was what thinking about Duchenne muscular dystrophy did to a mum. Thomas understood that; I ought never to forget that he was the man who got me. Thomas understood the sadness in my smiles when Lola petted and teased my boy. I always watched over him, it was my job, my joy. And Thomas understood, deep down, how glad I had to be that his girl wanted to reach out to my baby, even for a moment.

A few days later, we endured a lockjaw-inducing dinner. A meal sucked up through clenched teeth.

Lola needled and carped at everything I said. As I offered her potatoes:

'You know I'm off carbs, right?'

'No, I didn't.'

'Well, I am.' A look. 'I don't want to get fat.'

And, as a nineties dance tune played on the radio:

'Tune!' I cried. 'I used to love this.'

'God, it's really annoying.'

And, as I confirmed to Thomas that I was indeed wearing a new top:

'Wow, you love shopping, don't you?'

'No more than most, I imagine,' I said.

57

'How do you afford it?' A beat. 'That top … yes, I think Lizzie HJ's mum has the same one. You've met her, haven't you, Dad? God, she's so pretty it's sickening.'

And, as Thomas reached out to touch my hand:

'Don't look, Stevie, old people alert!'

And, as Stevie pulled back one arm and pointed with the other, his favourite Lightning Bolt pose – aimed straight at my loving chest – I said:

'The Olympics should be pretty incredible. And the Paralympics.'

'Yeah, but they're spending all that money on it and clearing out the *favelas*.'

'I know, you're right but—'

'The games are just so the better countries can show off to—'

Thomas smiled. 'It's OK, Lolapoo, relax.'

If she were mine I would have made sure she did more than relax. So much sharpness, such spite; you could catch a nerve on it, trip up and gash your good intentions. Why did he not *notice*?

Later that night, I was no longer in a receptive mood. I wanted to get the hell away. I wanted a cigarette. But Thomas was ready to share his stories. He wanted to tell me more about what mattered to him. So: Dad George dead, Boise, Idaho, America. George could drink a bottle of vodka for breakfast and defend a rape case before lunchtime. (I popped a mint in, started listening.) This combination of talents gave Thomas the cold sweats to this day. He had died over thirty years before and Thomas still felt weird; cheated that it was a car accident that got him – he had been in a taxi – rather than the burst liver for which his Tommy had spent his whole childhood preparing. His mum, Sal, a Brit, was not much inclined to live in the land of pumpkin pie and prairies. She fled sniffily to England, only to return, in crumpled Chanel, to Idaho, because that was where George was buried. The pull of that car-crash love, beyond pride and maternity and oceans, was such a shock to that practical woman that she never recovered. Thomas still retained some pride in this familiar yet foreign half of him; the US was the sassy, stacked superpower the whole world secretly fancied so he flashed his generous half-Yank teeth as he said:

'Imagine. Us in Boise, Idaho.'

'Can't.'

'Big fishing country. The Rockies, Pioneer villages ... fuck-all, really.'

'Thomas! I do believe that's the second time I've heard you cuss.'

'Is that right? Ah, that's not me, that's American Thomas. Tom ... Wassernacker. He swears like all—'

'Oh, shut the fuck up and come here ...'

'Darling! I do believe—'

'Hush now.'

There were bright stabs of joy, daily, despite the teenage parrying. Thomas seemed to be taking to Stevie faster than I had hoped. Going over and above; under and around too, drafting new ways for us all to be. It was a Wednesday evening, and I was to idle in the bath while he took the kids to the summer drive-in, showing *Grease*. As it happened, the hospital called first, needing me to cover, but his thoughtfulness was no less magnificent.

As Thomas started up the engine, with Lola and my son in his car, my mind buzzed. I wanted Stevie to love culture, even if it started out with some shiny, big-quiffed, 'Summer Lovin''; that night he would at least learn something about the beauty of transformation. I read books and watched plays, which some people found surprising, but that in itself surprised me. High Desford was not a complete cultural desert – not compared to Elm Forest, the small, scruffy nearby town where I had spent my early years.

Even if it was semi-arid, I had studied and sought out thoughts, dowsed for words and meaning, drunk it all in ever since we had moved here. If I had not been made a nurse by vocation and were I not Stevie's destined mother, I would have written. All the blinking time. I certainly read. Some of the first lines I ever committed to memory, apart from Neneh Cherry's 'Buffalo Stance', were from Ophelia's loco chatting which we had to recite once at school:

'Lord, we know what we are, but know not what we may be.'

So good. A bit too much sense for real madness, but that seemed to be the point. (We thesps of Class 4C probably did not greatly enhance the meaning with our am-dram gurning and tied-lunatic lurches.)

Thomas and the kids left for the movie before my shift. However, St Foillan's then called again to explain that they did not need the cover after all, and that the first call had been due to an administrative error, so I opted to hang around alone at Littleton Lodge.

I waited for them, wondering: what must it be to live in a home such as this, with a creator of homes such as this? It would be more than ordinary dreams could offer to see love in every lintel, every stairwell, every last nail. I leaned against the wall of his study; the petrol blue paint still smelled of the cost and challenged the eye in just the right way. He was clever. But more than that he knew how to plan for the way lives would be lived within his spaces, how to build, yes, *love* into an angle, to create unity and harmony, or division with a layout – a true domestic God. What power! I imagined myself as part of the house itself, a quiet corner or window. I moved upstairs, smoothing the balcony with my hand. I did not know what had been done or how, but interventions had been made in the original building so that the below flowed into the above without a stutter. I pretended to myself that I was doing my old pausing-to-admire schtick, but I knew I was in fact going straight to where I had to be: Lola's bedroom.

I went in, looking over the made bed, the chair with her stack of ironed clothes that got done by the lady up the road twice a week, the wardrobe and the desk. Tess watched my every move from her frame, the sun lighting up her milk-and-honey mouldings, frozen. I opened the wardrobe door. All the wispy skirts and half-cocked dresses, just smart enough to pour scorn on the mottle-thighed proles, plus a trifle or two of vintage, to my narrowed eyes the whole predictable cache of competitive irony – *Behold my sweet regurgitated rara! My jaunty 10p fedora! I, so young and so untender … and so tediously well-off!* All of it in colours tied to studied trends, the shapes following sanctioned fashions. Uncharitable, perhaps, but clothes that focused so much on the now and the then did little to move me. Whatever the year, my dress had always had something loud to say about sunshine and breasts and hip-to-waist ratios, even at a younger age, even in the coldest weather; moreover, I had never been so slight. Girl should eat more. I leant into the back of the wardrobe, groped and looked down – nothing but oak and dark space. I withdrew, closed the door and moved to her window, to its unobstructed view over the garden. The best view in the house, really. She was loved. Did she know it?

Finally, I did what I had come to do. I opened her bedside table and sifted. What was inside? Pens, coins, a phone charger, a plastic-sheathed tampon, a couple of hairbands, a notepad, five or six GoGo chocolate bar wrappers, an empty purse maybe. Girl's mess that did not invite.

Next drawer down: hairdryer, brush, dental floss, that sort of thing. Diet pills (ah!) half empty, more tampons, B vitamins, a few unused soaps, hair oil, foot cream. More debris denoting female effort.

I straightened, looked at the dressing table. Not sure why it caught my eye; perhaps it was the only exposed hint of disorder in that cleaner-controlled room. Peeking out from the third drawer down was the corner of a patterned head-scarf. I reached for it, pulled the drawer out. The headscarf billowed up into a silken cloud of ironic paisley. There was a small block of something underneath it. I dug my fingers under, pulled and … yes, Golden Kings cigarettes. We smoked the same brand. If Thomas had the first idea … I planned to have a word, put her straight. A drawer of secrets, then. More scarves – none I could imagine her wearing – and when I pushed through to the bottom, a blue book; an A4 exercise book with a dolphin postcard taped to the cover. The dolphin in its sea was a similar blue-grey so that it seemed as if the creature were swimming out at you from the depths of an ocean which was balanced upon the word HAWAII. Also on the book's cover, in large neat underlined capitals:

DONE LISTS

There was one entry – DONE LIST 1 – several pages long.

I read it; of course I read it. And then I smiled, dropped my head.

Just a child, I reasoned. A girl alone with her pen and her angry, angry words. I got it, we all needed an outlet. Angry child, angry words. Love would win.

Everything was wrapped, wedged and replaced. Five minutes later the three of them were pulling into the drive. I had texted Thomas about the cancelled shift; Stevie almost skipped to me in his KAFOs.

'Stevie, careful.'

Lola did not look at me. She would not meet my eye and when I examined Thomas he also seemed to be holding tense words an inch behind the jawline. Our backs to the kids, my expression asked him the question; he responded with the slightest shake of the head.

We readied ourselves for bed. I listened to one message – it was always the same one – then I deleted the seven missed calls, put my phone on vibrate as usual. Enough already.

'So now, what was that earlier?'

'What do you mean?'

'The atmosphere.'

'Nothing.'

'Really? But—'

'The kids had bickered a bit, that's all. Nothing big, everyone's just tired.'

It did not take a mother to know that his sixteen-year-old girl and my five-year-old boy would get nowhere near arguing, but I said nothing more.

Soon we were locking limbs around each other, never *that* tired, not then. But even as we stroked our bodies brighter and pushed on through to that grasping, eyes-shut, giving, gasping place where no child could ever find us, I wondered. Lola had *changed*.

It was as if she could read, in my eyes, what I had read in her room. But of course she could not and, in the end, I did not let it keep me from tumbling into the grave-deep sleep of the satisfied woman.

When I woke, I felt the childish urge to skip the whole breakfast routine and slip us out of the door. But Lola was the teen, and moody by definition. I was not. I swung out of bed, leaving Thomas to snore, went downstairs to my bag to get my phone and – before I had tripped the wire that triggered the brain-alarm '*Stop, in the name of your flaws*' – I was reaching for the pack of cigarettes, giving it a hopeful shake. I had been almost certain it was empty, but in fact it contained one final stick of tobacco. I ran the cigarette along my upper lip as I breathed it in. I weighed it in my pinch. I rolled it between thumb and finger. I held it between my lips, closed my eyes and waited for the dirty billow of longing to overwhelm me. It did not come. Moved by this lack of feeling – triumphant even – I dropped the packet into the dustbin.

Over breakfast, silence was broken only by exasperation. A wall-faced Lola, with 'Screw You, Darling' graffitied all over her. Stevie upturning his bowl in a rage because his KAFO had got wedged between the chair and table:

'They so annoy me, Mummy!'

Thomas soothed us all but my embarrassment soared as the milk dripped to the floor and then, after a quick wipe around, I gathered my son so we could totter – *clack-clack* – out of their smart door and drive home.

'No, she totally hates me, I'm serious. Huh-*ates* me!'

That weekend I pretended not to listen through the old serving hatch as Lola complained into her mobile for long minutes, muffled by a cushion; you could make out the tear stains on the silk. I sprinkled radishes through the all-Littleton Lodge salad. The lettuce, cukes and curlicues of pea shoots made a fine bed in their bowl. I'd left Thomas and Stevie in the garden, devouring the pièces de resistance: cherry tomatoes plucked straight from the vine.

'I know, how could she say that to Jess and not have told me?'

I figured she had to be talking to Ellie. I tore up a few more butterhead leaves, picked five minutes before from the Waite patch. Lola went on:

'Ellie Motte-Ryder is a complete and utter bitch.'

I rummaged for a jug, found one so well designed that it almost annoyed. I glugged some olive oil into vinegar, added mustard, seasoned and whisked. She had not seen me, could not hear me, did not know I was there.

'I can't believe she said that!'

It still needed parsley. I slipped out of the back door to the herb garden, snapped a stem or two and crept back in.

'No ... Oh my God, did she? Well just kill me now.'

The herbs in a colander, I turned on the tap, only for the water to explode in a great gush.

'Hello?' she called.

'Only me,' I said.

'Got to go,' she told her phone.

No time to waste. I walked into the sitting room where she was curled up under a throw, limbs unstirred as if under a layer of custard, no matter that the windows were open and it was 78 degrees outside.

'Can I get you anything, Lola?'

'No thanks.'

'Nothing at all?'

Darling White is rude. She'll get fuck-all of me.

Lola did not speak, stared straight ahead.

'Nothing?' I repeated.

'Perhaps a new life?' She would not be seen to cry, refused, but her voice caught, a downward glance.

'Ah, now ...' I moved closer, ready to sit. 'Why don't you tell me about it?'

She raised a hand before her face, hiding her eyes, blocking me out.

'Actually, just a hankie would—'

'Sure, let me get you one.'

I hurried back to the kitchen; I had to keep trying. I loved to care. Nursing was love – that simple and that complicated – love, time-stamped and dished out to strangers. Caring for your sick child could be similar but it did not vary with precisely the same frictions and erosions and unwanted quickenings and surprise softenings, with the rough incidents that abraded you when tending the wounds of the unknown many. Your love for your child was relentless, and joyous, and painful. But all of it – nursing, caring, loving – there was nothing better, nothing else I ought to be doing with my life.

Grabbing my handbag, I pulled hard at a corner of cotton and there, once again, was a packet of cigarettes that I did not remember buying, was sure I had not bought. The box was light. I shook it, flipped it open and there, once a-bloody-gain, lay a lonely smoke.

Ah, got it now, Lola. Her Golden Kings, all of them, were for me.

I snatched up the hankie, pinched the cigarette between my fingers, held it high and walked back into the sitting room.

'Why are you giving me these when I'm trying to give up?'

She said nothing.

'Why, Lola?'

She shifted so that her feet tucked further up under the creamy blanket and lowered her gaze to the floor.

'You seemed really stressy without them. Just trying to help.'

'That's the only reason?'

She looked me in the eye. Looked away.

'OK ... Well, thanks for the support, or whatever, but I need to kick these things. I will quit, too. Here.' I passed her the hankie.

'Thanks.'

'And don't you even think of trying it.'

'No way,' she advert-flicked her hair to one side, patted an eye. 'That's never going to happen. I'm not stupid.'

'Well, that's fine but—'

Clack-clack. Stevie was coming in, with Thomas close behind.

'Mummy, we've got tomatoes for the salad, look!'

'Thanks, sweetness.' I got up, trying to give Lola an 'our secret' look. She was staring at her nails.

'Let me show you, Mummy. Let me show you the plants, let me—'

'OK, OK,' I said, with a sunny nod at Thomas. 'Someone's had a lot of fun! I'm coming.'

I turned back to Lola once more, but with a wave of her wrist she had already commanded the TV to amuse her. We three walked up the garden. Quite some garden too; long and wide beyond anything I had ever imagined when I had first walked down this street. A lavender farewell by the kitchen door, alongside pots of herbs: rosemary, purple-afroed chives, thyme, mint, a stately bay tree. We walked on, passing the shed, through lawns fringed with a whole production of blooms, past the willow tree and onwards until there, before we reached that murderous pond, we breathed in the must of tomato plants.

Stevie tugged me closer to what was left of them. 'Here, Mummy.'

'They're beautiful, aren't they?'

'I wish we could live here so I can eat them every day.'

I said, 'I'll buy you some nice tomatoes, sweetie.'

'But I want these!'

Thomas was saying nothing. My eyes must have spoken despite me, and the look he gave answered at perfect pitch, did not shout, did not whisper.

'Can I dig a muddy pool?'

Thomas laughed. 'Sure, why not? I'll get a trowel.'

I chose that moment to leave them in the sunlight, Stevie sitting straight-legged on the grass in his dew-smeared KAFOs, with Thomas making a whole mudpit of mess in the place where his good things grew, and all for my boy.

Unwatched, I wandered back towards the house with sassy step, arms swinging free, pausing only to lean into the boundary shrubs and pick a trumpet of buddleia. Black and a flash of crimson fluttering out: a Red Admiral weaving up into the sky, first I'd seen for years.

I moved through the French windows into the cool of the kitchen. Lola's phone drawl drifted to me, a sharp note in the August air:

'Yeah, she's still around. And her son ... I know ... Yeah, she's basically a pretty big slut.'

My foot paused mid-step. I was rinsed down by disgust and anger, all washed over by something icier: cold shame. Shame that I had even tried with her, shame that I had failed. I turned and grabbed my handbag from the counter, slipped into the dining room, ducked sideways through the conservatory, out of the side gate. I had to have it.

I ran, a mad tiptoed sprint, halfway up the road. Just a couple more final puffs.

Her conjuror's trick cigarette glowed as I lit it. Lola knew, she had always known. The fags weren't some anarchic take on Girl Guide charity. She was a Millennial, she had been told her whole life that the nasty things were multi-talented killers. I inhaled deep.

First the cellar, then this. She clearly wished me a slow death.

Almost impressive. Not too shabby; no sugar-candy Mandy, this one. But dislike could do more damage than tooth-rot. No matter, *la!* I would sure as hell win her over.

One, one coco full basket.

She would change. We would be just fine in the end, Lola and I. Because that was how it was going to be. Love wins.

On the Monday evening, I engineered an excuse to stay over at Littleton Lodge when Stevie was with Demarcus and Thomas was dining with clients. I needed time alone with Lola. I would cook for us.

Food, though, was turning from my gift into our battle-ground. Most days Stevie ate anything, but Lola? She *was* a tricky one. That night I offered her spaghetti, with either bolognese or a tuna and tomato sauce, but she 'wasn't feeling' pasta, so I offered grilled chicken and potatoes, but she wasn't feeling chicken, or potatoes, so I offered a sea bass fillet, not feeling it, sausages, nah, sirloin steak, nah – she wasn't feeling any meat at all. By this time I was feeling the need for air, so – *back in a minute!* – I left her in front of the TV and grabbed my bag, which now held a fresh pack of cigarettes, put there by me alone.

I smoked. Then, with my deliberate failure already stale in my mouth, I hit upon a meat-free inspiration: everyone loved my Caribbean vegetable curry. I aimed for Pattie's West Indian Food Store a few streets away, bought what was needed and wandered back.

There was no sign of Lola downstairs.

I snatched up a knife and cut out the scowling. There would be no asking, nor pleading; no telling, no pandering now, just dinner on a plate. I needed to calm my blood and get this sauce to bubble; it would taste almost as good from Thomas's overpriced pot. I diced the onion fast – *chuk-chuk-chuk* – grated the ginger, then fried them together nice and slow. I whistled as I chunked up the vegetables, inhaled a savoury puff which seared my skin as I poured liquid over. A breather.

I padded to the back door. Time for the flavours to mix themselves up, for it all to meld together and break down a touch. I considered another cigarette but remembered Lola's gift of suffering and pushed the urge aside, for now. I went back to the hob, added coconut milk, stirred and covered.

Soon come.

After at least twenty minutes, I decided to seek her out upstairs.

Lola was in her room. She was sitting up on the bed, Facetiming some friend, and when she looked up I saw it: that naked, honest hatred that she had not been quick enough to hide. So then, Lola.

I stood, rock steady, in her bedroom doorway until she killed the call.

'I'm making a Caribbean vegetable curry for you …'

'I'm not really feeling—'

'What aren't you feeling now Lola?' I said. 'Curry? Vegetables? Or simply the Caribbean?'

A twitch at her mouth. 'Well. No. I was just going to say I wasn't feeling that well.'

'Oh,' I said. I waited for the sympathy to come, but it did not.

Two seconds passed. Three.

Then from cool flat nothing the magnesium sparked and flared, and Lola reheated a smile:

'Hey, want to see my new skirt? Try it on if you like!'

It was a black and turquoise patterned mini, and it was pov-chic and it was witty-tacky and it was small as hell; it would never have fitted over my rounded old black backside, even at her age. She threw it down on to the bed, a polyester gauntlet.

I did not rise, I did not move; I paused, made admiring noises.

'So yeah,' she said. 'Not bad for High Desford.'

'It's lovely, Lola,' I said. 'Anyway, I'd better check on dinner.'

'I told you.' That hot metal stare. 'I'm not that hungry.'

I met her long gaze, eye for eye. A flexing of time, and of wills.

'OK then.'

I walked out of the room. Lola got up and followed. I stopped by the stairs; she stopped.

'What?' I said.

She moved closer.

A loud purr, gravel. A car. Lola edged me forward along the landing, seeming to hear something that made her cry out:

'Why? Why do you need to be like that?'

'Like what?' I said, literally on the back foot.

'You act like you hate me the whole time!'

She was shouting now, a full-throated yell.

'What? You can't be—'

'It's true! No. You talk like you like me, but—'

'Lola!'

'You—'

'Lola—'

'Hi, Darling!' called Thomas.

And, poor silly girl, in that one weird second she heard not Darling, but darling, and she rushed to the top of the stairs.

'Hello?' called Thomas.

But I was still moving forward and she pushed, pushed at me, then more shouting, screaming, a heart-jerking lurch – she was *screaming?* – and then my arm flew out somehow, anyhow, but she flailed, flew backwards.

Down she fell, a tripping, twisting, puppet's dancefall right down to the bottom of the stairs.

I looked at Lola lying there, one arm up in a question mark above her small fair head, one arm down, legs bent. A beautiful catastrophe: her broken swastika of a body.

Lola

DONE LIST 2

You've got to be joking, right?

They'd been together for a few days and he wanted to fucking marry her? Well, at least that's never going to happen now.

Trust her to try to spoil the most important time of my life, ever. I have the most unbelievable, amazing, freaky-deeky news. We did it. How fucking crazy is that? No one can know. I've always wondered if he felt like that about me deep down and turns out he does. He really does. And the weirdest thing of all is that he does not realise that he is more or less a total god to me. Especially now.

But of course Darling has to ruin my life at the same time. Did she mean to push me down the stairs? What was that? I've told Dad she meant it, of course, over and over … but deep down I'm guessing the silly cow would not have had the bollocks to risk prison over me. I heard Dad coming back and got distracted so, who knows? She may harbour a criminal intent, it happens. OK, so I did sort of want to catch her out, make a scene – but not <u>that</u> much of one! #familiated

Between you and me, kiddos, I might just have got it into my stupid skull that I could try to fly, as high and as far as a bouquet tossed over a bride's head …

Anyway, I'm alive.

I don't want Darling White in this family.

I've tried to do us all a favour, give her the stinky fags she craves. Everybody would win that way. If Dad had caught her smoking, that would have caused a total shitstorm, or at least made him wonder about her. Much better than me grassing her up, which she would have soon wriggled out of.

As for my own medical issues, the reality? Sadly for our situation it was just a bit of a bang, just boshes and bruises, as Dad says. My ankle is sprained but it will get better soon if I don't put weight on it, apparently. Pity. Getting rid of her would be well worth a few broken bones.

What's wrong with everyone? Turns out Anna must have wanted to get with Will herself that night at her party and that's why she didn't want Caro to blow him in her parents' plastic disco tub. Like that should be the main reason!

Anna won't admit it, but how do I know? Because she called me a while back – all upset – to say that, apparently, Ellie and Will have a thing going on that they kept totally quiet, from before Mungojaxx. Ellie told Jess that they were getting serious and that she did not trust me any more. She doesn't trust me! The total bitch must have been lying all those weeks ago when she said Will and I would 'make sense' together. I can't believe that Ellie was going for him when she *knew* how I felt. Anyway, tough, too late now.

What a crap start to the summer. Prizegiving was crap – who cares if I got the Kendal Award for English? No Dovington boys showed up – and the day before was rubbish too. I've had bloating forever and no period to show for it because my cycle's all haywire, just shot to hell. Also, how did I manage to permanently lock myself out of both my internet banking and Facebook in the same hour? I must have tried a hundred versions of *Lolaisafitty#123* this morning while keeping my brain on life support by mainlining that old film Dad says Mum loved, *Four Weddings and a Funeral* (like if I watch enough well-advised jiltings, it might just rub off). I was sure my password was *Lolaisafitty#123* last time. Total mindfart – from now on it's all *fuckadoodled00*.

Seriously: my name's Lola and I'm a crapoholic.

Nothing is the way I thought it would be this summer. It's messed up. Things have to get better when I start college – and I won't miss all that school stuff. And what is even wrong with the teachers? They kept it up to the bitter, annoying end, making us do those 'Leavers' Sessions' a few weeks ago when I had already done my exams and all but got the hell out. We were <u>gone</u>. But no, they dragged us back in to have Jonesie go on about using the internet or crossing the road or whatever #lifelessonsforlosers until he tried to jazz it up with history bant and get all funny about Napoleon and 'divide and conquer' while under the desk we all whatsapped ideas on how he could ~~alli~~ alleviate his obvious ongoing sexual frustration (best suggestion: strawberry jelly and a gimp called Duncan).

And now I've finally left but my freedom's being ruined: that lot think I'm a megabitch because I first told everyone about blowjobgate, screamed it all out laughing at Maccy Ds as planned, and Caro got way over the top upset when she found out because Ellie had freaked at her. Anna, who was every bit as much to blame as me, is playing innocent now so Will doesn't hate her and she's loving it because Ellie is also freezing me out for being a 'stirrer'. Now I know the real reason – Ellie reckoned she and Will were <u>it</u>. She has no idea. Also great to put it all on me, given that they both say all the time that Caro's such a total dick. She clearly wanted a bit of a dick … ~~Anyway, if you don't want people to know you behaved like a complete slut, don't do it, right?~~

Like I said – messed up. But never mind Ellie, or Caro, or even Anna. I've got bigger things to worry about and no one I can tell.

AT was getting on my nerves earlier. There is no point in me going over and over the same old stuff. I barely see the point in what I'm writing, except that not talking about it for an hour every week keeps her in all the grandad shirts she so loves and all the seed snap biscuits (why?) she seems to think her clients (patients) might find both health-giving and non-threatening (hey, a little therapy quiz – if you could be a biscuit, AT, what kind of biscuit would you be? … Oh. Sorry). All of it, a complete waste of space. Just like me – snap.

I used to like Will. OK, bollocks. I really liked Will, I have liked Will Benton for an age. Over eleven months. Ever since he rocked back from a whole summer sailing around the Greek islands looking so tanned he was practically black, about a foot taller and a whole shitheap hotter than anyone else. So sue me: I still really like Will. I want Will Benton. But – and I still can't believe this – he was-or-is sort of with Ellie Motte-Ryder who used to claim to be my best friend and it probably started because their mums sometimes share the school run because of his sister and bloody boys just don't have a clue, do they?

I don't know what to believe. Is he with her or not? He's too old for her, for starters – I'm much more mature than Ellie. They <u>can't</u> be together. I tried to work it into a random chat I grabbed with him outside Maccy Ds, made a joke of it. I said something like:

'So, what you're into Ellie now? My friend Ellie?'

He said: 'Nah. She's a nice girl, but no. Nothing much going on there.'

'Oh yes. You're saving yourself for Caro Francis …'

'I told you, if you say that again I'll—'

'What?'

'Spank you. Oh shit, gotta go …'

Then he wandered off and I realised that Caro, Ellie, Anna and me were all pretty much the same to him, to all of that lot. Interchangeable. Just the Harbrooke Girls.

How the hell can I make myself stand out? How can I make him see me?

Not that he would want me, unless he was very drunk. I mean, my face looks all right with enough make-up on and my hair's OK if I dunk my head in serum, but my figure is way off, just too blah (hey, wonder if Dad would let me swap AT for a personal trainer?) and my shocking lack of tits will, let's face it, render me pretty much loveless forever.

Oh my God, that basically makes me the flip side of the Caro Francis coin! Will might have a point …

No, no way. Got to stop hating on myself, gonna get me some skills. You never know when you might need them #dontstopbelievin #dirtyglee. I've looked online at Freeporn.com to work out how Caro didn't drown when she gave the blowjob, as that might be something I need to know. Your parents never tell you the stuff you really need to know. Your Dad doesn't, anyway. The closest I could find were two women in a pool with this big oily guy. It went on for ages and no one laughed (how can they not laugh?) and they all kept going mmm-mmm but anyone could see it was fake and there wasn't enough of the promised 'underwater action' to show you how to breathe right with a thingy in your mouth and no wonder this stuff has to be free.

I could just ask Caro. Lol.

No, don't want to be like her – a one-off. Got to make Will Benton want <u>me</u>.

Total fucking aArmaggedon. Life is over. Dad's planning to propose tomorrow. He told me when we went to see *Grease* and it was totally unfair because we ended up having this weird hissing argument because of everyone trying to watch the film and having Stevie on the back seat. I don't think he meant to tell me then but he was really stressy and then he just said it. Then the stairs thing happened so I thought that would cool everyone the fuck down. Now he's said he's still going to ask her, tomorrow. He keeps smiling all the time. I feel sick.

You see? He's a dick, but funny. He actually called earlier:

'I know what you've done,' he said.

'I know what you've done,' I said.

'Your nan,' he said.

And we laughed (Will laughs really loud, it's hilarious) and I realised right then just how much I hated Ellie Motte-Ryder.

Maybe I should get a private detective on to her. We hardly know anything about the woman, after all. Where did she come from and what does she want with my dad? Look at them together. I just don't get why that would work. Or maybe I should track her – a quick fiddle with her phone would sort that one out. I don't know, no frickin idea what to do, but I've got to do something.

So boring in bed. I should have suitors coming to fill my room with flowers like they do in black-and-white movies. I think I'll soon invite Anna and Caro and – fuck it – Will over with the other Dovington boys and Jessica's group. They won't bring flowers, but Will could smuggle in some prosecco (or perhaps some of the good stuff smuggled out of his dad's old law textbooks lol). Plus Jess and Caro really get on – Jess has gone Switzerland on this whole thing – so I won't look like such a bitch any more #onelove and Anna would never dare make a move on Will anyway and I'll teach bloody Ellie not to twoface me. Napoleoned all over.

I'm not staying in bed a minute longer, never mind what they say. Dad says Darling's the nurse and they simply want to make me better so this is what I must do, but all <u>she</u> wants to do is <u>feed</u> me. No, I do not want any more chicken, or calypso rice, or callaloo bugaboo whatthefuck. Thanks all the same, but no.

She told me, like it was this big girly secret, that she doesn't always eat all that stuff normally but that coming to us is like coming home. Subtle, Darling.

She's being weird. What's more, she's brought my sickness back on.

Straight after I fell, she rushed down to the bottom of the stairs, told me to lie still and said my legs felt broken. I <u>knew</u> they were both fine. She might have broken her gammy old legs, but I am young and pretty springy. Resilient. I am a dancer (sort of). Only a sprained ankle and bruises and who can say fairer than that? I can't fully put weight on it yet but I can't just lie here any more.

I am so much smarter than she is. I wear her down with any argument. That's because I treat argue like a transitive verb (come at me, English A*) – I don't so much argue with her as 'argue her'. You can see her shoulders droop when I keep it up for just a few minutes.

Know when you are beat, Darling.

Can't stop thinking about that call with Will earlier. He's so different on the phone, he's actually quite easy to talk to when he's not surrounded by all his wanky mates. It's really weird, it's like he got how I felt about everything without me having to say that much. So different from when I last saw him with Ben and all that lot, less up himself imho. I worried about saying too much because I didn't want to sound pathetic, but he didn't seem to think I was a total loser or anything at all. Amazing. Maybe that <u>was</u> all just in my head.

You see?

She's learning (too late, mind) that I <u>matter</u> around here. Dinner tonight was actually not horrific: tuna niçoise, with the fish just seared so it was almost ~~sus~~ sashimi and balsamic vinaigrette on the side, exactly the way I like it. I thought Dad must have got it together for me, but no, it was Darling. Giving up, or sucking up? To thank her I fucked all their plans up nicely for pudding:

'I'm so glad for you guys!'

'What?'

'He asked you, right? To marry him?'

'What … oh! No, I don't think I'm supposed to know yet.'

'Oh, shit, sorry. Awkward! I'm really sorry …'

Oh yes, I'm pretty good at the pratfall, the accidental-on-purpose stumble. Silly bloody mare. Next time I'll argue her so much she'll stab me. Or – as she's probably not actually a gang member – she'll dish out a quick slap. Dad'll still hate her. And no amount of fishy bribery could ever smooth that over – she would have to drown me in balsamic before we waded out of that one.

No, just no. He'll never marry her.

Achievements

1. Already got over leaving school with probably no GCSEs and then probably ruining my life, unless Dad's right and I'm being melodramatic. #winning

2. Shafted the proposal, just in time. I don't want to seem like a heartless bitch, I'm definitely not, but who doesn't get pretty worked up about this stuff? I know I'm not two, but Dads should be married to Mums, end of. In fact, if I hadn't gone and killed my mum then we'd be the perfect happy family.

3. Watched more porn in one day than my dad probably ever has in his life. #accidentalgrossout

4. Did it! Darling said something pathetic about always losing her purse and earrings and stuff and I pretended I cared and said, 'I at least know how to stop you ever losing your phone, give it to me.' And she actually did and gave me her password too when I asked because Dad was standing right there and we were all smiling, and I activated Find My iPhone for her, played around with our phones a bit and then she thanked me! Stupid or what? #familysharing #oldpeoplefails #iseeyoubaby #unironichashtag

5. Argued with Dad until we both cried. (OK, he didn't quite). That <u>never</u> happens. But the whole time he thought I was sulking in my room afterwards, I was on the phone to Will. <u>Yes</u>.

Darling

WEDNESDAY, 10 AUGUST

The poor girl kept saying that she was 'mortified' (her dad's word) that she had spoiled my surprise, but I was too happy to care. I finally understood her, unhappy child. I had seen her book and knew her sorrows and would not need to trouble either again. Leave her to her angst and bother, I had *love*, love at last, to make good.

My babylove, meanwhile, needed me as much as ever. Have you any idea how much it costs to access regular hydrotherapy? A hell of a lot. We had a great girl there, Sally, who was only about nineteen and full of giggles herself, never mind my Stevie. Each Wednesday she put his proximal muscles through their paces and she advised that I should look into getting her on the NHS while we were still in the earliest stages. I told her I would. It was a real postcode lottery when it came to things like funding hydrotherapy, as any DMD family would tell you.

So on such afternoons we changed into our costumes, me as well as Stevie, and I assisted Sally by supporting my son, who hated getting too much water in his face, and filling her in on his progress; together we helped him strengthen his still-good muscles.

That was just one of the special activities Stevie needed. Our weekly list was uncompromising:

- Make sure Stevie does his daily stretching exercises every morning
- Go to the doctors
- Go to swimming classes, Monday and Thursday
- Answer emails and update Stevie's Wonders on his progress
- Give massages to ward off cramps
- Take him to hydrotherapy with Sally on Wednesdays
- Clean and dry the KAFOs
- Coordinate diaries with Ange, the childminder
- Update his health app with calories consumed etc every day
- Avoid fractures
- Read more about Duchenne
- Avoid fractures, avoid fractures, avoid fractures

It was unlikely that Stevie would ever become incontinent, although he did sometimes have trouble getting to the loo fast enough in his KAFOs. If the disease followed the route it normally did – but who knew what breakthroughs might come before then? – then the list would extend to include complex arrangements around ventilation, antibiotic courses and anti-flu vaccination, anaesthetic avoidance, steroid use, standing frames and the management of every last discomfort. Some cases even needed spinal surgery, but I chose not to think about that. Discomforts would be managed, long lists would be completed with love, and that would be enough.

Lola. Dear Lola! Lola was moping in plain sight because she presumed her clunky sabotage (I was no fool) had spoiled my surprise, but quite the opposite. I hated surprises when it came to the most important things of all. I liked to know where I was. So after she spilled the beans, not only did I know – *he wants to marry me* – but I could get that special secret kick out of knowing. I could prepare; become ever-ready and energised, like an old battery about to be put to use. From that day on I intended to walk taller and with that knowing sway that only the luckiest women had reason to adopt as they moved through the world. From that day, some ponderous wheel turned in me that meant I would never smoke again; I breathed in the pristine future. *La!* I would be primed, polished and ready to shout out my love in reply to his question. I did my toenails, my nailnails. I managed my body hair with extra care and monitored every inch of me for readiness. I prepared to be *thrilled*. Every time he pushed back something else, everyone else, in order to spend time alone with me, whenever he suggested a stroll or a dinner, I knew that my stomach would be sure to shiver, to *shimmy*. I planned my proposal-acceptance outfit, my selfie-for-two hair. I was just like Lola, standing on her great stage of the future, except the spotlight was on me, on the two of us and it was *happening*.

A gift of stomach-twisting delight. And all thanks to the lovely Lola.

It was Friday night. I had opted to make my poorly step-daughter-to-be (shh!) a real Jamaican chicken noodle soup. Saturday Soup, my mum used to call it – *but la-la-la it taste gud all week long, Darling!* She made it with a scrawny, scrumptious chicken back, but they didn't grow on trees round here (even if the neighbours' maverick Buff Orpingtons did keep trying to roost in Thomas's horse chestnut). My muscular broth was therefore a next-generation, localised version that used chicken wings, but Stevie knew no better; he loved my Saturday Soup. It *might* have been more than a little delicious, but most of all I think he loved the time it took me to chop hard-arsed vegetables like dasheen and to knead dumplings; time he could spend perched on a high stool at the breakfast bar, watching me cook.

I had planned ahead and got everything I needed from Pattie's that morning. Lola was still in her room. Not that she would have had any urge to descend and see how much love went into my pot, but I cooked as if those silvery eyes were upon me all the same.

I washed a pound of fresh chicken wings in vinegar and cut up chunks of yam, sensual green cho cho – *yuh know to dem Spanish it mean a woman's parts? Serious!* – pumpkin, the dasheen and cassava. I browned pale flesh and diced, chopped and crushed. I stirred. Then, the authentic cheat: a packet of powdered chicken noodle soup chucked into the mix; that was just how it was done. I brought it all to the boil as Stevie coloured in a farmyard scene from his book in which froufrou chickens featured. No moral dilemmas were raised except whether, as the pigs were purple, the cows should be green. Thank heavens for being five.

Down to a simmer. *Soon come.* I skipped the cassava as Pattie was all out – they had gone bad too fast – so I upped the quantity of yam. One Scotch bonnet was thrown in, instead of the advised two. I could hear her, my mother, chanting the same mantra for every single recipe:

Yuh put a likkle bit in, tek a likkle bit out. Mek it yours.

I made spinner dumplings and chucked them into the bubbling pot, gathered Stevie into a hug. Soon enough it was time to finish with coconut milk and serve.

Lord, Darling, it smell gud, *yuh see?*

Though simple, Saturday Soup was one of my best Mum-given gifts. As I prepared to serve it to my step-daughter-to-be, our motherless girl, I knew I was passing on more than nutrients, or piping nourishment, more than the knowledge behind creating an exquisite hot-sweet-sour-salty broth. More than bestowing the time it took to cook it, or care to ensure that vegetables and poultry were of equal succulence. More than my heritage, or even my mother's voice with its kaleidoscopic wisdoms. There were women, and then there were those of us who chopped and blended and stewed together ingredients of all kinds, whatever they might be. Those of us who made the very best of even the butcher's scraps of womanhood. I was telling her to watch and learn.

Later that rainy midsummer evening, we dived with soup spoons into our brackish Caribbean pools. Lola returned to her room straight afterwards, Stevie hung around for seconds and then was enticed up to bed by nothing less than a hot chocolate in the much-coveted 'big-man sippy cup' that Thomas drank coffee from in morning traffic. Peace, and the freshening *pit-pit-pat*. Once it stopped, the two of us sat alone on the terrace in the hot washed air. There were stars out, of course; stars that I liked to think of as clearer and larger, as nearer than normal, wrong though I may have been. He deserved his big stars for us.

We were drinking red wine from the cellar, a label boasting some chateau, some reputable clos, good and grimy. With hushed bursts of laughter and pausing often to marvel, we strolled our memories around the small but dramatic landscape we had created since coming together: the supermarket meeting, the meals out, Lola's fall, my first ever evening here and the now-fixed cellar door. I thought about telling him what she had done, locking me into that dark and dust, now that the time was right – *see, look at us now, no harm done!* But instead I stared upwards and soon we were taking the mickey out of ourselves for how few constellations we could name:

'Orion's belt?' I ventured.

'It doesn't look like that though, does it?'

'It might!'

'I think that would be a pretty tight belt.'

'Maybe he buffed up, went on a diet, or something …'

'Darling,' he stopped us.

And it began.

The words. As they were said, we knew we would be the only ones who would ever hear them. That was important: old magic. I could not ever repeat them; I would not ever share them. They were words that would not just bind us forever though. Nothing so safe and sacred. They were words that made things in me come a bit undone. Words with plain and unequivocal meaning that I could barely comprehend.

'Yes,' I said.

We merged in a kiss, then he pulled away and went to get another bottle of French wine, an older date, a dustier label; he returned barefoot and whistling. It was as if I was fresher to him even than the rain on the grass beneath our feet and this made my heart crack. Not sing, not heal, not soar: crack.

'I have never fucking felt like this,' he said, as he poured.

'Nor me.'

'But we do.'

'Then … "I do."'

Soon we were twisting ourselves around each other, both of our arms and feet the same slate blue by the light of unknown stars. We drank in silence a while longer.

'Hey,' said Thomas, looking up. 'This means we'll be a blendered family.'

'I think you mean "blended", darling.'

'That's what I said, Darling. Just one mixed up, happy mess.'

'Yes.'

Crack. There, in that moment.

'Hey,' he said again, growing more American by the minute. 'We'll need a new house, a better house. One that's right for Stevie …'

'Oh, sweetheart, I would *love* that. But don't stress yourself, we have plenty of time.'

'Why?'

'Well, we'll take a while just to be engaged, then to plan a wedding. No one marries fast with kids, right?'

'We do,' he said.

'Do we?'

He pulled back – the lightest catch of breath – then folded me tighter to him.

'Every moment counts.'

I tried to thank him but the words were too heavy in my throat.

I could not rest though, could not leave it alone. I had lied to myself that I did not mind her puerile scribblings about me; I thought I might somehow be able to ignore the rich source of information about what she had done. But few of us are so strong; I was not. I could not unknow anything, so now I wanted to know *everything*.

Before I had even concluded the thought, I was back there, alone once more in Lola's room while she was at a friend's. Thomas had gone to a meeting and Stevie was consuming some loud entertainment product featuring late teens bouncing around in primary colours.

I could not hold out a moment longer, I needed to know what had been DONE. As I reached down to the drawer, I knocked the make-up mirror, which toppled on its stand, then landed and smashed on the cream surface.

I grabbed for the broken glass, stupid with shock. A second later I felt the pain cut through. I watched as a drop of my blood fell to the floor, soaked into carpet and imme-diately leached outwards.

I gathered myself, ran for a cloth, the stain remover and dustpan, and cleared it up fast. My skin tightened and prick-led and my hearing strained for the familiar *ker-chunk* of the front door.

Seven years of bad luck, in old money. Mum had known them all: the spilled salt, a pinch of which had to be thrown over your left shoulder, the ladders to be walked around unless you were a *foofool*, the spotting of single magpies that could ruin your day and threatened worse still for your life. Superstition, which had fallen somewhere between folklore and religion in our house, was not to be ignored. What bad luck might come, and for whom?

I gave the carpet one last sweep, then finally bent to the drawer. There it was: her DONE LISTS, now with a DONE LIST 2 completed. I read fast, then again.

Then I tucked the book away, knelt on the rectified floor and wondered. The trick would be not to overreact. So, she was following my phone – it hardly went anywhere beyond the town centre and back, nothing to hide on that score. Best not turn off the app, or she might suspect I had read her book. And therefore learn that I had spied upon her unabandoned pleasure in telling herself she had lost her virginity (presumably) to someone – Will himself, was it? It was not entirely clear – as if she dared not quite believe it. Funny, though: the big event did not seem to have slapped a smile on her face anytime that I had noticed.

My phone went again. I checked: my usual caller. I would never block the number. It scared me more not to know when the calls were coming, not to know when I was being contacted. And who knew how far they would go to find me as soon as the calls stopped getting through? No, you had to be tough. If you could not block it or switch off the phone, you had to switch off key parts of yourself instead; that simple.

By the time I rose from my knees, I knew I was up to the challenges ahead. Time well spent, worth a few broken shards. One should always go into a marriage with one's eyes stark staring open.

A blast of sun, a heatwave at last, falling around 21 August, Stevie's sixth birthday. I was on high alert all day – he was hyper, a pent-up danger to himself, a jack-in-the-box tightly coiled, just like his dad. All it had taken was the brief visit from a few of Lola's friends and a couple of licks of the choc-olate buttercream on his cupcake (I had skipped the silver balls – last thing we needed was a trip to the dentist on the hottest day of the year).

My boy loved it all. Unfortunately, he loved the cake and me at the same time, and grabbed me with his chocolatey fingers. Lola laughed out loud, a startlingly natural giggle, and whipped out the phone to capture me next to my son, smears of dark icing on my new yellow dress: we had all given in to his delight. At last. Having opened presents chosen for their limited physical impact, Stevie moved on to shrieking and trying his best to perform a splinted, slow-motion career around the garden.

'Careful, Stevie!'

Laughing, he moved behind the bushes, back towards the miniature orchard of apples, peaches, cherries and pears.

'Relax, Darling,' said Thomas.

'I know, I know,' I said. 'At least we knotted up the swing.'

'Mummy, look!'

Stevie stopped and returned towards us holding out his hand with extreme care, his mouth a silent scream of shock. A&E, I thought, some apocalyptic bump or graze I had just missed.

'Look!' said Stevie.

But no, it was a ladybird resting on the base of his thumb.

'Ladybird, see?'

'Wonderful. Pretty,' I said. 'And did you know? They're lucky.'

'I am lucky, aren't I, Mummy?' said Stevie.

And I coughed hard and nodded; barked with some sudden bad tickle, turning away so that not even Thomas could see my eyes.

Another celebration. Lola whupped all her GCSEs: 10 A*s and a B, Thomas whispered down the phone, while I wondered why he was whispering.

'Come over,' he said. 'She wants fajitas and ice cream, which even I can manage. See you here by seven-ish?'

I brought her flowers, a bright fanfare of tulips, and a not-very vintage mirror, to replace the one I had shattered while dusting. And a congratulations and good luck card, as she was to start at her new college within the fortnight. She was in no mood for any of them:

'How do you know, I could have failed everything?'

'Your fa—'

'Of course she knows, Lola,' said Thomas. 'Now be happy, you should be really proud.'

'Hmm,' and she left the room. I could see my own face in her mirror.

'Gutted about the B,' he said low. 'Ten A*s and all she's talking about is the B in Physics, I mean … you know.'

'Kids are so tense, these days,' I said as the front door went.

'Gone for a walk, clear her head,' he said. 'She's also scared about starting college, don't forget.'

Lola returned and we tried to enjoy the fajitas, even as she tried not to. Neither of us needed to say out loud that it was not a night for me to stay over, so Thomas dropped Stevie and me back to my house. Third along in the row of squat terraces. Didn't look much from the front, but there were flowers somewhere in the darkness and I had only just painted the gate.

Thomas had already pulled away again by the time we walked in and I saw that our kitchen window, around the back, had been smashed.

'Stevie! Wait, stay there …'

The black hole gaped at us, a jagged sneer. Light. Should I put it on? Would they spring dazzled from corners, attack us – were they here?

I forced my arm to move and reached back for Stevie, standing in the already lit hallway.

Lights. I pressed the switch, turned, and saw it. There was a red mass near the table, among the shattered glass.

A cricket ball. It had come through our window and rolled into the far corner. We backed on to the smallest edge of the smallest park, Addlington Road Rec. I phoned Thomas:

'Our window, someone's smashed it.'

'What?'

'There's a cricket ball so—'

'Oh, fine. Listen, stay there, I'm coming back.'

He stayed on the phone with me for the five minutes it took him to turn around and collect us. Although I was failing to recall one time I had seen the assorted ruffnecks in the park putting down their spliffs to bowl a single over, by the time we were settled once more at Littleton Lodge we had decided to call the glaziers rather than the police.

At last, a kind surprise: we were to marry on 24 September 2016, just three months after our meeting outside the supermarket.

'Insane,' I had said when he told me that we could use a client's country estate, that the folly had a licence for weddings, and that there had been a cancellation and wasn't that so completely perfect because he loved me *à la folie*. And it *was* perfect because I understood enough French for that, but still I had breath enough to say:

'It will barely have been three months. Are you sure?'

'Never been surer.'

'In three weeks! Can we—'

'We can.'

'But—'

'Just the people we need to be there. Or the four of us. You're in control.'

Nothing more. He was giving me everything:

'I don't deserve you.'

The dress was a cinch, I had always known the one I would get. From the bridal boutique in the Old Town; a size too large around the waist, but otherwise perfect. It was taken in, accessorised at first with only anglicised amounts of bling, soon increased to more Jamaican levels – more diamonds, more white gold, more diamanté, sparkly shoes from London – when I felt Mum peering down in dismay at my dull taste. *La-la-la!* she would have cried. *Spice it up a bit, girl!* A bit of twinkle also mesmerised a restless, whining Stevie.

The next part was the hardest: who to invite. Thomas was easy – his mum lived in the Idaho nursing home minutes from where his dad was buried; she wandered along disinfected corridors hoping she might end up in England on days when she remembered where she was from. His sister thrived in New Zealand but, despite having three children under five, was no more a masochist than an air-mile millionaire so would not come back for years yet; no one else of the same blood mattered. Friends could come, could not come; Thomas insisted that he would have all he wanted either way.

Not so easy for me. I had told him: no mother, father, sister or brother. I had friends, of course, but those for whom I cared most were scattered. Then, through vexing tears, I told him that I had in fact lost touch with all wider family. *We* had to be our own nest. No, I did not want lesser-spotted aunties chirruping around me when my own mum and dad had so long ago fallen off their perch. As for my friends, I could not risk seeing an ounce of doubt, disbelief or cynicism in the eyes of those who should be wishing us well; I might buckle, even under just an ounce of it.

On I wept as Thomas held me, listening and still. I had been sure, anyway, that neither of us were worried about drawing up lists of attendees. We were dizzy with ourselves; wanted only us, witnesses and us, no one else to exclaim their judgements – So soon! So fast! So black! So white! So, kids? None of it, not on our day.

Just us.

I used the invitations that he had bought in our wedding colours – ackee (or dry prairie) yellow and Idaho sky (or Caribbean Sea) blue – as a wedge to prop up my uneven table back at my house and we invited only his neighbours, Guy and Allie, as witnesses. An acclaimed potter and an actor, each more talented than sane, they tended to appear over the fence during the odd crisis moment in their creatively lived suburban lives. Thomas and me marrying would make the merest colourful dot for one day, a single Hirst spot to roll into the corner of their wall-sized Caravaggio. Guy could double as our photographer, being a visual type. Sorted.

In three weeks we would be one.

The Thursday before the wedding I had a hair appointment. Having endured a nondescript weave for a while, I decided I wanted to go back to my roots for my wedding; literally to the scalp, with long, narrow braids surging from it. I had always liked them: the visual drama, the Medusa connotations, the sheer amount of female skill and effort that went into creating each plait – I sometimes had a sisterhood of one Trinidadian, two Ghanaians and a Bajan working my head all at once – the femininity was woven into you, the cultural history made part of you. Plus, it really was just fun to whip them around your head all day long.

Nothing less would do for my wedding day. Plaits were the don of hairstyles. However, the elaborate do tended to attract unseemly interest: strangers, people on buses and manning tills would reach up unprompted and touch my hair.

'Happens, innit?' agreed Trish, lead plaiter for the day. 'Get ready. We gonna make you look *fresh*!'

I was right in the window, my least favourite seat. All High Desford could walk by and watch me getting my hair done. Part of the beauty of transformation lay in its mystery, a fact that I wanted to yell at the young men who walked up to the window, tearing at burgers and proceeding to stare at me like I was ITV.

'Bugger off!' I mouthed at them.

They were lucky I was not Trish, who had slipped away to get a better comb. Trish was fierce. Trish would chase them down the street and bawl them out until they begged for a beating instead.

They must have sensed it, as when she neared the plate glass they wandered off, trailing stale mince, masticated bun and the aroma of half-baked disappointment.

I had, since my teens, been amazed by the hoohah surrounding the fertile black female. We were seen as either-ors: diva or drudge, Dahomey Amazon or post-colonial night nurse, lightning rods for the whole ho/madonna issue. We were each of us a continent of contention.

'Lena! Joy! Ameyo!' yelled Trish. 'Our two o'clock's arrived – bring me the good scissors and some more Pink Oil.'

Our hair alone was the most politicised on the planet – how does she wear it? Like she wants to be white? Like she's blacker than night? Is it real? Is *she* for real? Who does she think she is? And how can we tell her that she's not it?

And oh, our bodies! They were a battleground, but one all too often advertised – not least by ourselves, and a drop more than the rest of the multicoloured ocean of modern women – as a holiday destination. We were touted as dark recreation: a hilly climb of big bums, big tits, big lips – a caricatured sex safari in this porno age. Or maybe a meaty foreign takeaway. And did you want fries with that? I might be from Basingstoke but to some, black and white, men and women alike, I was Mother Africa on her knees.

Much later, Trish raised a mirror to the back of my head:

'There you go, all done. Beautiful. Gosh, man, can't believe you're getting *married!*'

'Am I exotic?' I asked Thomas back at home, head sore after six hours of talented pulling. 'To you?'

'Yes,' he said. 'Exotic. Erotic. Erratic … and just *you*, and I love it. Why?'

'Oh. Nothing,' I said, exhaling. The worst answer would have been the lie. His honesty was the special sauce on life's all-beef patty, and that night his loving eased me until way past midnight.

Saturday. Wedding day. Stevie was in his tiny suit and wet-wiped KAFOs and Lola slouched in a peach bodycon number she had insisted on pulling on at the last minute; she would end up looking naked in the photos, or disappearing altogether.

On a warm September day we stood by a folly that was weeping flowers, set in a garden that stretched on and on. Lovely to excess; I swayed when I saw it. My dress, which pooled into a satin sweep on the ground, had a low cutaway back, something I had never worn before. In wearing it I offered him an untouched part of myself; no one would ever know me more.

Yuh gon marry a man yuh jus buck up on inna supermarket? Yuh tek care now, yuh jus be careful.

The ceremony was to be short and secular. The air was taut, suspended.

The vows did not in themselves make me cry. The words were good and right and true; nothing could make me want to smile more. But when I thought about it, stood right inside the fact that Thomas had secured a full seventy acres of green space to surround us – trillions of well-anchored grass roots and who knew how much lucky clover? – then the waters rose and my throat worked harder. I looked at Lola and saw that she too was crying and this made Stevie cry and next thing Thomas's eyes did not look so dry either. All of us, weeping by our lake – on this sunniest of days, the dampest wedding of all time!

We walked back up the long drive, just the two of us, with Stevie and the others going ahead on some glorified golf buggy, draped with bunting and chains of silver bells. The diamanté Converse tucked under my dress had been a last-minute decision, but a good one.

'So, Mrs Waite,' he said.

'So, husband,' I said.

'You are so … *God.*'

'You look exactly like you did on the day I met you.'

'What, twelve weeks ago?'

'Uh-huh,' I said. 'Taken aback and terrified. Happy. But definitely terrified.'

'Because I just *knew* ...'

'Yeah, right.'

We laughed ourselves quiet again, frightened of breaking whatever it was that had woven itself about us with our vows.

'I did know,' he said.

'I love you,' I said. That inaugural moment: the first time I had gone first.

'I love you, Darling.'

A kiss. Then:

'And I have a surprise for you!'

I tried not to jolt as he pulled me close and whispered it with a few pecks, kissed it into my hearing, but it happened anyway. By the time we had walked back, twenty-five of our 'loved ones' would be there, waiting to celebrate our union.

'But—' I said.

'I know! You said no family, and mine can't travel anyway,' he said. 'But. Every wedding needs a party.'

'But,' I said. 'I have no family and my friends aren't—'

'Relax,' he said. 'Husband here. It's mainly my closest colleagues and friends, now *our* friends; just those who insisted on being here to see us happy.'

'But—' I said once more.

My phone, in my ivory clutch, began to buzz.

This was it. Now, here, this was it.

'Oh God.'

Thomas stopped walking, reached out his arms to pull me to him.

'I didn't mean to—'

'Wait! Please.'

I fumbled for the phone, my French-manicured finger-tips faltering as it vibrated.

'Sorry, someone's trying to—'

'Who, today? Leave it.'

I nodded and pulled out my mobile.

I was moments from the collapse.

'Darling?'

'It's fine, I just—'

'Forgive me. I knew you would fret if you had to arrange it yourself. But how could I miss the opportunity to show off my bride in that incredible dress. Look at you!'

In seconds everything would unravel. But he looked so glad, so proud I could say nothing but:

'Thank you.'

Thomas held open the door of Haresfield Manor's main reception room. I walked in, not to shouts of 'surprise!' but to the curious and well-meaning faces of Thomas's acquaintances: mostly white couples, a young Indian family and one portly Ghanaian lecturer.

I scanned every face. No sign.

I breathed out in a thin stream: not here, not yet. No worthy bride could begrudge her other half this celebration, not with 'Celebrate' actually playing through the surround sound and Stevie raising and lowering his superlegs in time to the beat all over the dancefloor. I pushed Thomas towards his clapping colleagues. He had not wanted to keep a secret, or even risk a surprise; he had only wanted to create memories for me, for all of us, without creating stress with the finicky details.

I looked about me and, pausing only to nip into the restrooms and swap the trainers for kitten heels, I tried. It should not have been so hard; there was all that managed delight, that polite bliss all about us. The excitement of the wedding reception was meant to prepare you for the abundance of family life, they said. But we were already living that so the night was, I had decided, more of an affirmation within Thomas's – now our – circle. That we were a we, and they were a they, and we were all of us an us.

At least for one night.

My phone buzzed again and this time, emboldened by bridal champagne, I did turn it off. I could never be found here, in this grand and distant house.

'Your wedding day,' I told the mirror above the sinks, and turned to go back into the room.

Stevie was charming everyone. He was pumped on icing and kept dancing and leaning to the right and wobbling to the left and guests flinched and raised hands to their mouths until everyone learned that he was just having a bloody good time. Lola missed the near-impromptu speeches – who had ordered speeches? – and seemed to be having an evening-long make-up crisis in the loo. The speakers crackled now and then and the top tier of fruit cake – *Only tree week til yuh marry im? Yuh goh soak the fruit in rum as soon as yuh stop saying yes, yuh see?* – had slid an inch off the base layer of chocolate sponge in transportation. But I told myself to remember that this was love à la folly, a ridiculous, beautiful eighteenth-century rotunda of a folly, which had no doubt been amazed to find itself all gussied up with *syringas* for Idaho and *lignum vitae* for Jamaica, and that it was a kind of fuck-me-love-you-forget-them-here's-to-us sort of a day.

I tried to forget my silenced phone.

We celebrated like every bride and groom we had spent three weeks planning not to be. We ate from the manor's Elysium Package menu; we toasted and were toasted, we drank and were drunk. At midnight, we nearly forgot to catch our long-distance taxi ride home. The new Waites. We had gone off-message; become all cheese, euphoric. A happy family, putting down the tips of radicle roots that could break rocks.

We departed to waves of well-wishing from a small sea of strangers. My buoyant husband led us out, his daughter drifting behind him. And Stevie, swimming in exultation: the happiest life of my day.

I checked my face in my phone camera, to make sure I really was here. There I was. A glossed-up, glitterish front-page bride, a cut-out-and-keep best version of me. I wanted it to last forever.

Lola

DONE LIST 3

Nightmare over. And just begun.

It was never supposed to happen. None of this was supposed to happen. She was never supposed to go through with it. I'm still in shock.

Who has fucking wedding chicken these days? No one. I know that and I've never even been on a restaurant date yet, unless you count Maccy Ds, not like all those amazing places Dad gets all fancied up to take her to. Chicken. Why not serve it in cardboard buckets with a ketchup sachet while she's at it? I don't mind that she's black but I do mind that she's such a fucking cliché.

What a wedding. I could not believe that my dad had invited even one of his and Mum's friends to their stupid reception. What was he thinking? No one wants to see some old guy clinging on to a big ugly embarrassing mistake while his daughter watches, no one.

It's not as if the guests were even their family. Where were all the black people? Not even a brother or sister. Thought they all had a load of brothers and sisters, but the woman has no family. Absolutely none, not adults anyway. That is meant to be a black thing, isn't it? ~~Hey ma sista blahblah-blah.~~ No, fuck it, forget it. I don't like what she does to my head.

The oldies totally missed the point. They think I cried at their wedding because it was all so lovely, because Darling was so beautiful, because I was so happy to have a mother figure at last, because we were so blown away to now be a family and ten more different colours of steaming crap.

I did cry, but not for that.

I cried because I could not believe my dad – my dad – would go ahead and marry someone like that.

I cried because none of it was fair, or right, or asked for.

I cried because I would be kept outside of everything important again.

I cried a little, at one point, because I nearly chipped a tooth on a sugared almond. Hey, DW, if you were a wedding favour … #clichémeup

I cried because I could – now, why now? – finally picture my mum's face, outside of photos, when I still sometimes panic that I have forgotten how to see her. And she looked hugely pissed off.

I cried because I did not believe in love any more.

I definitely did not cry because of the way dear Darling's discount dress shimmered in the rapturous sunlight, setting off the crystals cascading down her bloody bodice …

I was just really fucking unhappy. I even called AT from the loos.

I realise now that Will was the person I should have called first.

Harrowing. Just so you know, kids. Don't do it.

Will called me, again! This time it was nothing to do with Caro or Ellie or all that, he just wanted to talk to me.

'I've been thinking about you,' he said.

I couldn't believe it, I said something completely stupid like:

'Really?'

And then he said he had heard my dad had gone and married the black woman.

Then – it was amazing – he said exactly this:

'You don't deserve it. You're too fucking gorgeous to have to worry about all this bollocks, seriously.'

I said I wasn't and he said:

'Oh come on, you're fit as. I've got bloody eyes.'

And I didn't know what to say so I said:

'Thank you.'

We talked a bit more about our summer plans and the other festivals coming up but the whole time I could hardly talk straight. Gorgeous – fuck, did he actually call me 'gorgeous'? We chatted on and I was worried he was getting a bit bored until I said:

'You'll never guess what she's called.'

'No idea.'

'Darling White.'

'Ha! You're taking the piss, right?'

'No, unfortunately. Although technically she is now Darling Waite.'

'Mm, technically,' he said. 'Don't worry, babes, stay strong. Listen gotta run, OK? See you later.'

And he rang off and I just sat for a bit, thinking.

Oh my God, Will Benton thinks I'm gorgeous.

Everyone thinks they are being such <u>devoted</u> parents, not going on a honeymoon.

But honeymoons were made for people with kids who do not, ever, want to hear their parents screwing. For the love of God, Dad, go already. #endthetrauma

I hear them having sex all the time, here in our house and I tell them, all the time 'you kept me up last night' and I ask them, 'Why don't you go out for a change?' It just doesn't work. I know Mum is not here, I know that, but she may as well be – all the things from their time together are still here, all over the place, hoping for lifelong protection. And I'm here and I'm part of her and they're always up there, going <u>over the top</u> together. It's like Darling <u>wants</u> me to hear them, but I can't believe that's true, or <u>I'm</u> screwed.

People think that bulimia is a laughing matter. It is <u>not</u>. It sounds like a good idea, at first, if you want to get slim and not change a thing. That's just how it gets you. Personally, I used to think of it as 'the lazy girl's diet'. The foolproof, have-your-cake-eat-it-and-lose-it-again regime. No matter that your stomach's sore and you can't even taste the chocolate or chips or scotch egg or whatever for the panic washing around your gums, the gross bitter taste of digestive juices and total <u>fear</u>. You will have to rid yourself of it soon or it will be too late. It will all have been for nothing, worse than nothing, a big step backwards, another horrible pound on. Then the scales lie anyway and you've gone up two pounds because you are bloated and retaining water, so you have to eat more – until you are virtually sweating out the calories – to throw up more, get more sore and bloated and then you end up needing the <u>release</u> when all you wanted was to be thin and pretty, never mind 'gorgeous'. Nothing funny about that.

Wow, was I in a bad mood before! #stopthepityparty. I've just given Will a call – he does seem to like talking to me, I don't know what I waited for all this time. We chatted for ages. He gets the whole Darling thing and said it must be really quite shit for me now. I said it was and he went, 'It's fucking outrageous. Babes, are you OK?' And because he asked like that I got all teared up and said 'No'. Then he said, 'I wish I could do something to make you happier.' And I laughed instead and said, 'That would be good, don't suppose you could kill Darling for me, could you?' and we joked about that for a while, just some dumb stuff. He's <u>so</u> funny and he kept calling me 'babes'! I think we really could become a thing. OMG I can't even think about it.

So yes, I need to cheer the hell up. Like AT says, I can choose what becomes of me and what I do with my life. #inowpronounceyoumrsbenton #asif. Seriously, I already have a fair idea of what I want most of all, which is not a bad start. But for now, do not adjust your sets, kids, here's what I have DONE:

Achievements

1. Managed to hear not a single wedding speech by pretending I had a crisis with my eyeliner, my hair, my period, my shoes. It would have made me puke (lol) to hear Dad going on and on about that woman.
2. Lost the homage-to-KFC wedding breakfast. Also my Sunday lunch and a midweek dinner or two. Missed some

lunches at college: that's my new college, the place no one here cares about because of the bloody wedding and because it's free. It's OK. No really.

3. Only just stopped myself from running screaming on to Hotels.com waving Dad's credit card, on at least 27 occasions this week. #ifyoudontgetaroomiwill

4. Talked on the phone to actual Will Benton for over half an hour this week in total. Even managed to flirt, pretty badly. This is unheard of.

5. Decided what I have to do. Need to stay strong. Finally stopped crying.

PART II

Darling

My first week as a step-mother saw Lola staking out our shared territory as hostile ground. I waved white flags, made peace offerings. I tried to weave in and around her and her father's lives like a colourful ribbon, and to give generously of myself and a well-managed Stevie. Nonetheless we remained unwanted.

'Ohmigod, what *is* this programme?'

'Actually, no, I'll be at Chloe's for dinner, I did say.'

'Really, do people still wear those?'

'It's OK, you wouldn't get it.'

'Urgh, gross.'

'Joking!'

'No, I didn't mean it like that.'

Snip, snip, snip and soon the ribbon was in shreds.

'How *do* you wash your hair, anyway?'

I cut back: 'You know: shampoo. Water. Washing.'

'Oh. Right. I like it, though.'

If the snippety sentiments were bad, then proof of premeditation was worse.

The execution was often faultless. My innocent glass of red wine, which had been resting on a side table for a moment, was somehow knocked over when I popped to the loo, marking the carpet beyond repair and marking me out as a clumsy liar.

Music which had always been played at a reasonable volume or on headphones was now, whenever Thomas left the house, played over the house speakers at just one notch below intolerable, a challenge to me to dare disrupt her home space. It kept my nerves on edge all day; a face-off more disruptive to my headspace than the actual decibels.

My wedding dress still hung inside my wardrobe door. I planned to dry clean it and pack it away, perfect as it was, forever. When I turned it around to marvel once more at the beading and the sweep of short train, it appeared that a chunk of material had been cut out of the hem. Too neat to have been caught by a rogue heel. I had not checked but would, surely, have noticed such a tear. The best version of me: ruined.

I *did* panic then, no use denying it. Lola's relentless shittiness was trashing my good step-mum intentions. She was doing a dozen secret things that only a madwoman would call her on; they ate away at my nerves like acid, corroding our new-forged relationship. Ultimately, they could not fail to dissolve the bonds between her father and me. Our scheming little Lola was to marriage what *aqua regia* was to a wedding ring.

Eh go so.

One evening, having endured blaring music and so many snippish comments that I wanted to tan her snooty behind, I cried to my new husband:

'She hates me! And intimacy without love …'

'She's just a girl!' said Thomas.

'She'll have some massive nightmare meltdown as soon as you're out, I swear.'

'That was a one-off. She's delighted we're married.'

I needed not to panic, it was not my style. I was a nurse; I would treat the patient, Lola, not the disease of step-relativity, or its sometimes vicious symptoms. I would look after her.

Days calmed, nights turned over. I decided that a wonderful marriage was always destined to be so, but still it never hurt to start off on the soundest possible footing. Which meant that Lola and I *had* to be friends.

I was putting considerable effort into giving this asinine notion a chance. Following an afternoon of hydrotherapy with Stevie, I pulled her aside:

'So, Lola.'

'Hi.'

'I guess you might be feeling a little bit strange now that we're married.'

125

'Strange. That's one word for it.'

I settled clasped hands on my knees. 'What's another word?'

'Shit!' This was Thomas, back from the garden. 'Sorry, but I just got blood on the chair, look. Nearly put a nail clean through my finger. Damn!'

Lola and I rose and hurried to him, both wanting to get there first, to help more, to offer greater comfort, to be needed more. And any words we had been waiting to share were lost somewhere between the cupboard that stored the antiseptic cream and that grand and silent mindscrew of an Aga.

I bought her a little top from the market that I was sure was her size. It was a mint green vest with spaghetti straps and teensy tassels at the bottom, the sort of thing girls loved to wear for summers in Gran Canaria or Kos. Thomas thought it looked great, but I could tell by the magnesium glint that Lola hated the tasselled mint green top, hated the very idea of mint, hated my green taste. This stupid whim, this foolish insult, would disappear into her wardrobe, never again to emerge. And that is just what happened.

'But,' I said to Thomas. 'We won't have any babies together.'

'We could.'

'Don't—'

'OK, no we won't. We have babies. But your *new* baby is being delivered in two weeks. It's a wedding present, a honeymoon baby (just without the honeymoon).'

'What?'

'She's beautiful, she's silver and she's called Mercedes. Not new, actually, more of a toddler, maybe. But yours.'

'Oh yeah, here comes my chauffeur in his cap.'

'Didn't have the budget—'

'You got the personalised number plate, right?'

'I nearly died of shame buying one, but yes, that too.'

'You *are* kidding. Aren't you?'

'The whole deal for you, boobaloo.'

'No. Tell me there's no Merc, no way.'

'I even bought you that key ring. Way too girly, disgraceful, but …'

He held up a crystal and silver heart from which dangled a key.

'Tommy! What can I say?'

'Just say what Lola thought I didn't hear her say on the phone the other day. "Fuck *me*!"'

'Then … what she said. And please do.'

Jamaica was near to us, within the walls of my childhood suburban home, but as soon as we stepped outside on to the tarmac and rain-spattered grit, it was ten thousand miles away. When I was eleven, we made plans to visit for a fortnight. They must have saved for months, even with their good jobs. My mother, Grace, had worked as a nurse practically from the day they touched down at Heathrow. My father worked in planning for the council.

We were all packed to go to the airport. It took us a week to pack the car, box by bag, with good things for Auntie Pearl, Miss B, Auntie Marcia and Auntie Claudette, things they could not get 'back Home' but would marvel at – like entry-level Bordeaux, Quality Street, supermarket Cornish pasties and crumpets. A few items of clothing from Marks and Spencer. The surprise bras, kept secret from Dad, were the absolute highlight. *Yuh tink Claudette is a C or a D? Metink a D, she can grow into it, yuh see?* Then that window-rattling laugh.

Even with my luggage allowance all used up for such gifts (*Yuh can wear yuh cousins' tings*) I could not wait for that Friday-night flight. *Soon come*, said Mum. We got into the car early and sat chatting while Dad went around the house to do a final check of door and taps, to unplug every last appliance and do all the other eleventh-hour chores that would inevitably mean it would be a nervous race to Heathrow despite our best efforts. *Soon come.* Meanwhile we listened to the car radio, chatted about how hot it would be, how relaxed, how strange and yet familiar to a British-born girl, how beachy and brill, how *Jamaican*. After a while we turned the radio off to spare the battery. We talked about the many sometimes tenuously connected family groups over there: a beginner's guide to who was who, what was where and why. *Soon come, girl.* I had started to bounce in my seat with eagerness to get away by the time Mum finally said she would just check how Dad was getting on.

But Dad was gone.

Gone as in dead, passed clean away on the floor of the bathroom. Heart attack, they said.

'I knew,' Mum said much later, when words began to return. 'I saw that damn fat magpie on our windowsill this morning, and I *knew.*'

It took us a week to face unpacking that car. And we never did go to Jamaica.

I heard Lola, though she did not hear me. A loud retching coming from her en suite as I passed along the hallway. I turned back to go to her, reached her door and about-turned once more.

While it wasn't my specialist area of nursing, I figured that the right food had the power to heal all ills. The great thing about Jamaican food was that it celebrated every pod, root and gourd of the gotta-live, gotta-grow island bounty: fruit and vegetables that had themselves been nourished by gold sun, green goodness and black soil, in that fantastical corner of God's good Earth. Mother-food, prepared with passion and peppered with the same love that also did you the honour of kicking your ass. Caribbean food *healed*, no doubt about it. In the right hands, it could work wonders.

Lola needed fresh, junk-free, tempting food. I could only think of one offering worthy. Jerk chicken. I would make it exactly the way Mum said it was 'back Home' in Jamaica, with no ready sauces or shortcuts.

A true jerk dish was made with three elements: the dry rub, the marinade and the dipping sauce. Each of the three jerk elements married together to make the spicy whole; each was irreplaceable. There was, of course, the fourth main element: the chicken, this to be free range and from the best butcher in High Desford. The shop was a short drive away, which gave me yet another chance to slip into my new silver friend, Mercy.

As I walked out to gather my ingredients I stepped over another leaflet from Bright New Britain on our doormat. Now here was a political movement headed by a man who wrongly thought *he* was wronged – *an him de biggest batty-mout' of dem all!* He was leading a group, two dozen respectable faces atop a whole stomping of bovver boots, all of whom wanted their Brexit to be hard and white and red and cross and biting. I finished reading it, jangled my keys at it, put it in the waste bin. I would not recycle it; it was already recycled.

Later, I set out my stall on the worktop, measuring out the right spices, from allspice to thyme, into neat white porcelain dishes. Using a wooden spoon, I worked all the ingredients into each other in a large bowl, until they were thoroughly blended. Rub done.

I trimmed scrappy bits of fat, sinew and skin off the chicken quarters, then got to work washing them in lime juice. Then I worked it all over: pressing oil into flesh, rubbing in spices for long minutes until it was fit to leave in the fridge for at least four hours.

Next, the sauce. Good people did bad things to protect their own family jerk recipe – my only sin was to swap out some chopped escallion, as I was short, for half a chopped onion.

Yuh put a likkle bit in, tek a likkle bit out. Mek it yours.

As for the killer kick, I added two fresh, unapologetic Scotch bonnets; we four Waites, this new Anglo-Caribbean entity, were all on full-heat rations now.

Then I just needed patience, to wait until the dish was done. *One, one, coco full basket,* as my mother used to say. *Bit by bit, things will eventually come good.*

Later, the chicken went down a storm, and from her bathroom – silence.

But the evening had another surprise in store.

She walked in on us. And she meant to, I know it.

Lola walked in on us having sex. Over her father's shoulder I saw her, an empty expression with full eyes, watching like she was taking notes. Racing towards the moment of climax, I could no more stop my husband with a warning movement of my body than I could have stopped a high-speed train. For the longest millisecond my eyes locked with hers, then I had to scrunch my eyelids.

'Tommy!'

With cheeks like punched peaches, she shrugged herself around 180 degrees and out of the door:

'Oh. Sorry.'

'Shit,' said my husband to the trailing ends of blonde hair.

I said nothing but pulled some cotton up over my chest; a modesty come too late. I was wrapped up to my chin, but strangely I felt colder. Time to put the duvet back in its cover; autumn was coming in.

Red-pink and black. The whole night I dreamed of shutting doors and of a ringing in the darkness and of poisonous lies that pranged me awake. Hot, I sidled out of bed before 5 a.m. and went straight to my laptop. The site was launched in seconds. Articles, ads and announcements. A baby boy. The wedding plans of the local carnival queen. Discounts on pest control. An upcoming car park refurbishment. I was scrolling down 'Obituaries' when he came in:

'What are you reading?'

'Nothing.'

'The *Elm Forest Herald*?'

'Yes, just … old habits.'

'It's really late. Really early.'

'I'm coming,' I said, powering down.

We went up and got back into bed, but I made sure we checked the doors were all locked first.

One of my biggest flaws was that when I was in love, I got jealous. Like crazy jealous.

My new husband – *We should have been more careful, Darling* – made the decision to spend even more time with his sulking, skulking girl. Thomas and Lola popped out to the shops together, had under-their-breath conversations together, headed up to her bedroom together for urgent door-shut chats.

Like two pea in a pod, yuh see?

I was tempted to engage but did not know whether I should join in or intervene. Neither: she was simply showing me how she wished to treat our marriage, deep down. She would ignore it, belittle it, side-step it, and constantly brief against me to a loving paternal ear. That was how it was going to be and it was intolerable. Yet Thomas simply wandered on behind her, along the path of least resistance. I might love him, but my love was never blind. I was not blind.

My Stevie noticed nothing, Lola acknowledged nothing and sure enough a week drifted past without Thomas and me having a meaningful conversation, or for that matter sex, for the first time since we had officially got together. My body felt the loss long before my mind. By day four my hopeful feet were flirting in vain, pointing, tiptoeing, kicking up across the kitchen, wiggling their tough little digits on the sofa. By day six they were dragging, two plump reluctant bridesmaids supporting my jilted legs; then my chest joined in, growing heavy, but too scared and dull to burst with its boiling yell for conjugal relief. In the end, my throat constricted and a panic seized my gorge such that I began to cough, too hard, as if to dislodge a terminal itch, which in turn left me wheezing and still stranded on my unhappy thoughts a good ten days later.

Still, I could not say it. I would not *ask* or it would mean nothing.

Things had to shake the hell up. For a start, although the house itself was more welcoming than its eldest child, we urgently needed a new theatre in which to play out our daily dramas. Littleton Lodge was not working right for us, already. Rooms were now too close, others too far away, and who after all held which keys to what? The sooner we could build our own house, the better for our mangled newfangled family. The sooner we laid out plans that made the most of deaf walls and lengthy corridors, then the easier I would breathe. Maybe a doer-upper that had teetered for decades on the edge of dementia, with landing floorboards that groaned louder than bedrooms; perhaps a newborn white and glass box. Either way, we needed a home with no plastered-in memories shared by only two of us.

That morning I made him up a tray with poached eggs on toast, a flute of Buck's Fizz, coffee and the property section; I laid a snipped autumn rose on the tray and slipped on my silliest silk wrap (Lola was still sleeping). Then I served him with one steady hand as I whispered sweet house-for-next-to-nothings in his heating ear.

The following day we registered with three estate agents. And my feet no longer dragged.

It was late morning and feeling optimistic, I headed to the supermarket. As I arrived, this guy was standing just inside the electric doors, to the left. I clocked the eagle tattoo at the base of his shaven head; that slowed my entrance. As I wheeled my trolley in he said, loud enough for half the first aisle to hear:

'Great. Fucking ebola.'

I froze. Then I twisted around to say something cutting, or badass, but he was already pulling out his phone, staring at me.

I swished away from his muscular disdain, towards the oranges. He was telling me I was not welcome in such a place; that I should be at the Wednesday Picton Street market with the other darkskins; that farfalle pasta, refined homewares and organic semi-skimmed were nothing to do with me. All in a look: the most skilled racists know that it is an assault with a blunt weapon to wilfully confuse skin colour with a wholesale culture.

Not enjoyable, but he wasn't the first.

Then he started talking louder, growling at his phone like he hated it:

'Could be,' he said. 'Fuck knows.'

He turned towards the open doors again and his nape tattoo faced me straight on. Not many could have an eagle that size, right there. He was too heavy-set though, surely. And he should have thick, dark hair …

'I'll call you back.' It was knowing, that voice, complicit.

My stomach seized; it had to be him.

I started away up the long aisle. Did he know me? He would follow. I took a few steps more, but walking on felt fearful, far worse; I had to turn back.

He was gone.

I looked around, towards the tills. Gone. I edged forward a few steps. Could not see him. I wheeled my trolley past the end of the first aisle. Not there. I walked along it, gathering a few items as I went, did the same in the next aisle and the next. When I had amassed enough to tell myself I was no longer afraid, I queued, paid and packed my bags.

Lola was going to sleep with Will. Of course, I knew that she had already slept with him once, but I overheard her on the phone making a song and dance of it, as though she had never told her friends about the first time. She was obsessed with the boy: this don of getting hot-tub nasty, touted about as a future lawyer-husband – amongst these demanding nubiles anyway. Lola planned to 'get with' him when his parents were out. I was in no doubt that this callow youth would be delighted to be got with. There were also some unsubtle mutterings: 'bringing some stuff … or "the Wolfe"

… yeah, in his dad's old Something & Wolfe Criminal Law, bant … yup, let it snow' as if no one over twenty-five would know slang for cocaine. I was in no doubt that I should forewarn, prevent, put a dirty great spanner in the teenage works or at least say something moderately wise … but what? She had made it quite clear that she did not want to hear anything that came out of my fat-lipped mouth. So, wrong though it was, I said nothing – and figured it might do her good to have a hobby outside of the house.

When Will day arrived, I knew it was Will day because Lola flitted around, birdlike, asking about her purple bra, a lacy, knowing, tart's carnival of a confection that I had seen out drying and which had to be her best, meaning the one in which she might do her worst. She folded the bra, still damp from the clothes horse, and fluttered around the kitchen as if she might have something to ask, or say. She flew away from the dinner table after pecking at a few peas and a bite of fish, so that she could prepare for the party for at least an hour longer than usual; she would be staying the night at Jessica's. She may as well have worn a 'Today, I Will' T-shirt.

I did not share my suspicions with Thomas though – What boys? What booze? What blow? There was no catastrophe-free way in which that could help. When she shut the door and soared off to dive-bomb some unmade (or housekeeper-sterilised) bed, we were alone at last. Just us newlyweds, give or take a six-year-old trying to rap the

Ben 10 theme tune. However, Lola had been trying to liquefy our precious golden circle for weeks; I was pissed off about it, too. My brain rocked and fizzed, my temples were brewing a headache; I spent the rest of the evening on my muted laptop while Thomas worked in his study.

Lollapalooza, he called her. My Lolapaloo. It was starting to grate.

Dark

She needs to know the word. What is it?

'Ten, nine ...'

He had come into the kitchen, as usual, patted her head, given her a peach from the garden. Stroked her cheek, asked her how the day had gone.

Now he is in the toilet. Shouting numbers. A flush.

Specks of dust hang like babyweeny bugs in the sunlight, but they all jump as he shuts their loo door.

'Seven, six ...'

He is coming back. The pantry is waiting.

The front door is closed. The windows are closed. The roof is heavy and – strange – still on: even though everything has gone bad the house is not rising up, roaring open like a big dog's bark to save her. The door to the pantry is open and it is the only place to hide that is not 'out of bounds'. She goes in.

'Two, one. Coming!'

(Ready or not.)

She has run out of numbers but he is here anyway, with his heavy lips and heavy words and red eyes – red as hell, robot lasers burning her back for all the time he smacks her – with nothing that looks right in them. And worst of all, the forced glass. The cold red smell.

What is it called, this thickness of the dark in the daytime? She has not yet learned any words that can describe what this is.

Lola

DONE LIST 4

Dad is spending <u>so</u> much time with me right now. He's back again, there in my darkness; tall and solid like those old lighthouses that stop you from smashing yourself on the rocks. Hey, no way! I just worked it out – I should have played smart and thought ahead to avoid all this and set him up with AT. Dear old <u>Alison</u>! Bit of an age difference maybe, probably the wrong kind, it's hard to tell her exact age because of whatever that thing is she does with her hair. Still, at least <u>he</u> could never say his wife didn't understand him. #dadjokesrock

I think AT is married though, but she's never actually said and Dad certainly doesn't know. Maybe to someone <u>symbolic</u>. The gender wouldn't matter but she would probably be happiest with a nice undertaker or midwife. She would need some life or death meaning to get all worked up about. I'll never know – part of the whole shrink/psycho deal is probably to keep herself private and anyway I don't really care about old people's love lives. Enough of all that at home.

College is not what I thought it would be. It's just not. I thought it would feel <u>outstandingly</u> grown up and a bit like a younger uni, but it is full of chavs (sorry, but it is) and the teachers are pretty bad. One guy's classes make Bonesy Jonesie's feel like they were the hottest, most fascinating date you ever had. Also, Anna had said she was coming here, a couple of people said they were leaving school for college, but what, did they <u>all</u> go and change their mind over the summer? I keep telling Dad that I think I made a horrible mistake. He keeps telling me that the college has a great reputation (what, is it No.2 in the finally-no-school-fees download chart?) I'll get used to it, apparently.

But what happens if I never do? What then?

So, I googled 'Chinese water' meaning chestnuts, because I've been wanting to know how to make that stir-fry Bron's mum used to make, but Chinese water torture popped up in the list so I clicked on that instead and read for ages and was sort of freaked out and forgot all about vegetables. I told Dad, but Darling was there too and she laughed really loud, although it wasn't meant to be funny.

Drip, drip, drip. Some problems are exactly that. I am

trying but I cannot overcome the rub of ever-flowing <u>issues</u> on to, right into, my head. Drip, drip, drip. Brutal.

Where's Darling anyway when I need her? She's off taking Stevie somewhere medical as usual, in the Merc I still can't believe he bought her. She goes nowhere but to Stevie places. The boy has to go to the doctor's <u>a lot</u>, like once a week, more. Poor little sod must be really <u>sick</u>.

So, I slept with Will again. Second time since 23 July and the tent at Mungojaxx. #virginholidayslol #woofrickinhoo. God, I had the giggles when we nearly kicked the tent down by mistake, but we had been drinking the vodka I'd nicked from home and smuggled in disguised as tonic water. This time was better. Less malcoordinated and not at all funny and <u>warmer</u>. #happy2ndbangaversary

I should have felt changed straight after the first time, but I didn't feel any different. But twice: does this time now officially make me a High Desford College hottie? At least I am no longer one of the epidemic numbers of virgin-but-legals at Harbrooke House and Dovington #sadfuckersareus. But I don't feel different exactly. I may look different because Darling told me I looked 'wired' when I got in at eleven this morning.

This time <u>was</u> different. Will actually asked me over to his house, for a start – his parents were out. We went pretty much straight to his bedroom. He didn't kiss me right away though, so I felt quite awkward and just chatted on too much for a bit, told him about all the ways that Darling was driving me completely batshit. I actually told him:

'I act like it's OK, for Dad, but it's not. I can't stand having her around the place. She is basically ruining my entire life!'

It felt <u>really</u> good to say it at last and better still, Will gave me this massive hug and agreed:

'If you ask me, it's totally out of order. Still want me to kill her?'

And I laughed, but then I said: 'Seriously, if only there was a way we could break them up.'

And then we started to talk about what we should do, like I said, 'Get her to start smoking again so that Dad dumps her' (I'd already had a go at that one, of course), or 'Steal money and credit cards and stuff so Dad thinks it's her – and dumps her!' He was great about it, he kept pulling me closer to him and then he pulled me right on to the bed – OMG I could hardly listen to him properly, but he was going:

'Well, maybe we don't even need to do that. Maybe we should just see what we can find out about her and go from there.'

I asked him what he was talking about and he was all, 'Well, she's black, isn't she? And from Elm Forest? Bound to have nicked a car at some point, or to have a criminal record for something at least.' I laughed and went, 'You're really not supposed to say that.' And he said 'Well, you know what they say – behind every racist joke there's a fact.'

And then I was gutted because he got up off the bed and went to his desk to show me all these papers, this stuff he collects from some political group. I wanted him to lie back down but he got a bit into it, showed me things like black people are loads more likely, three or four times more, to go to prison. I didn't know what to say to that. Then he carried on joking around and he was saying that with a stupid name like hers it would be easy to get the dirt on her and that he would talk to his dad because he's a lawyer and it would be a piece of piss, he knows all the police in High Desford, everyone, and we'd soon have her banged up. I was so nervous that his parents might come back before we did anything that I just kept on nodding and laughing. He did lie back down in the end though and then he kissed me (and a lot more, obv).

So, everything on the Will front is looking amazing. And although only yesterday I was worried he would never want to do anything with me again, we totally did it. As for Darling, obviously I don't really think we're going to find a way to send her to prison, but it did also get me thinking. I mean, we still don't know anything about her. No family showed up at the wedding and she hardly talks about her life at all – how weird is that? – and Dad walks around in a dream world like it's all just 'dandy' #fakeModernFamily and everyone's happy.

I _am_ happy about Will and me at least. But it still doesn't exactly feel like I thought it would. Maybe it will take some time to kick in …

Also, now I've started with all this sicking up.

Achievements

1. Will is my main achievement, without a doubt. It's so great, he really does seem into us. Into me. #yayformiracles
2. Lost the easiest 4lbs ever, without even trying. The usual. Also mucho helped by the little leftover half-wraps of ~~coc~~ stuff someone's been giving me. Burns mega calories. True dat!
3. Actually went to work with Dad, to a meeting in London anyway. We stopped off at Mum's grave because it was nearby (she died exactly a decade ago, weird) and I waited for him at this all right café next to the cemetery. We loved it. Beat the shit out of most of the places around here; at least they played decent music. He said it was loud, but we loved it.
4. Made Stevie laugh for about an hour by blowing bubbles into milk through a curly straw. Darling's face when I tried to do it through my nose … #grossouttheoldies
5. Spent a whole day without speaking to anyone I liked at college. Asked Dad straight out if it was too late to go back to Harbrooke House. He said I'd be just fine.

Darling

Mid-October settled a better mood upon us. It brought Braeburns and the last of the beans to the garden and I started to feel more hopeful.

I might have been wide of the mark, but Lola seemed happier. Admittedly, not often when I was in the room. But surely she had to be coming around to the idea of me, or at least sliding into a muted resignation.

One, one coco full basket.

She would never treat me as a parent, I knew that; I had come to her when she was too old. But nor did I plan to be some big sister; I was too old for that, and too traditional. I also respected the unique place of her late mother. Once you had been raised by a Jamaican woman you were never in doubt of the power of a mother; not every one of my early days had been perfect, but I'd sure been mothered to within an inch of my life. However, I felt I might be accepted by Lola as a caregiver. Someone to nurture her. I knew by now that she needed me more than she would ever let on.

One morning, she said:

'I'll have some of that spicy chicken again for dinner, if you're making it …'

Caught off guard, I overdid it:

'Yes, sure! Good girl, you hungry then?'

'Yeah, I really am, today.'

'Great,' I said. 'I'm sure I've still got all the spices … Good, great, I'll cook you up some more; it might take a little while. What do you need right now?'

'Oh, I'll just make myself some eggs,' she said.

'Great,' I said.

There now, yuh see – even hope taste like chicken!

And then, the strangest thing. Instead of heading to the kitchen she went back upstairs again. She had this pink towel turbanned around her head, and she stopped on the third or fourth step and turned to look back at me, just for a second before she went on up again, and I felt with both horror and relief that I might cry.

But I did not let tears fall and our day continued to unfurl, fine and quiet as a fern.

In the early afternoon, I started separating the spices into their little white bowls.

As I was measuring out the ground cloves, Lola came down again, still thin in her thin summer dressing gown, still a towel around her hair.

148

'There you go, I'm making your favourite chicken!' I said.

'My what? Oh,' she said. 'Actually, I'm going out now, sleepover at Ellie's.'

'I thought you weren't talking to Ellie.'

'I am now.'

'Oh, should I—'

'Please don't get stressy, I'll eat it another time.'

'I don't "get stressy". It's fine.'

She wandered away, shouting: 'Dad! Can I have a lift?'

So: not so much wide of the mark as a whole bus ride away. Whatever had been in Lola's eyes when she looked back at me that morning had been lost by the afternoon.

She and Thomas left about half an hour later, and almost as soon as they'd gone, the phone rang. We usually ignored the landline but it had rung and rung as if it mattered. I picked it up and said 'Hello.' There was no sound coming from it. I waited for another second, nestling the weighty receiver closer.

'Hello?'

Nothing. Or almost nothing; breathing, faint but there. There was someone on the other end of the phone.

'Hi, hello?'

I was alone downstairs. Stevie was playing upstairs.

'Hello, can you hear me? Who's calling, please?'

Only more breathing, heavier now, which made me feel that they were moving closer. I waited a moment more then went to hang up, but before I could, they were gone.

The next day, I found a parcel of poison. She let me find it. She *made* me find it: the paperclipped clutch of flyers – and what? Aide-memoires? – that she clearly needed me to see. She had asked for help, a brazen trick, as Thomas prepared to take her to another friend's house:

'Oh, Darling, sorry, I left my charger upstairs. Dad's coming … could you?'

Unthinking, I had trotted off to her room – step-parents did that – and there lay her charger, sitting on top of the papers I had been sent to her room to see.

Such appealing colours, made to clash in such an ugly way! That dark red-pink and orange; the sun setting on kindness, perhaps, or a new dawn of bigoted fuckery. Of course the colours caught my eye, they were meant to, and I retreated with the charger prongs digging hard into my hand.

I said nothing. But after the two of them drove off, I bounced straight back up to her room, because sometimes it was just too tiring to resist the script.

Also, sometimes words spoke louder than actions. So, in that screwy bundle: every Bright New Britain leaflet I could remember seeing, untorn and untorched. Plus, bizarrely, a flyer for a Law taster day at Durham University. A photo of a boy, standing next to a man who looked as the boy might at fifty, leaning towards the *battymout*'-in-chief and clinking pint glasses, somewhere that looked like a hotel carvery that had been brightened up with a job lot of horse brasses. A copy of a newspaper article featuring women in matching dark red-pink and orange T-shirts, with what Lola might call 'Alpha' eyes and 'headfuck dreamgirl' hair and skin slapped in product to keep it fine-pored and clearly as white as possible. More newspaper cuttings from Bright New Britain praising those who had steered the country away from the Continent, away from the waiting immigrants (Migrant? Refugee? Tricksy, PC words!), away from darkskin disaster and deviousness and ruin. An actual photographic print of a selfie, complete with white border: Lola, and possibly the same boy, half turned away. A BNB flyer for local elections in Elm Forest, only fifteen minutes away.

This is why, she was saying. This is *why*. And there is no way around it or through it or under it and you will not ever make me love you. This is our truth, she was telling me. This is it, Darling, this is it.

I needed air, after that. What was going on with her?

Slate skies outside, with a wetness in the air that only Britain managed to do well, that sort of arsey, grudging rain. The wind powered around the garden, the best sort of mad weather, far superior to snowdrifts and torrential rain. The pathetic fallacy of the troubled mind, for me more honest than the sun.

My pulse was only now starting to slow. There had been more, in her room, too much: I had bent to gather an upturned cup and some clothes from under the bed and felt the brush of plastic on my fingertips. A minuscule bag, with traces of what I knew had to be cocaine in it. Or rather the residue of 98 per cent cutting agent if the prevailing wisdom was anything to go by – not even the vices were true any more.

On the windiest days, or nights, I looked into the wheeling sky and remembered who I was. But who exactly was my step-daughter?

No, I could not afford to doubt. Love had to always win. I would not tell Thomas about either the drugs or the little bundle of hate she had sent me to find; he would overreact, kick up an almighty fuss that would help no one, I knew it. The girl had no mother: I would simply have to give her more.

My mum used to give me treats, intimate delicacies that only she could know how much I would savour. The first swollen purple fig fresh from the garden, plucked out of that corner of Negril which flourished behind some garages in RG22. An expensive not-on-the-sofa pomegranate. The third pancake in, when pan and wrist were well warmed up and before the buttered oil burned, the lemon and sugar all ready to go. Fresh cockles, bursting bright with vinegar and peppered in two shakes, from the most crowded stall on Clacton holidays. Or best of all, while our Sunday guests and other family might hope for the succulent 'oysters' from our roast chicken, Mum and I would know that she had already sneaked me all the real treasure: the bony, gnawable chicken neck, the hot liver, dusted with a bit of bog-standard table salt. My tongue thrilled, my heart was too spoiled and sated to quicken at its own good fortune. Even in the most trying of times, always the chicken neck, the giblets.

It is only since I have had Stevie that I have realised how important the just-for-my-mouth things were. How much I was loved.

I could offer Lola some history to adopt: one of our best-loved family drinks. Not that Jamaican Christmas favourite, sorrel, I could not bear the smell, but pineapple punch. This I did not need a book for – I could still taste the tart simplicity from the barbecues of many White summers.

You blended pineapple juice with condensed milk, cinnamon and nutmeg. A little water, if you wanted, plus a dash of vanilla (the cheaper essence was my favourite, nothing too rich and fancy). You near-froze the pineapple juice first, really chilled it out, then served over ice. The true family secret was to add dark rum for all except the youngest children, one good splash to give it that punchy kick. I would pass on that though for Lola, so as not to upset Thomas.

It was those little private tastes of things – sweet fruit and salty insides – that knitted families together. Lola might feel angry at present, but I would take care of her.

After all, this family was my community now. Every other night on the news they would talk about 'the Black Community' as if we all – from Somalis plucked wet from the Med to third-generation Tobagonian barristers – hung out together in a warehouse made of breeze blocks somewhere off the North Circular. Sure, the collective mattered, more than ever. But without us Waites, I had no real family, no people. I had to make this family work.

Thomas didn't notice things, though – couldn't help with some things – and I had my hands full with Stevie, and sometimes I knew I was missing things. Not parties, or theatre trips, or coffee mornings: to hell with all that. I missed things around Littleton Lodge, at home. I would go off to watch Stevie walk through water for Sally and when I returned things would feel different, the air would have somehow changed. Things did not always add up.

I could hear her, that violent lowing as she threw up into the toilet bowl. Had to burn. I called out:

'Are you ill?'

'No!'

Then I saw it: her phone on her bedside table. Before I could think, it was in my hand, about to lock any second. I tapped, there it was: Find My iPhone. Before I could stop them, my fingers were doing the smart thing and in moments – *fuckadoodled00* – thanks to Family Sharing, I was following her right back.

I replaced the phone. 'Lola?'

'No, you can go, I'm …' The predictable pause. 'Fine.'

'Lola, open up, please.'

A much longer pause. 'I don't know what's wrong with me.'

It would soon be time to confirm to Thomas that his daughter had a more serious problem than even we had realised.

It was a Wednesday. I wanted to hop into Mercy and drive to a cobbled market half an hour away, get Thomas the most unusual French cheese I could lay my hands on, a proper nutty stinker, and perhaps a round of that artisan bread we hadn't eaten for a while. I needed cash: we were talking seriously out in the sticks and no one ever wanted to be the Nubian nube who thought the world should bend to their metropolitan plastic. A twenty had been tucked away in my purse. I stared at the empty leather, bemused. Dropped? Spent and forgotten? Or had it been stolen?

Would she, though? Thomas was always dishing out money to Lola. What was all that about? Sure, I gave Stevie play money, a £2 coin to go up to the nice lady and buy the balloons, but Lola, these young girls. They sucked money up with no shame.

Only 7 a.m. It was hard to stomp quietly but I did it anyway. I tramped without a sound into Spare Room No.1, which I sometimes used as a dressing room to hide unseductive wriggles into some newlywed whim of lace constriction. Might I have been …? No. Bollocks. I was sure – in my bones, in my *blood* – that Lola had taken my money.

A purple double-take: on the pillow was a belladonna-dark wisp of *bra*. Not mine. Lola's over-here-boys little purple bra, her colours from the 'Will day' joust, poking out from under the duvet. I strode over and snatched it up. Real silk. The girl meant business. I had worn efficient, roomy, stretch-cotton triangles at her age. Working bras to promote well-behaved bosoms, not wanton scraps of fancy. Proper brassieres. *Büstenhalters*, as we girls had once joked in deep hausfrau voices. What was wrong with them all, these girls today?

No £20 of mine though, on the bed or anywhere.

Yuh nuh water yah money plant today? No? Go find a likkle baby spider.

I did not mind the money, I had given her more without hesitation; but I minded the taking, the lie.

The following day I found a puff of candyfloss panties floating around in Spare Room No.2, next door. She was spreading her goddamn underwear all over our home, and for what?

'Thomas!'

'What?' He had shuffled through, perusing some plans.

'This. Is. Not. Acceptable ...'

I held the pink spun-sugar knickers high on one deeply unhappy finger.

'Well? Well?' I demanded his outrage.

'Are they Lola's? I'll ask her to—'

'Don't ask her anything! Tell her! No more knickers everywhere!'

'OK, Darling, but—'

'And tell your messy-messy daughter to stay out of my purse while she's at it!'

'Darling!'

But it was too late. I flung the fairground attraction undies so that they crumpled beside the laundry basket and stalked downstairs, in time to see Lola step inside the front door. She was dressed in another tuft of breezy nonsense, this with some battered velvet blazer thrown over it, looking up to where we had been standing as if waiting for Act II to begin. Her millpond expression told me our words had all been absorbed.

Words like acid, burning my tongue. I wanted to spit it all free, feeling not one year older than her in that moment, wanting to ask if she'd thought to get dressed that day, if she'd mugged a tramp for his jacket, and if so could she please use *his* cash to buy herself a big old can of none of your goddamn business? But her look, that odd placid look, cooled my mouth.

My feet would not move, so I let her pass me on the stairs – *yuh know that's bad luck, gyal.* I was not sure about all of my mother's superstitions. But even I could feel it in my water, read it on our upheld palms: Thomas and I had seriously different parenting styles and that could only spell trouble.

I confronted her; I had to.

'Lola,' I said. 'I found some Bright New Britain material in your room. How long have you supported them?'

'I don't,' she said. 'A friend of a friend was here, left it here or something. Don't get stressy.'

I said, 'I don't get stressy. Do you agree with it?'

Just like that, straight out.

'No way. No,' she said.

'What about the white powder?'

'What?'

'There was a bag with what looked like … Are you doing cocaine, Lola?'

'No,' she said. 'Probably from sweets, or make-up or something.'

'It was cocaine.'

'I wouldn't know.'

'What if Stevie had found it?'

'God, all right,' she said. 'But it was all someone else's, so please don't bother mentioning it to Dad. Not that, or the leaflet thing. Please, I'm begging you. I'm begging you.'

'OK,' I said. 'I won't.'

And, although I knew better, this cold girl had begged until I had melted, so that was that. For now.

'Lovely day for it!'

The marathon was to be a homespun slapdash extravaganza. All nineteen girls rocked up at our door, in the black, white and pink T-shirts that they had designed themselves: 'Stevie's Wonders – Defying Duchenne Muscular Dystrophy' on their fronts (they were educated girls) and '26 Miles Signed, Sealed, Delivered' (they were retro-funky girls) on the back. Thomas and I had rigged up a sort of finishing line with a wide baby-blue ribbon from the local department store. Better still, Guy and Allie had rallied a number of the other neighbours to congregate alongside the photographer from the *Gazette* for the 1.30 p.m. ETA.

At 1.23 p.m. they rounded the corner like the unstoppable force they were – young women on a mission. Bucket in hand, they managed to smile and shake down strangers for cash while striding forth at well over my personal top speed of 3 mph. Amazons of compassion they were, strong and slender and *hyperactively* kind. They came nearer and closer until, with Stevie waiting by the chocolate-box ribbon, they let their well-oxygenated lungs explode into a song about how lovely he was.

Stevie, my baby, was beaming, unsteady with excitement and singing along at immodest volume. I thought about patting his shoulder but the *Gazette* man was already taking potshots at our merry band, so I merely looked on, fond and proud for posterity. Stevie's favourite SW, Aoife – a minxy little redhead with socially conscious and welcoming bosoms – was singing right at him as they crunched into the gravel and – *la!* – broke through the tape on to our doorstep.

'Woo! Hi there, little one …'

Glasses of iced water knocked together in congratulation; there were selfies with Stevie; there was cereal bar scoffing and loud laughter all round. These girls. These hearty, generous girls. They really did seem to love my boy; perhaps it was the dimples. They had smashed their £5k target and as they left to clamber into someone's boyfriend's minibus, they rattled their bucket and swung still lively haunches while waving goodbye to their cause and mascot, trailing a faint salt-and-urea air.

We fizzed for a good hour after they had gone. When would the paper come out and hadn't they walked for a long way and wasn't that a lot of money raised in Stevie's name and hadn't all the neighbours got ever so excited?

An mi, Darling. Mi suh proud.

The whole day I stayed happy, and stomach-sick. All of us in the papers: our faces, our names, our house. I had wanted to pull this event off for Stevie, but who else might I have brought to our door along with those delightful supporters? My son, though, always my son: I had pushed

160

down the fear and strangled the worry and roared those young ladies over the finish line louder than anyone. In the end, Lola's reaction made it worth the trouble twice over. She was shining, on this unusual day. She was enjoying my son more than ever. To watch them together now, at least from a distance, you could only see an age-distanced brother and sister.

Shame she still hated my guts.

She was just so *rude* to him. My mum would have given me a look that shut me up for a week if I had dared to be as feisty to my father. As ever, it was Mum's voice in my ears when Lola roared and slammed her door:

'I'm not doing it!'

An him workin' all de hours God send to keep her in her highty-tighty ways. Chupid chile. Nuh ha no manners.

I tried to be the bigger person. Even, steady and unfrightening, I tried to give Thomas full emotional support in my role as secondary parent, the same as he did for me with Stevie.

But they tested it, *she* was testing it!

There they went, off once more into their exclusive little huddles. I overheard them in her bedroom after the door had been slammed shut, in operatic fashion. There was that spoiled mezzo soprano:

'I'm not doing it, Dad!'

The bass murmur, hard to make out.

A top E, or F, that made the windows quake:

'How many times do I have to say it? *No!*'

I tried to creep closer, get a front-row seat, but then Stevie came up, tugging at my hand and asking me when we were going to the doctor's.

Lola, a handshake away from some connoisseur of racist literature – but then weren't we all? – surely had to be starting to need me soon. She never *needed* me. Any tiny chick of hope I had nursed, thinking I might have made some progress, had long been drowned in the shallows.

Just the thought drove me out of the house; I had to get some air.

I was off to the shops, alone. Stevie could stay with Lola for a while; the two of them were gabbing so much that they did not look up as I called goodbye.

I shopped. Pattie's chicken, Gloucestershire Old Spot chops, cheese-stuffed peppadews in their oily tub, pomegranates from a Lebanese stall. It was busy; High Desford on a Saturday was always buzzing with some unexpected entertainment. This time a man on stilts, in a yellow T-shirt and super-length striped trousers, was bending, with no little skill, to throw his employer's brand of sugar-free sweets into a ripple of waving primary school kids. Stevie. I should have brought Stevie after all.

I made my way through the throng, pausing to snatch a sweet from the air as it flew towards my face. Strawberry, his favourite, with a grinning red-maned unicorn on the wrapper. I turned to go back home.

Nipping left, I cut through an alleyway that would save me five minutes of elbowing crowds. I had reached almost halfway down when the way ahead darkened. Men. Three of them, standing abreast, blocking my path.

I looked behind me. Nothing, no one. I edged on. With the sun behind them, the men stood in shadow. I could not make out faces but the middle one was him. The man from the supermarket. Darren Hodson. I knew it now. All three were coming towards me, marching on me as one. Dry mouth, acceleration of heart, dilation of pupils, constriction of blood vessels, of throat. Fuck, help me. The men barrelled towards me and I froze.

Help.

A rustling of muscled polyester, I was elbow-hit, turned hard, my shoulder my hip my shin my chest my side, tumbled in an angry whirlwind of men. A last ankle-shove and they had pushed past, leaving me slumped and shaking, facing back the way I had come. Hands on knees, panting, I watched the three walk away, now in single file, taking strides towards the old white lady coming towards them. Still frozen, I watched them flatten themselves against the wall to let her pass. I looked down. My handbag had dropped, but I still had my purse. The sweet, Stevie's red unicorn sweet, had been crushed into the mud. Tears started before I could turn away.

When I got back I was still rushing, still flooded with hormones from my shocked brain, shaking as I turned the key in our lock. Relief, and loud music, lifted me as soon as I walked into our home. Too brilliant, that embracing sound: Stevie Wonder himself, 'For Once in My Life'. It took the tremor from my shouted hello.

Nothing back. On the floor there was post. Junk, pizza flyers, white envelopes. One dark red-pink and orange envelope. I bent down: *Ms Lola Waite*.

Leaving it on the floor, I stalked through the hall until I could see into the artfully ramshackle snug where I had left them. There I saw her dancing, with Stevie, my artless boy, standing there looking up at her.

'This is you!'

I did not burst in. I hovered unseen, needing – despite that garish envelope; because of it – to spy on this rarest of moments. I very much needed to see her being kind.

Be nice! Poor mawga likkle girl got no mommy.

Stevie was kicking out his KAFOed legs, laughing so much he could barely stand. Now Lola changed: she jerked, convulsed her limbs, converted her carefree shimmy into a rocking, straight-legged lollop.

'This is you, this is!'

Then she leaned in low to him, face up close to his. The music played on, deafening – I could not quite hear what I am sure I heard, but I swear I *felt* her say:

'This is you, isn't it? Is this you, Stevie the wonderspaz?'

I marched in.

'*What* are you doing?'

They both looked up.

'Oh we do this, we silly-dance sometimes,' she laughed, as if it were nothing at all. 'We're just playing around. Why, what's wrong?'

'He can't get too tired,' I said, an acute pain punching somewhere around my temples. Maybe I had taken a blow to the head. It had been so fast.

'I'm not tired, Mum!' Stevie shouted over the blaring soul.

I was tempted to stomp over and turn the radio off. But I had to deal with the sharp, digging ache now at my ribs – a stitch? Worse? – and the pain in my temples. I could not think in all the funky clamour; but then I truly did not know what I might do if my thoughts knifed through that clatterbanging of confusion.

Overcome, I retreated to the kitchen, tried to think. I had not been mugged. What could I report except that I had been 'roughly pushed past'? The man, I could not now be certain he was the same man from so long ago, not at all. He had the body, the air, but they had all been one burly blur. Best forget it. Best tell Thomas a version, an unworrying account that would end in a hair stroke, a cheek stroke, a bear hug, calming sex. My husband was not made for too much reality. But for now, me. I had not been hurt, had I? I lifted my top, and moved my right hand to my stomach, only then to see that it was balled into a fist. I opened it – the broken sweet, my mud-smeared palm. Why had I picked that up? I dropped it where I stood, examined myself with my dirty hand. No, no bruises or flesh wounds. One thought did pierce me though, one cutting certainty: from now on I could never leave my boy alone with that girl.

Lola

DONE LIST 5

Darling came back from town and yelled at me just for dancing with Stevie or something and later she was talking to Dad and it turned out that these three guys had pushed her over in some dirty little alley. No need for her to yell at me like it was all my fault, but I suppose I have to admit it did sound quite bad.

I could be wrong, but I think she was trying to make out to Dad it was something to do with her being black, which is all a bit obvious. They probably just wanted to mug her for her cash and iPhone like everyone else. No need to go for the major sympathy vote, Darling. Still, I suppose it must have been pretty upsetting, the way she shouted. I think I'll ease off her this evening, that should cheer Dad up.

There you go: just when I was starting to feel sorry for her, she goes and pisses me off again, a fucking masterclass in piss-off. I was trying to talk to Dad, had him on his own for a change and then she needed some stupid thing urgently – probably to use his credit card – and next thing I'm left standing there in the lounge like a dick while he goes and helps her, then I spot them having this long kiss and she walks past and gives me this look, like 'See?' and I hated her like mad. I know I sound nuts but I do get cross, really incredibly angry sometimes. I can burn up with it if I am not careful. Never mind red mist, it's a volcano – reeking of sulphur, a purifying fire. #poetsdoknowit

One good thing is that I've stopped moaning on to AT quite as much as I did. In fact, I am thinking of shutting up for good – it only causes more issues. Up until a few weeks ago, I used to say, 'It's not fair!' and Dad would always reply 'Life's not fair!' as if he was teaching me some kind of great valuable lesson. Now I am starting to realise what he was driving at, but he did not go far enough.

'Life's never fair, Lola,' he should have said. 'Life's <u>never</u> fair.'

Don't slash your wrists yet though. All I mean is that lots of good people – people in hospitals and charity workers, or people helping with the homeless and that – are <u>trying</u> very hard to push things in one direction, but the shitty crowd still swing it too far the other way. They must do, because life just never seems fair. I hope I grow up to be wrong. Or maybe I'll go ahead and grow up to be one of the shitty crowd!

Am I getting depressed? I feel like I, or maybe just my thoughts, need to be fired up and moulded into something new, like metal. My ideas need to take a hammering to get into the right kind of shape. It feels like some kind of destiny, that I must be pulled onwards, like my mother. Who can do that for me now, though? There's only Dad. Or Darling lolol.

I don't know why I think of all this crap. I should be thinking of my 'outstanding' GCSE results, my 'brilliant' future, blahdiblah. But I get like this sometimes, this must be what AT means about getting low. I try to lie to her about it, to hide it. After all, she's a pretty good shrink and I don't want her to think that all her years of hard work on me have gone to waste …

I want to be funny about that but I don't know how.

Worked it out.

If you make yourself ill enough, you will become ill. That's the truth of the matter.

Will said something odd but brilliant about Darling on the phone. He said he'd gone and spoken to his dad and they had done some digging and that Darling 'is definitely not to be trusted'. I can't believe he actually talked to his dad about it. Is that a bit weird? That he actually got his dad to check up on her? To be honest, I thought he was joking when he said all that stuff before about how she was bound to be a criminal. I never thought he was actually going to try and investigate her! He was loving it, of course:

'Told you, Lol!'

He calls me Lol sometimes and if it were anyone else I would be annoyed but he just makes me laugh so much. So then I asked what Darling had done and he was all, 'Don't worry about it, but take it from me: she's trouble.' I tried to get it out of him and he just said, 'I can't, but she is known by people. She has form, believe you me.' And he actually sounded pretty happy about it, so I didn't want to push it any more at that moment. I'll find out soon, I'm sure. But it does feel like things are all moving in the right direction. Any day now, we'll get to the bottom of what she's done so that Dad can realise she really was a massive mistake. Then life can get back to normal.

This morning Darling sent me a Facebook request. Bit awkward, much? I don't want her to see all my private shit. Let her request sit there a while and let's see how long it is until we both forget about it.

People can be so obvious. It's disappointing, lazy thinking.

Pretty much like my actual so-called friends.

Et tu, Ellie? Again, seriously? Even though we were sort of getting on once more and she said she never really liked Will that much and that she got off with this uni guy on holiday anyway, she is now being majorly OTT about the fact that Ben Wischer invited <u>her</u> and all my old school friends to his brother's party, but not me. 'I feel sooo bad, Lo, really!' She could just <u>not go</u>, as Dad and even Darling said. She could tell Ben Wischer that we've been friends since Year 5 and that I have gone to a Sixth Form College, not died, and that he could invite me too or go fuck his preppy self. Lazy, see? Thinking with no passion, no fire in it. But people have school (or college) to worry about, or their craptastic jobs, or they marry my dad … They're just far too busy to think, I suppose.

I've tried to phone Will back, a few times, but he must be blanking me too now. Fan-fucking-tabulous. Caro's whole friendship group still all hate me for telling everyone about her 'going with Will behind Ellie's back' – duh, hello? What do they think Caro did in that hot tub, then? Clue: she wasn't scuba diving down there. Plus, I didn't know for certain Ellie and Will had anything real going on, which they <u>actually didn't</u>. Plus, I can't believe Will has not stood up for me once, not even to Ben about the party thing. I really thought he liked me. #geturdumbasschixhere

Ellie insists that she is cool with me but she doesn't want Will and his mates – especially not Ben Wischer – to hate her. Weak. Basically saying that I mean nothing as a friend. How invalidating, right, AT? Thumbs-up smileyface! #fml

I am quite specially talented at being friends with people who hate me #jointhequeue. Need to sort my life out.

So anyway, all this has made me think of something from just before we broke up from school. We did this dull-as-fuck trip to a gallery with literally no one talking to me on the coach and no phones allowed and so my head was like a washing machine before we even arrived. And the one thing that made me stop wondering when we would get to the gift shop and whether they stocked vodka (I could just see them selling out of handbag-sized novelty bottles in that place, with *The Scream* or something on them) was Hieronymus Bosch. Yes, I can spell that, what am I, twelve? Twisted bodies and weird troll dudes and arrows and tortures and all the reds and browns and no, I thought, my head does not look quite like that, even when I'm in a massive rage. Like I said; more wet and spinny. I only stopped and stared at the painting because that was how I always thought it should look, stuffed full of tortures and revenges – like this human volcano sort of place. Mind you, I don't suppose God's judgement, which was what it showed, is supposed to be the same as revenge exactly, but how would I know? Anyway, the painting looked like I thought my head should look, but the more I talk to AT or Dad about that stuff, the more I realise: my mind is white. White-hot and turning and slowly attempting to cleanse everything inside it as well as itself. Nearly pure, but not yet. I'm trying but it is *hard*.

OM fucking G. I spotted a prescription slip for her pill in their room, Femu-something. <u>The</u> pill. It had not even begun to occur to me she might conceivably get pregnant, she's way too past it to have a baby! What have I been <u>thinking</u> this whole time, what have I been <u>doing</u>? This really is no joke. An actual baby, could you imagine?

Darling has got to go. There is no point me being a wimp about it – they <u>cannot</u> stay together. This new life is making me sick, it's all got so much worse with her here. I don't know much, but I know she <u>has</u> to go.

Achievements

1. Finally worked out that Ellie is just not worth it and Will's probably not worth it either. Although at least he had been trying to find out more about Darling before he started ignoring me. Also, note to self: will have to hide all my stuff better because Darling's such a nosy bitch.
2. Did not tell <u>anyone</u> except Dad and even Darling over dinner (to be fair, everyone else knows): Will's older

brother's girlfriend – who is reading Law ffs – kissed
Laetitia, Anna's sister – who is doing teacher training – at
a toga party, even though both boyfriends were apparently
there. They were wasted, but … what is going on with
everybody? #dontneedit. Then, better still, had to hate
myself longtime – and loudly – for being thrown scraps of
two-day-old goss by Izzy bloody Farmer. Lesbo kisses go
viral in seconds, not days. I have no friends any more.

3. Ta-da! At last, a real Achievement! I worked out how to
get him to want me again, like before … It really worked,
bigtime! Now I know how to keep him interested in me.
Feel like a goddess!

4. Finally worked out how you breathe with a thingy in your
mouth. But not underwater, yet. #nostrilsrock

5. Deleted all the Friend requests from people I never want
to be friends with. Oh, that'll be just you then, Darling.

Darling

I fought. Fought to understand Lola, fought to not fight about it with Thomas, fought to push everything from my mind: the phone calls, the stares, and now the alleyway. So far, I was not winning.

Still, I was scrappy.

'She acted like a cruel maniac,' I said. 'She is an active kleptomaniac,' I said. 'You don't know her; she is even taking …'

'… and so you see, I took twenty from your purse,' said Thomas, 'to give to the collector, and forgot to tell you.'

No sneak-theft then, I was simply wrong. But I was still shocked. My head had been rocking and rolling with thoughts of Lola's heartless dance for days. How could she make fun of my boy as she had? She protested a number of times that they had just been having a laugh together, and of course Thomas *insisted* that had to be true, but I knew what I had seen.

The trick was not to get too paranoid. Teens could do that to you. Tech could do that to you: make you think you had a need to know when none had existed before. Find My iPhone fever? No fear; I was going nowhere that I wanted to hide from her and I had all but given up looking at her movements on the app – she was always where she said she would be and mostly with friends or at home. Still, an interesting tool. It reminded you to focus on the present, not to let it get away from you.

I looked about me to see what else I might have missed. I had to refocus on my new family, us Waites.

Thomas was surprising me. He was talking to me more about Lola, the stuff that bothered her, the quirks and funny little ways and worries that would help me better understand his daughter. He *so* wanted us to get on. We talked once more about her history of bulimia, how he had first noticed it sometime around her thirteenth Halloween. He talked about how she missed Tess, no longer seeming to worry that I would feel any pangs at this (he was right to talk; and wrong). He even told me some of her weirder worries: that she got so morose sometimes she thought she might actually be a living painting of hell. Or was it that she was living in a painting of hell? That gave me pause.

I decided that I had to look after everyone better. I would cook up a storm for them, make something Caribbean again.

It bin a likkle while, innit?

I made Escovitch fish, a six-headed sea monster for Stevie: a swimming platter of seasoned red snapper, onions and peppers. The smell of it lured Lola down from her room. For the first time she was already sitting at the table as I bore this Scyllan delight aloft from the kitchen.

'Oh, it looks …'

She sat and stared out this fish that had been plonked on her plate with its head still on; a quick glance at her dad. I had saved her the most bright-eyed specimen.

'Come on now,' I spooned over plenty of the liquor. 'Dig in. Help yourself to rice and Johnny cakes and things.'

We dug in, Stevie waving his fork in glee, ever happy to be eating 'Grandma Food'. He did enjoy it too. Was that some genetically conditioned preference? Not unless he was also Italian, Indian and Chinese. Perhaps he simply liked the best food, food that made families talk, food that told family stories.

'Mmm, really good, Darling,' said Lola.

I looked up.

'Wow. So nice.'

What was this? I looked at Thomas. He beamed as his daughter heaped praise upon his wife's table. A fishy smell in the air. I looked at Lola. Impassive, simply eating.

'Oh, I *love* this, Darling!'

There it was: that magnesium flash that told me the lie had just exploded. I could hear what my husband was deaf to, that tone, mocking and plastic, the first resort of the insincere. It said, 'Here's a wall. A strong, fast-built wall, through, over and around which nothing you do or say can get.' It said, 'Screw you and your weird fish too.' 'Give it up,' it said.

I wanted to call her on it, bawl her out, but Thomas would have been hurt. Baffled. He would swear he could hear no malice – *hush dat wicked chile mout'* – and he would not have been lying. I had learned fast, these past few months; my husband was not attuned to that which it was not in his interests to hear. Had I yelled, we would have soon found ourselves on that steep dead-end path, the one bumpy with rocks for hurling at each other's heads. Far better to suck on stony silence, or fish bones.

Lolapoo eyed us with a saccharine smile.

'*So* good.' She would not stop.

I broke cover:

'Why *thank* you, Lola! Let me get you some more of the liquor.'

I shot up to grab the jug from the kitchen and slosh more tepid sauce into it.

Yuh gotta suck salt outta wood'n spoon, Darling.

Salt. There was a thought. A little sharpener, take the edge off all that saccharine. It could kill slugs, you know. But despite the provocation, I over-seasoned it with nothing more than a smile.

'Here you go, Lola,' I said. 'The very best bit.'

'Thanks so much, Darling.'

Nothing to do but join in, outnice her, force her into the shadow of my nightlight grin as I slopped the sour juice all over her plate. Who could be the best girl for Daddy?

I felt it keenly, minded a lot that Lola regarded me as other, less than, unworthy, inferior. Not a new concept. I had learned from a young age that there were those who would look at me and assume I was poorer, less intelligent, less cultured, a quandary solved upon sight; sexually incontinent, insanitary, ill-mannered and ill-educated for good measure. Not everyone, not most, even. But for those who saw colour and wanted you to know it, these were the cudgels with which they daily tried to crack your thick black skull.

As a child I had not seen it, beyond the playground. When I developed the narrowed gaze and broadened horizons of a teenager, just thinking about it made me want to swear, loudly and at everyone concerned. But as I grew I learned that simply swearing was a fool's gold tooth. No, I was duty-bound to confound. I took the fight to them, beyond them. I would call them out in French, in German and in Shakespeare; prove them wrong in Italian and Nietzsche; checkmate them in Chaucerian; demolish them in Dutch and Dante; crush them in Spanish and Latin and Maya and Morrison and Molly-freakin-yeah. Then I would sit back to watch their little faces, unable to compute, their clodhopping ideas all covered in darkest dismay.

I've been storing up words, lines, ripostes – and books – for many, many years. I've read libraries and read faces and I have learned and learned, and all in order not to be a teacher, or professor, but to be a true nurse. A nurse of nourished mind. The truest and the best, pure of thought and heart and mouth.

But this was my step-daughter, our girl. And she wanted me gone. She was itching to rub me out of the picture. But surely, as long as there was hope and chicken …

Gentle persuasion betta dan force.

True enough, not just of heads stuck in railings and tricky locks, also of teenage girls; of the love and the food you could feed them. Lola could not be forced into being friends, but perhaps I could persuade her with my dishes, maybe even save her.

Flavour cannot be forced into food. Take a fig. A plain, miraculous, green-purple fig like any one of those my mother plucked for me from the back-of-the-garages wall. I know nothing of how to grow them, no mulchy tale to be dug up there, but when it comes to the eating, that I know. A fig. You can cut it, when entirely ripe, with a kitchen knife. You will, in a deft chop or two, get quarters or halves of green-cream-crimson fruit that are perfectly pleasant and ideal for eating. But. Take your next fig. Now dig your thumbs in deep and tear it slowly in two, urge it open. There: see it come at you, see it explode into a riot of fruitfulness, become more than it was, voluptuous.

Persuasion always tastes different. Better.

This is what I wanted, for Lola and me. Not a sharp, swift reckoning, but a ripe response to my gentle inducements, a burgeoning towards what we could and had to be. Now, was that too much to fucking ask?

'So you see,' I said to Lola, standing a few feet from her father. 'I know his needs might seem to get in the way sometimes, but it is really important that Stevie feels valued and, well, listened to. We want him to feel as normal as possible, don't we?'

'Sure,' she said, still texting.

'Lola ...' began Thomas.

'*Yes.*' But she looked up, thumbs now still. 'I like Stevie. He's fine. Stevie is not the problem.'

She looked down again, eyes hard and glittering, thumbs jittering, feet joining in. Not *a* problem, was what we pretended to hear. We had all heard the truth, but not one of us said a word more.

The first Monday after half-term. I planned to give the house a good going over while the family were out. We still left Agata from up the road some cleaning, plus all the washing and ironing. She needed the money; we valued her taciturn efficiency. But I liked to make myself useful and it had been ages since I'd been given any work. The bank nurse managers for St Foillan's had been dead keen for a while. I had been 'popular' they had said at one time, 'a great asset', even 'one of the family'. Then I had moved a while back from paediatrics to geriatrics and the rest was silence. Radio silence, with a bit of static whispering about too many new foreign nurses, too few jobs. ('But of course *you* know how it is, don't you?' Foreign as I intrinsically was, or had become.) Thomas's view – generous, kind husband – was that I should kick back and enjoy looking after the family. Our family.

So, Monday: a day of deep-cleaning nooks, deep-filling a steak pie (Stevie, neither particularly Jamaican nor restrained that morning, had been vocal in his insistence), wiping up and wiping down, hoovering and plumping cushions. Then, on lifting up the pillow in the spare room, what should I find but another pair of knickers stuffed underneath, these screaming scarlet and stringy, a lairy net designed to pull in some thumping, jumping excitable catch.

I lifted them up: new, and worn.

I threw them down; yet another violation. Devil red and so scant they could only be Lola's.

Lola?

Yuh nuh like dem? Yuh tink she force ripe?

Never mind her sartorial choices. What? Why? Under what good circumstances would she have needed to remove her knickers here? What the hell? What the holy hell had she been doing? What the hell was she thinking? What the hell did she need to come here for, into this rarely used third spare room? What the *hell*?

A cigarette, just one cigarette, which would light up like the face of an old friend, burned into my thoughts.

'Bloody bloody no.'

I snatched up the hellish undies for the wash.

There it was again, the murky brouhaha of illness as Lola once more puked into the loo. I guessed that architectural ingenuity had not come so far as to prevent such noises being heard, rough and insistent and clear, on the other side of the bathroom door.

I was going to call her name and then I heard it: a cry so soft it was a whimper, a mewling. That shifting, just under my ribcage.

I needed to raise this, now, needed to set us on to a new path. As soon as I could, I cornered her in the conservatory.

'Lola,' I said. 'I need to talk to you.'

'What is it?'

'It's … you,' I said. 'You're not well. I've heard you—'

'Heard me what?'

'Being sick.'

'Yeah, so?'

That hard glitter was back in her eye; that arrogant jaw. I recognised it from the nineties, from the sugar-dusted parties at a friend's uni halls.

'Your dad's told me, of course. About your problems with this.'

'Oh what the—'

'Come on, he couldn't not, could he?'

She said nothing.

'And I know you're lying to me about the charlie.'

'*Charlie?*' Such acrid contempt.

'Well, yes. You are doing it, aren't you?'

'I …' she glared at the floor as if it had wronged her. 'No.'

'Look, Lola …'

'No!'

'OK. Listen, I know you've been going through a tough time, with your friends, and exam stress and the hot tub stu—'

Her head whipped up.

'What do you know about the hot-tub thing?'

Heat surged to my face; could she tell? Stupid, unforgivable of me to forget: I was not supposed to know. Only her DONE LISTS had revealed to me Caro's spec*tack*ular party trick.

'Have you been in my room?'

My lie of a weary sigh.

'Overheard you on the phone. I just want to help.'

It was unfortunate that she did not realise I could not see Thomas rounding the corner as I said:

'All this being sick is not good for you, you know.'

Then her father was there between us and in poured an atmosphere of hot bile. The eyes flashed dark:

'Maybe it was something I ate?'

My face grew hotter. Did she not know the efforts that I had made? Did she not know me at all?

Thomas, ever the man's man, was busy seeing, hearing and speaking no evil; racing off to a quiet life down Three Wise Monkeys' Lane.

'So, ladies.' *Ladies?* I was ready to combust: the fake cheer was itself a betrayal. 'I was wondering what you fancied doing tonight.'

'Out,' said Lola.

'Me? In,' I said, spiking my words with a pinch of spite, 'and cooking my husband something lovely.'

Lola walked off. Thomas hesitated, stayed. He hated the tensions that were building. Still, we all had our weaknesses; his foot tapped fast, seeking the accelerator. Stopped.

'By the way,' he said. 'When you've got a minute, I'd love you to look at my longlist of sites. For the house.'

'Which house?'

'Our house, one day. It will be … stupendous.'

'Wow, OK. Superb.'

'Then it will be stuperbous. You're my client, Darling,' he said. 'It has to be just how you want.'

I kissed him without meeting his eye and said:

'It will be exactly how we all need it to be.'

Of course, I tried to remember that his greatest weakness, now, was me. My happiness was his journey, his fuel and his destination, and it was only the gear-shifts that were proving tricky.

But Lola was managing to knock all the joy out of me.

'Dad, what time are we supposed to be going out?'

'Dad, do you like my new dress?'

'Dad, can I have thirty pounds?'

'Dad …'

Dad, Dad. Every time she said it, shouted it, whispered it, it was an in-joke bellowed across my ears, a gobsmack of victory. Not you, it said, never you.

Worse, she tried to put herself in the middle of my son and me.

'Mum, can I stay up?' Stevie would ask. 'Just until the news?'

'No, baby. You need to—'

'Oh, he'll be OK, Darling,' Lola would say. 'I'll keep an eye on him.'

'Mummy,' he would start up. 'I don't like this yoghurt.'

'But you—'

'He prefers the raspberry ones,' Lola would say, then in the next breath, 'Dad, can we go to see Auntie Diane sometime? It's been ages.'

Always shearing me off – *swoosh* – like some tatty old edge of silk. Always excluding me with a power so potent precisely because to all but me it was imperceptible. That invisible *kapow!* She was a superhero of bitchiness.

It was bewildering.

I came back from dropping Stevie at his dad's to find no one home. I had only been gone for an hour. Wondering, I tidied downstairs, moved on upstairs.

Some instinct sent me straight to Spare Room No.3, which lay furthest from our bedroom. Empty. The duvet, though, was crumpled. Something was wrong with this picture. Very wrong indeed; as a nurse, I knew. I went to her bedroom, stopped, listened. Not a sound.

'What has been *done*, Lola?'

Feeling feeble and brave and angry and curious, I went straight to the bottom drawer. Scarves, only scarves; the cigarettes had vanished and only the faintest tobacco must lingered. The book was not there, however hard I looked. Her DONE LISTS had disappeared.

Moved, of course. I had practically foghorned my discovery into her face, chatting on about hot tubs. Besides, that brain of hers could have devised a decent booby-trap – some broken hair or dislodged speck may have grassed me up ages before. Where though, where would she hide it?

I went to the wardrobe, flung the doors wide open. The once-neat row of clothes was all out of order, mishmashed, all over the shop: yellow against scarlet against turquoise.

The shoe boxes were still stacked, though each too small to stash an A4 notebook.

I pulled at the wall of boxes until they tottered and slid; nothing was slotted behind.

I stood, looked up to the shelf of day-bags and clutches, the magpie's haul of trinkets and belts. I reached in, lifting and replacing each item, reaching right to the back—

'Hi, Darling!' Thomas shouted. 'We're back!'

We. She was with him, could be racing upstairs two steps at a time. I flew back from the wardrobe, pressed the doors shut and sped away from the room.

'God, Dad. Cricket already?'

She was still downstairs and in a good mood. Girls were messy, girls were distracted; anything out of place would be mistaken for her own carelessness. But though I had not been caught, I had failed. No DONE LISTS found, no explanation found for the underwear I had unearthed in unused rooms.

My mind was becoming littered with the rogue scraps of nylon and silk and lace, clogged by them. They were giving me a headache, one which soon spread down to my neck. The stiff neck set my shoulders out of whack and when I tried to twist away, to pluck panties out of my dreams, a whole host of puckish undies would get away from me, hide in corners, the wicked things, until I was burning up, sweating with the chase. This fever was setting my sense of smell off-kilter; everything smelled of mouldy spice.

The next morning, I was infuriated and perspiring in light fog on Norton Road when I decided to give up, go home, lie down.

Lawd a massi, yuh head a tek wata.

I was back home by around noon and determined to hot-wash this grimy secret, whatever it might be. I would also talk Lola out of her rash new white habits, both of them – the cocaine and the politics. I was her step-mum, I had a duty of care.

I opened the kitchen door to discover two blonde girls I had never seen. They were laughing and cooking on my four-grand hob, bacon and eggs, and they were drinking the last of the orange juice. They looked a year or two older than Lola and were wearing nothing but the vaguest suggestion of cami-knickers and bra tops.

'Hello?' I asked, squinting. The kitchen looked too bright, too light.

'Oh hi,' they said in unison, as Lola wandered back in holding our wedding photo book. She did not introduce me:

'Hi! Isla and Christie came over after you'd gone to bed. Thought I'd show them your lovely wedding photos ...'

The voice was deadpan, and she lied with her choice of smile. She really thought I was that much of an idiot.

'Oh, and we cleaned the fridge up a bit, if you can't find some stuff. It was a bit ... messy.'

Always; that presumption of dirt. 'Thanks,' I said, wiping my forehead.

She turned her back on me.

Get dressed, I wanted to say. All of you, get dressed. My husband could be back any minute. You are not twelve and you are not innocent. So get dressed, or get the fuck out of my kitchen.

What I said was:

'Mind that you don't get burned. By the fat. It sputters.'

Then I walked out of the kitchen and a moment later they were all laughing, louder than before.

The fever stayed, for a while.

'Do you think you need to see a doctor?' asked Thomas.

'I'm not really sick,' I said.

'Then what's wrong? You're on edge at the moment, and you're burning up. You seem …'

'I'm OK.'

'… not yourself. Darling?'

'Honestly, I'm fine.'

The next time we made love, it felt like anything but. We had sex, because it felt too defining to say no, and I suffered, yes suffered, his brief shout of coming with a detachment that felt close to pain.

He slept and I did not – too hot. The least bearable thoughts kept me company all night.

All too soon, everything became clear.

I had been out, still feverish but playing it down, as you did when you had raised a boy to six by yourself. Sweating but not shaking, I went out to buy the Sunday papers and came back to find them both laughing. Her on the sofa, him standing, looking down at her.

'It will seriously only be twenty-five quid, Dad. Thirty at most.'

'That'll be forty, then.'

'Dad!' She was open and buttercup-bright as I walked through the door.

Her manner. She treated her dad not as I had treated mine, but … What? She forced him into the role of some close and over-attentive relative. An *uncle*. And how tanned she had got this summer, for an indoors girl. All brown leg and skirt. A rare smile, which faded as I walked in the door.

'Hi, Darling!' called Thomas.

'Hi, hon.'

Did she know? Did any young woman get how lost these self-styled big-men-of-the-world could become when it came to *our* sex? Did she *know*?

'Hi, Darling,' she smiled.

Lola and I were *enemies*; I could no longer deny it.

'Listen, love,' he said. 'I'm just popping to the cashpoint, then we can take it easy. Lola's going out. Can I get you anything?'

'No thanks.'

Lola had already risen, slipped out the other door.

'Hurry back. We've been so busy lately …'

'I know. Just us tonight, Lola won't get in until late. Stevie's sorted, yes?'

'Yes,' I said.

He went out of the door with a stroke of my waist and I sank into the sofa.

I was shivery, ham-thighed; the worst thoughts were having a fine old jump-up in my head. We needed an evening without her. We needed to talk. I sat, stretched hands clawed like a hacked-off cat, spreading to form a wide X, my fingertips now straining towards the corners of the ceiling. Then I relaxed, let everything slump. How could one's eyelids *pound*? My arms slipped down the back of the sofa, and now my hand was digging, delving in behind the seats. Almost immediately my fingertips struck something cold and hard. A dropped earring? My splitting mind yawned open with the seat cushions as I pulled out the prize: a plastic diamond stuck to the waistband of a pair of terrible, flammable, white knickers.

Then I was shaking and the *sweat* …

Oh God.

Puppa Jesus.

The snipey attitude, the roaming underwear, the drugs, the head problems, the sickness, the secret conversations in the bedroom …

I rushed to the front door and grabbed the handle, my feet wanting to run out after him and feel the pain of gravel. But I stopped.

I would not scream in the street for him. I had to face him down in our home.

I ran upstairs clutching Lola's underwear and shut myself into our en suite. I ran the bath hot. I sat on the loo for an age. I raised the balled fist to my nose. Worn.

The front door went. Thomas. Footsteps coming up and closer. Lola somewhere near.

With no work now, I was prone to baths around the clock; he never thought anything of it. But I needed Lola to go out. I ran hot water into the bath. Sat on the loo seat in my clothes until the bath was near full. Let it fill until it started to slop on to the floor, creating a chain of doll's house pools in the expensively dented tiles. Pretty. I turned it off.

Then I sat longer.

Much later, the door went again, a teenage shout. She had gone.

Staring into the dusk of our bathroom, my face bathed in sweat and steam but with no intention of undressing, I released the scrumple of pale polyester in my hand so that it fell to the floor, two hours too late.

'Thomas.'

My throat was chilled, scratchy, the single cool dry part of me. He had turned me inside out.

The croak failed to penetrate the walls.

'Thomas.' I lifted my body, my voice. 'Thomas! Thomas!'

A thudding as he ran to me.

'What the? Are you OK in there, what is it?'

I unlocked the door. Left it closed.

'God, open up. What is it, Darling?'

I did not cry. I ran a finger down the bathroom cabinet's glass. Through the mirror's steam a sliver of my face, shining; twisted metal. I opened the door.

'You,' I said.

'What? I don't—'

'You,' I said. 'You do things. This.'

My hand flew out, pointing to *this*, the seamy underwear, his daughter's, on the pock-marked tiles.

'What?'

'Whose are they?' I asked.

He looked down at them.

'Must be Lola's?'

'Yes.'

'Well then … so?' His voice was rising too, in pitch and volume. Something urgent was reaching arms around us, squeezing.

'So!' I said, louder. 'So!'

'Darling!' he cried. 'What is it?'

'You!' I was screaming now. 'You!'

He stared, as if nothing was coming through, the hot mist gone black. I dropped my voice to stone.

'You. I have found her knickers … *everywhere* and I've been out. There has been no one else here. Lola, *Lolita*, is that your game? You both plot together, hide things from me.'

'Darling? What are you—'

'You know what. Monster.'

His eyes. The way that they opened wide, their thousand-minute calculations; the way they glinted with a new light, the next moment extinguished. Her dad.

'What's wrong with you, Darling?'

His mouth closed and something in him slumped as if puppet strings had been cut. Then he walked out of the door.

Thomas was not in our bedroom. Where?

I could just take Stevie and go. But then in he came, still dressed in yesterday's black jumper, holding what looked like whisky, no rocks. Five-something a.m. The glare of artificial light was building; our whole lives at that moment looked unreal, over-exposed.

'You're still here,' he said.

'I've been here all night,' I said. 'You know that.'

He looked through me. Dangerous.

'I'm going now,' I said. 'So don't try and—'

'Go,' he said.

I stalled. Then he turned and left our bedroom. I rushed in, pulled a suitcase out and started pulling everything into it: tops, bottoms, shoes, mismatched underwear; all a mad dash.

It was killing me. Killing me to have to hurry without a sound. A flash of mirror showed me my face, crumpled and damp, so much dirty satin. I dragged the case to the door, ran across the landing and attacked the lock on Stevie's room with its key.

A hillock of duvet.

'Come on, baby, please, time to get up.'

No sound. I pushed at the unmoving bump.

Still nothing. A drop of my forgotten fever splashed down, soaked into cotton:

'Stevie? Stevie, Stevie!'

A stirring. 'Nnnn.'

'God, I thought you—'

I pulled him into my arms, got the KAFOS from the floor and, still shaking, started to strap him in.

'Nah, Mummy. No!'

The door swung open. Thomas was standing there with our suitcase.

'Thought you might need—'

'We don't need anything' – I rose to heave up the suitcase – 'from you.'

I kept on with the KAFOS, Stevie all the time wailing.

'What's wrong, Mummy?'

'Nothing, sweetness, come on.'

'But *why* are we, Mummy?'

'For God's sake, Darling, at least let him—'

A dam burst. 'Don't you effing tell me what to do. You! You effing—'

'I need the loo, though, Mummy.'

'This is so ... don't, just don't, woman. Listen to yourself—'

'Oh, I hear me. I hear me thinking—'

'Mummy!'

'How could he? Who is he, this man I married? What has he done? Why did he—'

'Mummy!'

A hissing, water. I looked down and saw the urine pooling at Stevie's feet, soaking his KAFOs, his pyjamas. I grabbed and lifted him.

'For God's sake, Darling,' he said again. 'At least change him before you go!'

'Out, Thomas. Get out!'

He backed away, a slight stumble, turned and went.

'Sorry,' I said to Stevie. 'Come on, let's change you. Sorry, I'm so sorry ...'

I did everything to make him clean and dry, dressed him in his softest tracksuit, tried to get him to doze for a while longer. We would wait until the house was quite still again. And then we would go.

A Thing or Two

Her first kiss.

She had heard that kisses were sweet, but never thought they meant like that.

No. No thank you. She does not think she would like a kiss from a real man. (Kisses were from boys, if you liked one when you were really old, maybe twelve. Not a man who has too much forehead and is all grown-up.) But he is him. *He takes another hard peach and a few brown cherries out of his pocket and puts them on the table and tells her that she would like a kiss, wouldn't she, and she says: yes.*

Now he is asking again. A second kiss.

She shakes her head.

'Come on, I know you do, come here, quick …'

No.

No, thank you.

No.

No.

No.

Lola

DONE LIST 6

There has been trouble in the night. Fighting. Stevie pissed his pyjamas: I woke earlier and texted Dad and he was still up … I mean fuck, really? What are they trying to do to us, her and her pissing son. I <u>love</u> my dad.

I suspect it's my fault though. Shame. I've been freaking her out a bit. People like Darling can't stand being ignored. She won't have bothered counting, but in the past 48 hours I've said no more than five words to her, including 'yes' and 'no' twice each. That's all the vocabulary she deserves.

I'm Napoleoning Darling, too. (Jonesie taught me at least one thing worth remembering.) I cut her off from our conversations with wide eyes and a baby mouth. Ga ga goo. Dad smiles; he is my unknowing collaborator. I ask him things only he can answer, like things that happened before her time, when I was a baby.

'Dad, did we live in Sanderson Road when I was two?' (And Mum was here.) 'Or three?'

'Dad, when I was little,' (and Mum was here) 'what was that story you read me at bedtime?'

'Dad, when I was a baby,' (and Mum was here) 'did I like, love, rusks? We tried some at Taz's sleepover and they're yum!'

Ga ga goo, fuck you.

She's got to go.

I've been giving her a hard time over her rancid over-hot food too. Not saying anything exactly, just what you might call 'making my feelings known'. I told Dad, straight out, that her crappy food was making me sick, that she had to be poisoning us all with her funky stews and junk soups.

Well, I had to say something! I know Dad hears me puking all the time. Got to give the poor guy some handle on my freakdom. And I might not have had actual food poisoning to date, but you can't be too careful. (Unless, I suppose, you're me, lol.)

She's still here for the time being, unfortunately; I've clicked the app and I can see. Although I bet she's not in the same room as Dad. Hold on, I just heard voices again. They can't still be arguing. Going to find out what's going on.

What the actual very fuck?

I mean, WHAT? The woman is crazy, seriously nutzoid. She really does need to sod right back off again to wherever the bloody hell she came from.

I can't believe it. I went up my 'secret stairs' and along to the far end of the loft, then back down again to the other landing door with the gap so I could hear what they were saying. Totally wish I hadn't. How can my dad have married someone who could think he was a paedo? She found some knickers and decided he wanted to ~~screw his ow~~ just gross. God almighty, what a freak (her not him).

Can you believe the cheek of that woman? Poor Dad sounded so upset; it was obvious even though his voice was all muffled. I actually want to kill her.

I'll never get back to sleep now. Might as well write some shit and make AT's day. Or maybe I should try to count lots of fit Wills jumping over a fence (he's not Dovington athletics champion for nothing). Please tell me he's not properly blanking me. Maybe he's changed his mind about us …

Will told me Darling was not to be trusted and he was right! He is going to go nuts when I actually get hold of him to tell him all this. Or he might just piss himself more than Stevie did, the sicko. Yes, he will, knowing him, but he'll also totally get why I hate Darling even more now (just when I thought I was about maxed out). He always says people exaggerate about all the 'nasty racists' and it's simply the natural way the world has worked out. White people made everything worth having, made all the places worth living in, which is why everyone else is piling into leaking boats to get here now. It's not racist, he says, people like him just don't want their country ruined.

I know I should get angry when Will says all that stuff – Dad would go ape. But it's hard, I am starting to think he does have some good points. It's like when his Oxford application went wrong. His parents were so fucked off about it and they knew it was tied to all those reports in the papers about letting in more coloured people and Muslims and state school kids and the 'one-legged-leftie-lesbians' that his dad reckons are getting all the breaks these days.

Just heard a door. I wonder if they are going to go the hell to bed soon, or if she is planning to walk out. He should really kick her out but I know he won't, he's too nice. He would die if he knew I had heard them arguing about it, and it's not like I know what to say to him about something so spectacularly fucked up. I'll keep my mouth shut and let her do all the damage herself.

Quiet again now.

Anyway. Will was totally cheated over Oxford (he is so goddamn smart and he doesn't even try). So I can kind of see where he's coming from. It's hard for boys like him – everyone thinks they've got it all and so they should share it with less impressive people, but why should he, really? The wars and corruption in black countries are hardly his fault, are they? But then again, I do realise that some little kids

actually do die at sea or get abandoned in shitty camps …
It's pretty messed up. But none of it's his fault. Darling goes
on, she reckons things are changing for people like her in
the UK, but then what would I know? I've only been around
for sixteen crappy years. OK no, it's not like I don't care at
all, but what the hell am I supposed to do about it?

Voices again. God, do they think I'm deaf or what? I can't
believe she is still here. What's it going to take?

OK wait, I need to back Dad up, I thought I heard them
say 'police'. I'm just building up the nerve a sec. I'll have to
tell her. I'll tell her that I should bloody know if my own
Dad has been abusing me and that she has to listen to me
when I say it isn't true. And that if she had found a pair of
knickers lying around … Well, I did do some naughty stuff,
all over the place. Will liked me to go in all the different
rooms, he used to say, 'I'm going to have you all over your
house.' None of it was anything to do with my own bloody
father, though, ffs! I was working my lacy backside off just
to get Will to like me again. Stupid dumb mutual fun, a bit
wild and crazy but not really bad. It was private.

Fuck her. Police, though? I need to tell her. Shit shit shit
this will be properly cringe. But it's got to be done. I will beg
her to please, please not tell Dad about Will, but to please
just believe me. Then we can both explain to Dad that she
made a big mistake and that I left that underwear lying
about because I am simply a lazy, messy teen. Normal.
Unlike her.

After that I'm getting the hell out of here. I need to see Will – maybe we can go somewhere far away from parents? I can fill him in about this latest Darling nightmare and, as I'll have taken one for the team, he can finally cough up whatever he knows about her. I'm sure he'll be only too happy. He seems to find her almost entertaining: tracking her phone with me, generally taking the piss.

Must meet with him asap tonight. Now I've got a real reason, so it's not like it would be asking for a date. I don't think Will loves me properly yet, but give or take the Ben Wischer party thing, he does seem to like me. So that's cool, isn't it? And he did say he'd help me.

Dad and Darling in love? That really _is_ fake news. _Love_ is probably fake news.

Could have gone worse. I heard movement in the kitchen and went downstairs even though it was super-early and confessed it all to her, sang like the proverbial canary on speed. I apologised, rather beautifully. I think it's done the trick. I can't hear any more voices now – Dad might finally be getting some asleep.

I'm still in shock that it could all blow up like that. I just didn't think. I certainly didn't think that Darling would lose the plot about some stupid pants. And I still can't quite believe I was silly enough to leave my knickers lying around!

Although, to be honest, the first couple of times I did down a fair bit of their gin and stuff too – how else could I get the nerve to do those things for the camera? May have been a bit too drunk, got a bit sloppy … maybe I did just race back to my room before someone came home and caught me. She must be totally exaggerating about the amount of underwear though – I surely can't have been so careless more than once. Or maybe twice, absolute max. To hear her shouting at Dad, you would think it had happened loads of times! Anyway, God, I can't believe I nearly got Dad banged up, or got Will and me into trouble, for that matter. Also, not great that when I apologised just now, I screwed up by showing her Will's photo – totally forgot she'd seen all his political stuff in my room! Still, what's she going to do? Now I've confessed about the amateur porn-star antics she should be happy.

I don't really care what she thinks of me but – *how* embarrassing. Still, bottom line is that she made this whole knicker thing into a problem, not me.

Anyway, she is sworn to secrecy now and has finally unpacked her suitcase. Which is a shame, of course – missed opportunity? – but at least Dad won't be doing actual time for a) being a paedo or b) beating the crap out of Will for corrupting his daughter.

Still, I hope Will might corrupt me some more if we get to go out tonight.

Maybe AT nailed it in my very first session, maybe my issues do go back to my childhood. They <u>must</u> do, right? After all, childhood is the only thing that has ever happened to me. There is something that has stayed with me, this whole time. I remember in the weeks before Mum died, every time Dad went out, this man came around and I used to have to sit and watch some noisy kids' show while they went upstairs to talk. It was so stupid, all that slapstick stuff I hated even then, and I never knew what it was called, which made it even more annoying – they always missed the opening credits. And Mum turned it up, really loud. I never knew the man's name and I never saw even what colour his car was, or if he walked to our house, or when he left, and I've never told Dad because Mum had said not to and it sometimes keeps me half awake at night so that I wonder whether I am dreaming now, or whether I was dreaming it then. Except I know that in fact I was not dreaming then and it was always daytime. She was having an affair – I once got bored of the cartoons and saw their sex and kisses in the landing mirror – and I've never told him. I think that might keep me awake for the rest of my life.

One question I still can't answer – why does Dad even want to be with her. Why?

I asked Will one time. He reckoned it was because 'black women are easy and they've got big nipples'. I didn't know what to say. He's always really funny like that, but that time I couldn't laugh, just felt sort of cold.

Could it be her nipples, though? I had a look online and Will's not lying, but surely there must be more to it than that. Mind you, I can't see what else is so loveable. It's not just about her colour. With Darling and Stevie, we seem to be having some horrible sad kind of Bob-Marley-comes-to-town (with all his ganjaed-up mates) moment. Hey, some of Dad's favourite singers and US presidents are suddenly black! He actually put on reggae the other day. Flipping reggae, WTF? Since when has he ever liked that? She's changing him, but then isn't that what they vowed to do when they said what's yours is mine what's mine is yours, etc? Thanks to her, we are now all mixed up, blended in every way. The United Waites.

Maybe it's not her nipples. But I can't think why the hell else he reckons he loves her so much. And more than ever I can't stop wishing that she would do us all a favour and just drop dead.

Great, Will has said he'll meet me at the Rose and Crown on the high street later. I'm worried there's no way I'll ever get in, even with my fake ID, but he has told me not to worry, he can get me in no problem.

Meanwhile I am staying in my room as much as possible. I don't want to look at Darling unless I have to. Still so pissed off about her weird stupid accusations, I could actually hit her right now. Some of the girls at school always used to say I had 'anger issues'. Of course I do, don't need a fucking shrink to tell me that. I killed my own mother.

But I reckon I was angry way before that. I must have been born angry and I've no fucking idea why.

Darling controls everything … all the power, all the sex, theirs and mine, and no doubt soon all the money. Our whole family. That <u>cannot</u> be fair.

Also, forgot to mention: as if last night was not bad enough, I found out that she told him to fake my sixteenth birthday cake. We were talking about cake the other day and he told me about that, feeling bad, while she was sitting right there. Just came out with it, like it was some cute little anecdote the two of them had shared. He's not a liar, like her. She's ruined my life. I loved his disgusting cake and it turns out it was all a lie and next thing she's lying about him too and what in the name of bastard am I supposed to do now?

He'll need cheering up later. I often try to, without him noticing. I've been asking him lots of good questions lately:

'Dad, what's a liquid asset?'

'Dad, when should you start learning to drive?'

'Dad, what is a silly mid off?

'Dad, how do you get a mortgage?'

I sometimes ask a load of questions in a row, just to ultra-annoy Darling. Dad loves explaining stuff – practical matters and issues of great, big-deal life importance. He seriously should have been a teacher. Sometimes it's like he's waited his whole life to explain stuff to me.

Goes both ways.

God, what a night.

Will was right, there was no problem getting into the Rose and Crown. I was sure they wouldn't let me in – for a start I can't find my best eyeliner and I look about twelve without it – but it was easy. Will put his arm around me and went up to this big scary-looking guy on the door. I wanted to turn around and go, this bloke looked like we shouldn't mess him about at all, but Will just said 'All right mate?' and the guy said, 'All right, Will, in you come.' And that was it. He didn't even ask for the fake ID, thank Christ!

It wasn't as scuzzy as I had thought it would be, inside. We got a table in the corner near the loos and Will told me the bouncer's name was Daz and I tried to joke, 'Well, if my father asks, tonight you're called Cassie, or Caz.' And he was all, 'Who the fuck's that?' So I told him I'd had to lie to Darling to come out, which really did make me look about twelve. But I was sort of secretly impressed because Daz looked like someone I would never dare talk to and about forty, but then Will knows a lot of older people and he is practically nineteen himself.

Then he bought me a double vodka coke and I told him everything. Well, maybe not every last detail, but I did say:

'Darling's gone too far this time. She called my dad an actual paedo.'

He spat out some of his drink and went 'What?' And so I had to tell him the whole embarrassing story, including that I must have left my knickers lying around after one of our 'Facetime Dates'. (I didn't say fucks because there was this nosy couple on the table next door and the man was quite fit despite the eyebrows but she looked like a teacher and it was all pretty distracting.) Will did piss himself and said 'What a silly bitch!' a lot, but then I said to him (this was so awkward):

'I don't think we should do any of that Facetiming stuff any more. I mean, I promised Darling I wouldn't. And even if … I really don't think we should.'

He said 'Don't be a twat, of course we can.'

And I didn't like him calling me a twat so I told him that I just didn't want to any more anyway, which was totally the wrong thing to say because then he said:

'Suit yourself. To be honest, it was quite funny watching you try to be sexy.' And then he did this impression of me.

And I was so shocked I couldn't speak, and he got up to get himself another drink – I still had my one, but even so he didn't ask. He took ages at the bar and he was chatting to this blonde girl with massive hoop earrings queueing next to him, for ages, and then he came back and he seemed a little less pissed off. So I tried to perk myself up and get him on a better subject and I asked him:

'Anyway, what is all this great stuff you know about Darling? What's she done?'

I thought he would be dying to talk about it, but he said:

'I can't really go into it, sorry. But you don't need to worry.'

So I pushed a little more and said:

'But if I know then maybe my dad will decide she's not worth the trouble and finally kick her out.' Which made perfect sense to me, but he said:

'She's just a trouble-maker, that's all. But it's sorted, leave it.'

And I was a bit confused, because I thought the whole point was for us to split them up, but then soon after that the bouncer guy, Daz, came past our table and stopped and said to Will:

'Is this her, then?'

And Will said yes, which made my stomach do an actual flip because he has obviously been talking about me to his friends.

The bouncer gave me this big smile – I think he might be quite sweet under the tattoos – and then he disappeared out the back door and I asked Will how he knew him. His answer surprised me, he said:

'He's actually a friend of my dad's.'

And I was like 'What?' (Will's dad is really posh.) But he said:

'I know! A bouncer from Elm Forest. And my dad. My dad defended him once – he was wrongly accused of something stupid – and now he thinks my dad is an absolute legend. Which is cool for me.'

'Yes,' I said, although I did not get what was so cool about it, until he said:

'Because obviously he's the best dealer round little old High Dumpford.'

I must have looked shocked, but only because I was sure the couple on the next table could hear every word. And Will laughed and just said:

'Don't do that face. Where did you think all that lovely blow came from, Father Christmas?'

And then I felt stupid, so I laughed loud too. But at least Will was back to normal and this time he got us both doubles and some crisps and started to joke around a bit more. Then, just when I thought he might ask me to go outside with him or something, he started to tell me that this Big Daz bloke was a handy guy to know because he was also 'pretty good with a cricket bat'.

I must have been reaching my most pissed point around then because I thought for one second he actually meant sport and said:

'What, Daz is a batsman?'

And Will laughed, like a <u>lot</u>, and said:

'Don't be moist, Lol. More of a problem-solver. Solves problems with his bat. Could even solve Darling for us.'

'What?'

'Sort her out. Hit that fugly face of hers for six.'

He was laughing, but then he went on about how Daz had been inside at least twice, and something gross about some guy he hit who ended up with his shin-bone poking out and imagine if that was Darling and then neither of us were laughing any more and Will was looking quite intense which made me feel suddenly way too drunk and a bit sick so I said:

'Just stop, Will, please.'

He got all annoyed and started flicking bits of beer mat across the table and saying:

'What's your problem? You're the one always going on about how much you hate her.'

And the next-door table were practically in our laps – he was sort of checking me out from under his eyebrows and the teacher was listening to Will's every word, I swear – and I did not want a scene especially as I wasn't even supposed to be in there and I really wanted to get back and so I said it was probably time I went home. I sort of hoped he might leave with me, but he just said 'See ya!' and leant right back in his chair. So in the end I had to walk back down the high street in my heels in the dark feeling sick on my own and I knew Dad would not even be in when I got there and that Darling would not give a toss where I had been.

So, on balance, not the best night. Horrible, in fact. Bloody wish I had not even mentioned Darling. How did I manage to screw that up quite so badly? #epicdatingfails #drinkdietcoke #fmfl

This morning I woke up and had to run to the toilet. Sick, sick, sick. I'm sure it's not my hangover. Let's cut the bull, we know what this must mean. I hate that dodgy old expression 'up the duff' (what the hell is a duff when it's at home, anyway?) and 'knocked up' and 'bun in the oven' and all those nasty little phrases which all basically mean you're fucked. Pregnancy is why they call it being fucked.

Just thinking about it makes me want to vom again. But if I chuck up any more I'll probably faint and then I'll come to and no, it really is not a bad dream. Oh God oh God oh God.

Pregnant, seriously? Why is my life falling apart all at once? Dad and Darling, wedding hell. Stevie. Ellie messing me about. The whole Will thing, which all of a sudden seems to have been just some cheesetastic, Ferris-Bueller-fail, rites of passage shitstorm. And now this?

He hasn't whatsapped me at all today. I'm not even sure how much I like him. Last night was so weird. How am I supposed to stop thinking about him though?

I have just been sick again. Why do they call it morning sickness – it's fucking 5.47 p.m. Not like my loopy, AWOL periods can confirm anything, but ... I don't want to think what will happen if I am definitely, without a doubt pregnant. Dad will <u>freak</u>, God, he will go nuts. But Darling might be able to help. After all, she is a nurse. What would Darling do?

Oh God. Just my luck if she's my only hope.

Achievements

1. Googled a lot about being pregnant. It is <u>not</u> good. #nonononothankyou
2. Decided to keep all my goddamn undies up and on from hereon in, aka forever!
3. Planned to walk all the way to Will's to try to talk, but bottled it and went and got myself a second piercing in my left ear instead. No one's said anything, so I'm guessing they haven't noticed.
4. Obsessed about cake for more hours than might be

normal. I'm not even your biggest cake fan. But it was <u>my</u> cake. #buttercreambitch

5. Cried and cried until I looked like a fucking frog. Darling heard and tried to hug me ffs. She's watching me a lot, at the moment. Like, a lot.

Darling

MONDAY, 7 NOVEMBER

I was here but not here. We were supposed to be leaving before Lola woke up, as soon as Stevie had rested more, so that he might wake to find me lying on his duvet and think the night had all been a bad dream.

We were in the hallway with our suitcase, good as gone. A padding down the stairs.

'Darling, can I have a word with you, please?'

She was wearing the pink playsuit I had first seen her in, when I had been put in mind of mythical creatures, but now with thick black tights and a slouchy cardigan.

'You need to go to the loo before we go, Stevie. That's it, go on.'

Then she told me everything: that she had been fooling around with the boy, Will, on their smartphones and got carried away, leaving her knickers and such all over the place.

'And so, what, you filmed yourself, for this boy—'

'Will. I'm seeing him, he's not just anyone.'

'I thought you guys fell out ages ago?'

'We did. But I got him back.'

'By showing him your bits?'

Nothing.

'Have you at least got the film, the files?'

'No!' she said, boggling at me, numbskull that I had to be.

'I only *meant* to destroy them …'

'Oh. No, it was mostly Facetime, it doesn't record, and the vid— Don't worry about it.'

'I do worry. I was right to worry.'

She looked around as if for exits.

'So, what's he like anyway? Is he worth it?'

She jabbed at the screen, cocky and pissed off, shoved her phone under my nose and there he was. A smugshot looking out from his conquest's phone with eyes that gleamed with knowing; not glaring, but no more pleasant. He was in the sort of suit that sixth-form Millennials found smart and was wearing the striped tie that I recognised from around town. No man, then: just your average, three-Shredded-Wheat, conquering since 1066 Dovington boy. He had been to our house once or twice during the summer. I hadn't twigged; he must have shot up. It was so clear now – when you recognised that tilt of the head, that leader-in-waiting smile – this was the same boy, then younger still, puffing his chest up next to his dad in the Bright New Britain photo that had been waiting for me in the bundle on Lola's bedside.

A wha dis fadda?

Dear God, that *was* it. She was in love with a boy who loved to hate darkskins. Oh, the conversations they must have had about her new step-mum! What havoc he could wreak on us all were he to practise his dark arts in court!

Wah gwan, gyal? Mi nuh swallah mi spit ...

'Good-looking fellow,' I said. 'Seen him before, somewhere.'

'He was here.'

'Perhaps, but I'm sure I've seen him in a photo. In your room ...'

Realisation can be a red flash, or more like cream coming to the boil; both happened at once in her complexion.

'Ah ... oh.'

'So he hangs out with Bright New Britain people?'

'I'm not sure "hangs out with" is right ...'

'But who does he know there?'

'I'm not sure, why?'

'Because ... nothing.'

'Sorry.'

'Hmm. And he's why I found your knickers lying around?'

'Yes, it must be, but you see I didn't mean to be that out of order. And I'm so embarrassed.'

I paused, weighing each of her words.

'No, Lola, I can buy that.'

She looked at her feet.

'Does your dad know about this yet?'

'Course not! And he can't, please, I—'

'It's OK, Lola—'

'Seriously! He would fucking freak if—'

'No need to swear, I won't tell Dad, it's OK.' Just like that, the possessive pronoun dropped. *Dad*.

'Let's just say I'm a slob. That I was acting all weird – nothing new there, right? – and that I'm a messy slob, so you got it wrong, all my fault. No harm done, right?'

I waited a second. 'You swear that's all there is to it?'

'Yes!'

'And you'll keep your goddamn undies up and on from hereon in?'

'I promise. Please!'

'Fine.' I sat down, as if weighing my options. I had only one: 'I will go and see Dad. But first I need a coffee.'

I was on my second coffee, Stevie was settled and watching cartoons, Lola was back in her room, and I still hadn't summoned the nerve to go and knock on my own bedroom door.

I had fucked up, big time. What did it say about me that I could doubt my husband so seriously, that I could pack our bags before he had unpacked his first explanation? Yes, I could tell myself that I had to be certain that there had been no wrongdoing, or that I had been protecting the children, or that I had been fooled by randy, selfish teens; but what I felt now was more than guilt, or shame. I could not have been crueller to my Thomas.

How could I go to him, now?

I was thinking of filling the kettle again when I heard his tread on the stairs and then he entered the kitchen. Dressed, skin grey.

'Thomas, I—'

He raised pink eyes to me, looked away. He took his phone off the charger, turned and walked; walked out of the front door without a word.

Heartbreaking, the things you do to keep yourself busy. It would have been unwise to phone Thomas at work, and he would not be phoning me, so to take my mind off that fact, I went back to one of the habits I couldn't give up. It was usually when Thomas was in the shower that I read the *Elm Forest Herald*. Now I could read it all day long, if I wanted.

I clicked on to the dismal news:

Local councillor Malcolm Fletcher has spoken of 'record support' for the political movement he represents, Bright New Britain, ahead of the weekend's rally. Putting the influx of new members down to a 'healthy Brexit bounce', Mr Fletcher spoke of his determination to ensure that 'real locals get real choices'. Despite earlier plans to retire this year, he has now announced a new campaign to target younger voters.

Targeting the youth, goose-stepping to the right, declaring what was real and what was not. It was no shock. I had long followed the rise of Bright New Britain, lived through the wild popularity of councillor Fletcher in my old home town. Now support for them was growing in High Desford.

Another new dark red-pink and orange-rimmed flyer had dropped on to the doormat that morning. Rather than tear it up, recycle it or use it for kindling, I thought I would take in the headlines:

BRIGHT NEW BRITAIN
We Won Brexit. What Next?
10 More Ways for Us to Take Control

The 'more ways' turned out to be the same ways as before – by rolling the country's horizons inwards – but strangely they did not spell out a clear policy in relation to abusing, intimidating or indeed pushing those rich in melanin. Or to stomping them as they tried to get home from their Saturday job, putting a knife against their screaming throat and telling them that they did not belong, had no right, that if they told the police, or anyone, they would die.

This was what the teens were being fed nowadays. The landscape Lola was growing up in once again trumpeted this hostility to non-whites (and, of course, the Polish, hauled up for honorary abuse). The vitriol ranged from casual burka-berating to unabashed anti-semitism. For the black people, the brown, and what some used to call 'cappuccino' complexions (and where had all that optimistic froth gone? What had happened to the cinnamon chai latte palatability of British race relations?), a chill was setting in in the villages, in the old industrial towns. It could not all be put down to the stone-cold terror of terror. This was more as if someone had left the fridge door open, or perhaps the front door to the UK, the same one out of which they now wished your too-big black arse would fall. Bit nippy, was Brexit Britain. All at once, everyone who claimed to have been forced quiet for years was a loud expert on what was wrong with all these *darkskins*.

Stevie wandered in.

'What are you doing, Mummy?'

'Getting angry, poppet.'

'Don't, Mummy.'

I put down the flyer. 'Not really, sweetness, just catching up on some reading. You go watch your cartoon and I'll bring you some porridge.'

I watched his tiny head retreat. Had he been born to become a non-word, a *darkskin*? No, but the people had spoken. Listened to *battymout'* logic and had their say. The bad old days of finicketying around, having to waste time noting the differences between East and West Africans, those from the north and the south of the country, continent, whatever; having to pretend a Cameroonian really was different from a Bajan was different from a Muslim was different from a Turk was different from a skint-bloody-Greek was different from a Jamaican – bloody exhausting! Or pretending that rap and bongo-bongo music came anywhere near art forms, or that any of them liked anything other than rap or bongo-bongo music, let alone were able to play proper British music like Mozart and Whassafella von Beethoven. Those days had ducked behind the horizon, for now. No more! They were all *darkskins* and the Poles built their bloody houses and became their bloody cleaners and …

'Is it porridge time now, Mummy?'

'Sorry! Coming, my love.'

I put the flyer into the old coal scuttle along with some other flammable scraps. We would put a match to it on a colder day and use it to warm ourselves.

To be fair, she did not look too pleased as she announced:

'Dad phoned, he won't be home tonight. And I'm going out too. With Cassie.'

'Oh, OK. Thank you, Lola.'

Message received; a blow for a blow. Where would Thomas be sleeping? Who would he go to, so angry: a friend, a hotel? A woman?

I dialled him at last. It went to voicemail, as expected. There was nothing I could say.

All evening I watched to see if he might change his mind, walk in on the three of us at dinner, or turn his key in the lock as Lola left and I tidied up. But he did not.

I went up to bed, knowing I would not sleep. While we Waites alone would have done the trick, insomnia was guaranteed thanks to the world's biggest story, happening just across the way in the US. As the psychiatrist apparently always told Lola, there was no such thing as an accident: I was meant to stay awake. Election-night coverage was starting to build and though I lay on my pillows, already overwhelmed by real-life dramas, every time I went to turn the TV off, something else went wrong so that I had to keep it on.

On and on through the night and wronger and more wrong it went until, finally, everything was going *right*.

The builder of a gilded tower was leader of the free world.

He came back.

'The thing that hurts most, Darling,' he said, from just beyond the kitchen doorway. 'Is that you didn't even come to me, try to talk to me. You assumed the very worst.'

'I know, I was crazy, literally, I was in this sort of fever and I couldn't think straight … I was scared, Thomas.'

He did not move closer. 'Just. Hideous.'

I felt my pulse pick up. He was not being himself, not responding as I had imagined all through that terrible night.

'You see, you kept on having these private bedroom chats; and then there was all her underwear. And once she shouted, "I'm not doing it, Dad …"'

'Did she?' His voice came as if from far away.

227

'Yes, angry, like you were forcing … something.'

'Ah,' he nodded, as though being careful not to break. 'I can't remember that conversation. But sounds to me like she was saying, for the millionth time, that she wasn't making herself sick …'

Truth *does* ring when you hear it. There was the most minute chiming in my ear. I released, so that the tears came:

'I'm so, so sorry.'

His head bowed further.

'Darling, I can't,' he said.

He walked out again.

I could not leave it alone.

My head no longer ached, but my mind itched. I sat in the conservatory, with my laptop and wanted to *know*.

Bright New Britain, from their earliest days, had tried to tattoo their hate on to our ordinary, decent lives. I knew better than most of what they were capable. I used to quake in my young bed at the mere thought of a close-shaven head – and then I had to watch ever-greater numbers of our neighbours slap the BNB canvassers on the back and tell them, 'You're all right.'

I feared, but I read; I had learned that ideas could save you. Save you from men who rose to power as men of the people and yet hated who the people, all of us together, really were. Men like Councillor Fletcher were driven to stomp all over anyone who called bullshit on the vivid sickly lens through which they saw the world. On the myopic things they did.

Once, as a teenager, I had stood up, shouted loud. It was the middle of the local elections and the papers were predicting a rise in votes for Bright New Britain, that they could gain a 'significant foothold' in the area. I couldn't let that happen. I could not let people be fooled, not by those claiming to be one of the people; I might fear, but I read. I had other ideas.

I had ideas.

I went to the Citizens Advice Bureau and asked a lady with plain spectacles whether I could get a grant to prosecute the BNB figurehead. She smiled. We talked for a long time, even though someone else was waiting, and I left with an action plan. That afternoon I spoke to a lawyer. By the weekend, Malcolm Fletcher's thugs, led by Darren Hodson, a man known for his prodigious violence and the eagle tattoo on his neck, had found me and punched me unconscious by the bins behind the pizza café where I worked each Saturday. I came to with a knife to my throat and as I screamed (the café was closed), I was told:

'Don't you go to lawyers, fucking ever. Or police.'

I did not. I thought I might. But the *knife*, you see.

I should have told Thomas the whole story, but I could not bring myself to, not quite yet. He did know that these days I still kept tabs on BNB, especially in Elm Forest. What did they do, these people, outside of the campaigns and the marches and the leaflets? What made them happy? Who and what did they love?

Luckily, the internet was made for people like me, who could not leave it alone.

There it was. A picture I had seen before, now archived forever: a younger but still old Malcolm Fletcher, in his pomp as Elm Forest councillor for Bright New Britain, greeting his new leader – *him talk such a lotta battymout' nonsense* – on a walkabout of the town. Two larded smiles, four eyes set on the greasy populist pole.

Would a girl like Lola love such politics, were it not for Will? I found it hard to fathom. Was his charm so very great? What did we ever do to you, lovely Lolapaloo, my teensy teenage Nemesis? What harm have I done you, except to love Dad, our Thomas?

But there it was. No use professing to be stumped. The world was what it was and she – with her laptop and her phone and her moods and her young lusts, her young unedifying habits – she was very much a creature of it. No point pretending otherwise.

For more reasons than one could shake a *juju* stick at, Lola bloody hated me.

Trying harder was tough as old goat. Thomas and I had spoken, briefly.

I was sleeping in the spare room. 'We' thought it best, for now. I had tried to make my signature curry – it was his favourite – but time had got away from me and it had been rushed, and failed; Pattie's end-of-the-afternoon stock had let me down, and we had all gone to bed half hungry.

It would seem that all laughter was conspiring to annoy me. Winding me up something chronic. I tried to shut my ears to the song-like twitterings of three girls from Lola's old school, themselves covers and remixes of the girls who had come the day before and the days before that. These girls seemed to be endlessly ferried in oversized cars, with mothers who did not linger in either the doorway or the memory, apt embodiments of their fast-evaporating magnolia and vanilla scent. Friends (and therefore mothers) who I knew she talked to about me, all the goddamn time – maybe even the friend to whom she had proclaimed me a slut on the phone. Moreover, what with all the lift-shares, I was never sure which mother went with which girl. Today had not yielded the only one I had loved on sight: proper old school good egg – genes of a duchess, laugh of a stable girl – fagging away on our doorstep in the most unHartbrooke manner and a bit late and just so extravagantly *human*. Collection today could be by one of those who, when you opened your own door, regarded you with polite incomprehension. Or worst of all, the one or two former business Boudiccas who were now totally *over* reproduction and bored as shite in the burbs, and who snorted condescension to get their kicks as if it were the white stuff of the good old days. And yet, despite knowing the PR Lola would be giving me, and despite knowing there was more to being Alpha than cultivating long straight hair and not eating a sandwich, I was supposed to smile and to not mind and to offer teas and healthy snacks and iced fruit-infused waters. (Lola made it quite clear: we were never to look like starch-addicted proles in front of these lovingly reared Lilies, these trained *orchids*.) I was tempted – just for bant – to slap a bowl of fried chicken on to their laps, along with some pineapple punch, in all their greasy, sugary, blackfood glory, but it would not have been worth the fallout.

One girl, product of the perfume-spritziest mother and a platinum-card father I would never meet, blushed whenever she looked upon me – every goddamn time – and never even said hello, not once. I didn't know whether that was a you're-a-parent thing, a you're-black thing, or a you're-such-a-bitch-to-Lola-and-you're-shagging-her-dad thing. To loathe me for all three might be overkill, but you just never knew with kids.

Still none of them could be quite as *singular* as Will. I had seen his photo, I knew he was interested in the BNB. It set my teeth on edge, but the problem was how to put it to Lola. When her friends finally left, I asked her outright:

'Your Will, Lola. Are you sure he's OK?'

'What do you mean?'

'Well …'

'What?'

'He wouldn't have something against our family, would he? Or rather, me.'

'What? That's absurd.'

I felt foolish but had to scratch the suspicion. 'You know, he wouldn't do anything to try and upset me, like make a silent call or break my window or—'

'What on earth are you talking about now? He doesn't know you, does he – and anyway he goes to *Dovington*.'

She spoke kind of fast and although it did not feel true, her words carried enough weight to make my shoulders sag.

'No. Of course not. It's just that … nothing.'

Lola said: 'Anyway, we're not … he's not "my" Will … Oh, don't worry about it.'

Then she scooped up all her things and moved to another room. The boy was clearly bad news, but I had no way of knowing how bad.

I was drawn again and again to Lola's Facebook. It was an impressive fabrication. A hundred 'Love you babes! xx' to girls I knew full well she hated, tonnes of pouting photos with the usual filters to make her look even skinnier, or faintly tangerine, as if she was at Miami Beach rather than High Desford's park on a wet Thursday morning. A cascade of photographic lies and half-truths. I knew this was symptomatic of the age; that a generation of girls were coming up the hill and would, like me, disappear over it in time, leaving behind them a gajillion bytes of filtered smiles at themselves and perhaps the odd hank of non-biodegradable hair extension. Social media as live, drawn-out, premature A-list obituary instead of *living*. Was that normal?

I tried, put it to him. It was the sort of debate you could joke about together, the sort of rhetorical question Thomas used to love:

'Don't be silly, Darling,' he said. He would not look up from his paper. 'She's just a girl.'

'Silly'; it smarted like a backhand slap. I longed to explain, that had she been the tiniest bit *kind* my heart would in fact ache for her, more with every selfie she plastered on to her friends' screens.

Defeated, I went to find my son.

'You be the stegosaurus, Mummy!'

As we played dinosaurs together, my phone buzzed. I let my son's tyrannosaurus rex mash up my peerless stego-saurus over and over until I sprang with a squawk and wrapped my arms tight around him, a velociraptor of love; game over.

I checked my phone. So, there it was, again.

What did the other stuff matter, really – the calls, Lola, Thomas, any of it? How could anyone ever doubt that Stevie was my world? I had thought marriage would change that. It had changed my world, and the wider world had changed around my marriage, but he was still *it*. I loved Thomas, but Stevie was the wondrous core.

I knew what my problem was: I did not think things through, I was too big on love. Too big. But then, why else was I on this sweet Earth? Love was what I did, who I was. I had long ago decided that you had to love who you loved: love them all, love them hard. Love them even harder when you were blended like us.

Intimacy without love, now that was the real killer.

I wandered upstairs, back to the spare room. Muttered low at my laptop:

'I'll give you "silly". Fuck ... adoodle ... d00 ...'

I was in.

If you looked hard enough on Facebook, in the posts, the messages, all around and about, you tended to find the bad stuff. The words that someone wished they could take back, though they must surely have meant them, at least for a moment. The inauthentic truths and authentic lies. The smartarsities. The game-changing clauses.

Buried under all the 'Love you babes! xx' in Lola's account was the bad stuff. The underground dirt without which she could not exist. The horseshit layer from which the verdant truth sprang. I hoped that I had got it all wrong, jumped the gun. But here were links to Will and through him to other men, young and not so young, to a group called BNB Futures which advertised in dark red-pink and orange. Go a click further, to her dad's page, and you would find albums of photos of the wedding, of us Waites, of our young son.

But that was not the worst of the bad stuff. There was much more in Lola's world: in fusky corners and up digital alleyways, tucked away as messages and ads and links and posts of all kinds. Not the kiddie-bad stuff, not the druggie-bad stuff, but dark all the same. Somewhere amongst it all lay the worst thing of all: a dark red-pink and orange box heralding an event, this same night, to which Lola had been invited. BNB Futures was having a ball.

And Lola's response?

Going.

From fireside gin to bathtub gin. A strange tinge to my drink, tonight, as if my thoughts had, over time, melted into the bitter fizz until everything tasted rank. I cupped it, weighed it; it could intoxicate me no more than my own foul and diluted logic. I could try to offer that to Thomas: an apology that was two parts explanation.

Still, I drank. I stared up at the ceiling. She was *going.* Tonight. I let the water go cold, pulled the plug for a minute, then topped it up with hot again. For four hours. I could not look away from the ceiling. I could no longer taste my gin. And Thomas did not come knocking once.

I went to her room.

'Don't go,' I said to Lola.

'What?' she said.

'Don't go, please. I won't mention it to Dad, but you really shouldn't be mixing with those people.'

'Have you been spying on me?'

'No, but … I've seen the envelopes arriving from Bright New Britain. It's Will's influence, isn't it? Bad news, Lola. Really bad. You need to stay well away.'

Lola turned her back on me, picked up a lip pencil.

'Think you must have your wires crossed, Darling,' she said. 'I'm just meeting up with friends. Anyway, don't think Dad is listening to you much at the moment.'

'Right,' I said, putting down the glass I'd brought up for her. 'OK then, play it that way, if you want. I'm only trying to look after you. Nice new piercing, by the way.'

I carried my hypo-allergenic pillow down the cold blurred hall to the spare room.

'Darling,' he had said when I had cornered him coming out of our bathroom earlier. 'I can't, not yet. We need to take some proper space.'

'What? Are you saying that—'

'Well, we kind of rushed together, didn't we? It was *fast*.'

'But not *wrong*?'

He looked away, so grey now, so tired.

'Thomas?'

I knew then I could not confide in him about Lola's plans. Enough bad blood to drain away, enough to explain away without the added confession of a Facebook hacking.

'All I'm saying is … let's both get a good night's sleep.'

And so, back to the spare room. I was settling the right pillow on to the wrong bed when I heard it. The raw-throated sound of retching. Enough, now. I walked next door to Lola's bedroom and pushed the door open:

'Lola?'

No reply. I opened the door of the en suite.

Lola was lying on the floor. She was quite still and in a flash I saw her just as I had at the foot of the stairs, but then she spasmed and began to writhe and moan. Her face was white and her head rested by a pool of vomit.

'Lola! Oh, you poor thing.'

I knelt to sweep her hair away from the orange liquid and take her head in my arms.

'What happened?'

'Don't tell Dad!' The panic in her voice was more shocking than the sight of her.

'What, I need to—'

'No!' A weak scream. 'Please, I—'

She surged wearily on to her hands and knees and fell forward just in time for the torrent to hit the back of the toilet bowl.

'Urgh. God,' she was gasping, fell back on her knees.

I looked at her, the gleaming cheekbones, the bruised lips, the eyeliner and mascara bleeding downwards in black trails. I waited for her to speak. The shadows shifted on the far wall. The moment stretched. She had a globule of spittle on her cheek and I wanted to wipe it clean away, but I did not move, I waited.

'You know I'm no addict or anything, but … well …'

'Go on …'

'Could something like cocaine make you sick?'

'You mean vomiting?'

'Yes.'

'Not normally, no. But it is really, really bad for your head.'

'OK, thanks.' She lowered that look, a senseless mumble: 'I thought I might have been spiked.'

I went to speak then swallowed it, waited.

She looked up again; two wide molten pools.

'You think it too, don't you?' she said, so quietly it did feel as if I had thought her actual voice.

'No, Lola. What?'

'I'm pregnant.'

I stayed very still.

'You're sure?'

At that moment, Lola leaned over again, in a perfect, miserable curve and dry-retched into the echoing bowl. I rubbed her back, thinking. The noise subsided and she came back to sitting once more.

'See?'

I nodded. 'Have you taken a test?'

'No, but … I'm scared. *Promise* you won't tell Dad.'

'Don't worry, one thing at a time.'

She rested her head on me until her stomach ache appeared to ease and there was no more heaving.

Then I said:

'We'd better get you into bed.'

'I was supposed to be going out …'

'Bed.'

I wiped up and saw her through to her bedroom. I busied myself putting away her ironed things so she could drag off her clothes unwatched and throw on the faded, oversized T-shirt she favoured, one of Thomas's cast-offs. For the first time, I tucked her into bed.

'Now *sleep*. Don't worry. Wait …' I rose, took an empty glass from her bedside, rinsed it and filled it from her bathroom tap, then returned. 'I won't say a word to Dad. And of course I'll help you with the test. Nurse, remember? Now sleep.'

'I'm in hell,' she said, then gave a dry laugh. 'And Will wasn't even worth it!'

'Rest now, Lo,' I said.

Then I rose and closed the door, certain that Thomas would have heard nothing.

I could not believe how pale, how *breakable* she had looked. And yet how angry at her lot.

Lola

DONE LIST 7

Yofuckety. I have screwed everything up big time.

I called Will. Had no choice – we were supposed to be going in this big group to this ball and I was hoping he might still let me go because his dad had already paid for the tickets. I had figured that if I went to the ball really dressed up (I spent ages finding a dress that I didn't actually look too whale-like in), then he might forget about us falling out. Also, I had to warn him that Darling had seen his photo and would probably tell Dad he was involved with Bright New Britain, who kept getting in the news for all those marches and made my father shout at the telly. Will said I should still come to the ball, if I liked (thanks), and that he would see me there and that he would get his mate Paul to give me a lift. Great – is he friend-zoning me? As for Darling's suspicions, he couldn't give a toss:

'So what if she knows who I am? You're having a laugh, right?'

'No, what do—'

'Christ, Lola, you <u>melt</u>! What's she gonna do to someone like me, that dirty liar?'

'I'm sorry, Will, shouldn't have mentioned her.' He sounded wound up and I didn't get why. 'I didn't think.'

'No shit.' The phone went silent for a moment. 'OK, forget it. It's not like I'm involved, they already knew her. No, it's good you told me, forget about it now.'

'OK,' I said.

'And I'll phone you next time, OK?'

'OK.'

Then we hung up. Bloody great. And then, best of all, I ended up vomming massively when this Paul was supposed to be collecting me and I couldn't go to the ball at all. My life sucks more than Caro Francis, the poor cow.

Shit-a-brick, how the hell have I got myself pregnant when I have only just started having sex? Surely that's a kind of special cruelty, right? Reserved especially for idiots like me who believe the lies of hilarious, full-of-themselves young men. I think they call it 'cruel and unusual punishment'. How can that even happen? ~~I mean I do know technically how, I'm not~~ <u>~~that~~</u> ~~kind of speci~~

I whatsapped Will to say sorry for not coming to the ball last night. He's read it but still not said anything back. I'm guessing we're definitely over.

I suppose I should be feeling my heart breaking in two, but tbh right now I just feel tired and embarrassed. And my stomach still aches.

Thank God, bizarrely, for Darling. She really looked after me last night.

I'm starting to regret having been such a bitch to her.

Darling wanted to tell Dad about what she calls 'my predicament'. That made me giggle, then feel totally sick. She can't can't can't can't can't tell Dad. I made her promise, straight up, on her life. It would <u>kill</u> him. I'm <u>sixteen</u>, still <u>his</u> baby.

What have I done now? Is this it, finally the thing that I cannot ever undo? Please no.

However, I have to go on. Tomorrow I have to be brave and go to the chemist. I think Darling might go with me.

Do you know what? Fuck Will Benton.

I've been sitting here for hours, hating myself for being such a dick and ruining everything. I got this message from Ellie, saying I should call her. Anyway, she told me that she was just trying to be a friend and that Sadie Connors was at this ball I had said I was going to with Will and she swears blind Will was all over some other girl last night. Really pretty redhead. They were practically screwing each other on the dancefloor. Ellie was even nice enough not to sound too happy about it, after everything. She said she just thought I should know, and I believe her.

You know what else? I kind of did know, deep down. Will and me are done.

Wow, WTF? Really?

Just went to talk to Darling. I wasn't exactly aiming for a humungous heart-to-heart but I did want to talk to her properly, for the first time ever. I had been thinking about Will and Daz and that beaten-up bloke with the horrible wrecked shin and before I could stop myself I was in the kitchen talking to her. I've got to put down exactly what we just said super-quick before I forget because it might be the most grown-up thing I have ever done (apart from getting pregnant ha ha not laughing).

I said, 'Darling you need to know something. If I tell you something, do you promise you won't go nuts? Or tell Dad?'

And she said, 'No, go ahead.'

So I said (I actually started shaking a bit, which was very weird and OTT of me), 'I just wanted to say that I haven't been totally honest with you. I was really upset after the wedding, just because of, you know ... And you know Will? You know those leaflets? He was quite into all that and I sort of went along with it, but not because I'm like that. He told me about his mate Big Daz, Darren something—'

She looked at me really hard for a second. Then she said, 'Go on.'

And I said, 'Will knows him from the pub and he and I got talking and anyway, long story short, Will got big into finding stuff out about your past—'

She was still looking at me hard as hell. 'Like what?' she said.

And I said, 'He didn't really say, just stuff you might have done. Will said he knew people who knew you.'

She was pretty tense and it all made me get teary and I confessed to her:

'I basically wanted to split you and Dad up, which I know is really really really terrible, but I just couldn't get my head around it all. The wedding and all that. And I really wasn't happy. Do you forgive me?'

And she said, 'Relax, Lola. I already knew all that.'

And then I just started crying like a total dick, but she actually put her arms around me and said:

'I forgive you.'

And I stayed there for a bit, but then I pulled away because it is not like we're exactly an episode of the fucking *Waltons*. So I muttered something like 'thanks, sorry' and came straight back up to my room to think.

It was a good move. As long as she doesn't tell Dad and make him hate me, it was a very good move, I think. Now we might just get on with each other a little bit more, and this matters because I think she might be the only one who can dig me out of this mountain of merde I am in.

It's weird. Pregnancy is like this mahoosive revenge, this judgement – I take it all back, Darling, please make it stop lol. #notlolling

At first, back in July or whenever, I really did just have a bad patch of making myself sick again. Happens – to me, anyway. Soon though, I couldn't bloody stop puking.

So here's how it is: after that little stint I did feel a bit queasy all the time (I figured that she couldn't cook for shit!). For a start, all that greasy cocoa butter stuff and other afro bollocks she fills their en suite with all stuck in the air, in my throat, but even with that and all the unnecessary fiery food, I was not fully fit to puke. I stuck my fingers down my throat because I just fucking felt like I wanted to let it all go, you know. I knew she could hear me and I did not care. I do it sometimes, it was the whole exams thing – deal with it. But the next day and the next day, I had to stick my fingers down my throat just to get a decent night's sleep.

But in the end I really did stop doing it.

And – spot the irony, kids! – I would give anything never again to yak the way I yakked the night I had to blow Will out just so he could go suck on the redhead.

For now though, please God, it all seems to have gone away.

Achievements

1. Agreed to go out with Darling to buy a pregnancy test.
2. Agreed that I would cool off the AT visits for a while. Rather than have her interfere, or have to flat-out lie to her, it would be best to take a break. It was Darling who suggested it and she is a qualified professional, after all. We won't tell Dad and I'll still keep writing lists, kids, don't you worry. Your inheritance is safe.
3. Achievement fail! Was thinking of messaging Will and accidentally hit dial, then hung up, so now I'll seem nuts. But I'm making myself not care. He's such a bell-end – you'd think he would have at least waited until after that bloody ball after everything we've done together. Did he ever give a toss?
4. Googled 'terminations'. Was too scared to click on a single page and then I deleted the internet history just in case.
5. I finally stopped worrying about being sick and thinking about Will for more than five minutes and started to sort of get the point of Darling.

PART III

Darling

We had a new understanding, Lola and I. And it was beautiful.

Hear dis. One, one coco full basket.

I could hardly hide the smile. I could hardly hide the hope. Not for the arrival of a step-grandchild, heaven help us, or for her to renounce her sins narcotic and ideological; not even that I might get back into the marital bed (Stevie had been reassured that my side of the mattress was 'getting fixed', which in a way it was). But my hope was that at last all my caring might be winning her over.

A it dis: Massa God nah let mi dung.

I have always been too big on love. And as any child of a Jamaican mother knows, it is impossible to truly love someone without wanting to nourish them. To cherish, yes, there is always that old wedding vow, but to nourish – you do that most of all for your child. To nourish is to nurture, to feed, to raise; it is Latin, and Old French, norrir, and nourrir, new French too. European then, but with equivalents and synonyms in every language. Little wonder: to nourish is to nurse. That most human of endeavours, that most primitive drive. From nutrix 'she who gives suck', which is something to do with an old word for letting it all flow, like time itself. Like love itself.

To love you *must* nourish. A pan-fresh Johnny cake, an untimed kiss, the milk of goddamn human kindness, whatever you can rustle up. But to love, you must nourish.

I would nourish her.

My thoughts were so full of all my plans for her that I almost stumbled over Thomas as I came in. He was standing in the kitchen, looking at me with cold eyes. Something felt wrong. Then he spoke:

'Who are you, Darling? I mean, really?'

I lowered the bags full of courgetti and salmon, fromage frais and steak to the floor.

'You know who I—'

'Someone rang while you were out. A woman.'

I put a hand out to the doorframe. Just to feel it there.

'She said that she had finally managed to find the number and could she please speak to Darling White? She said that she would really like to speak to Darling, that she was her sister …'

'But I—'

'That's right! But you don't have a sister! Except this woman, Jade, was quite clear that you do.'

'All right, Thomas, I hear you. Jade rang.'

I fought the urge not to slip back out of the front door. What? What had she said?

'Jade, yes, you're catching on. Your sister. The sister that you don't bloody have. What on earth, Darling? I don't even know who you are any more. I don't know if I can trust you at all ...'

'Of course you can,' I said in a whisper. Then I spoke up. 'What did she want?'

'Just to speak to you. She was pretty damn keen.'

All those phone calls, the endless calls to my mobile, and now she had broken through, in the end, despite me. But it would all be OK. Lola's change towards me was a sign. Maybe it was finally time to stop running scared.

'Look, OK, I do have a sister and I should have told you. But I didn't, because we fell out such a long time ago, years and years. I know I should have said, but ... it's complicated. Do you understand?'

'No. And I'm starting to think I won't ever know you, Darling.'

My fingertips, pressing so hard, could no longer feel the doorway.

It was time to tell him.

Jade. She was called Jade. She was my younger sister and those in the caring professions would say she was my own template for caring.

I had loved her long and well.

Even Thomas, surely, would forgive the lie. Would it shock him so much that I had erased one little sister? I could give him comfortable, probable reasons, find words that hit home. I now realised, all these months later, that I had no choice but to try. She would never, ever stop ringing. Ever.

Try harder, care more. We were all supposed to care more, weren't we, these days? That's what the news challenged us to do every night, when we were inclined to turn away; the cookie-enabled charity ads and the upturned caps on the street and the diligent door-knockers. Care *more*. It was a sound idea. If we all got to the point when we could not care less, then children would die for lack of love and good people would go hungry and bombs would blast the innocent and strangers would be felled in the street and the seas would boil, and … oh.

We *did* still care – didn't we? But me, I had always set out to care *more*. Not just more than average, or more than anyone else, but more than was convenient, more than even I thought I should, more maybe than the other person wanted. You were born into this, this caring. For some it was almost an affliction. It was born needing to be *needed* and so you fed it with good deeds – a neighbour's baby rocked to sleep on your young lap, a wrong forgiven, a playground mate cuddled until the scraped knee was forgotten. It grew. It could go on to grow until it had expanded to fill your life and all your work, as it had mine.

I loved Jade from the day she was born. Of course I did, big siblings do, and I had been prepared for her arrival with bucketloads of smartness and patience by my parents – *Mommy still gat all her time fuh yuh, gyal*. More than that, I had looked after my little sister even in the womb, fretting over our mummy, tugging her swollen hand so that she might please sit down, urging her to walk all careful and slow on the stairs. My parents had told their peers that I was so could-just-eat-her-up kind, so concerned for dear Grace, so caring – and I *was*, but I was caring for *Jade*, every second, before she had even been born.

I knew, before she arrived, that I wanted to look after her more than anything, to show her games and hold her hand and keep her in the light.

When she was old enough to move around on the floor, I would roll her in my special blanket, leaving her with her own tiny white rag to clasp under her sucked thumb; then I would tell her what was wrong with her. Some days she had German measles, other days chronic earwax, or a cut finger, or croup. On one memorable occasion she had undergone a near-fatal heart attack. Whatever the ailment, I would open my red plastic box with the white cross that Father Christmas had wrapped in gold and addressed to:

Dear Darling, the new nurse in the family xxx

As her nurse, I had been consistent and highly conscientious. Every fictitious injury or imagined ailment – *Whappen, Darling, poor likkle Jade done mash-up herself again? Yuh a gud nurse, yuh seh* – was treated in the same way: it got bandaged. Measles? Bandage. Finger? Bandage. Earwax? Out came the roll of gauze while I deafened my baby sister by blowing air into her completely clear ear canal with the nifty plastic syringe. Heart attack? Big fuck-off bandage.

Jade – *bless dat poor likkle girl* – never complained. More than once she fell asleep while being bandaged. Or she chattered happily and gave excellent patient reviews and insisted that yes, the bandage had made her feel instantly better.

I knew then I really was a nurse. I knew then that caring *more* made a difference and that as a result my love – more than crayoning, running fast, making gingerbread or writing stories – would keep my sister alive.

Yes, I had a sister called Jade and once upon a time I had loved her.

'So, this … sister. Why did you fall out?'

'Oh a stupid thing, really. A misunderstanding that just grew and grew until neither of us listened to the other any more.'

'What happened?'

I could only say: 'We fell out over some boy, that's all. Like I said, stupid.'

Thomas was looking at his feet.

'This will take some time to tick through the system. For me to understand why you don't trust me enough to talk to me about things—'

'Thomas, I—'

'So, this week I'll only work from home today. I'll go back into the office tomorrow. We both need a little breather.'

I kept trying so damn hard. I had to prove to Thomas that he knew me. Why had Jade chosen now, when I was trying harder than ever? I had to make this family work, come what may. Lola had come so close to real hatred. Hate has its own alchemy, it changes people, families. Changes love itself, of course, or tries to. She could never be allowed to get so close to it again. Nothing was more important, not my own crowding doubts or fears, no laws, or social norms, or superstitions. We had to work, come what may.

Maybe I could buy time, before working out how to keep Jade well away. I could no longer keep my concerns to myself. I had to step up, make Thomas listen about the company his daughter had been keeping.

I cornered him in his study and, while true to my word – I never once told him that his daughter had wanted to split us up – I filled him in on the rest: the leaflets, the undesirable mates, the unattended balls. Thomas looked as shocked as he ought to have looked, to give him his due. Then, as I grew in confidence and began to hint at the other reasons we had to watch her, he grew tired of looking shocked, told me he would talk to her, said that the political thing had to be some stupid misplaced curiosity and that it was also clearly over before it had begun as she had never mentioned it, and told me she was 'just a girl' and opened a cold beer before dinner. He did not find it amusing or even remotely ironic that it was a Red Stripe, left over from the night of the chewy goat.

'So you see,' I pressed the point home. 'You say you don't know me, but what about your own daughter?'

Thomas rubbed his head:

'No, this isn't us. Not in the slightest.'

'She wanted it to be.'

'Well it was never going to go that way, she didn't mean any of it. She's not like that.'

'Perhaps. But maybe you can see now how I've been a bit worried, distracted?'

He didn't nod, only said, 'I'll talk to her. But you do know she is a child, she is not me, Darling, and …'

'And what?'

'Well, I married you, didn't I?'

This, as if – despite me cooling my heels in the spare room each night – it should have been enough.

I awoke as I had the previous morning: alone and troubled.

It was the strangest thing: as my worries about Lola and me declined – pregnant or not, I would look after her – I started having dreams about Stevie and me once again. Always the same: my boy sitting in deep dusk, alone, until I appeared from nowhere to hold him. I hugged him hard, I had known that he was cold. This hug seemed to last an age and it was nearly all of the dream. However it was not all of the dream: at some point I looked up and there it was, this vast hand above us casting not a dusk but its own shadow, its palm facing downwards, ready to press down on us with great force. We did not flinch, we did not run: I always awoke before it could descend. Thomas, now apart from me and in the other room, would never know anything of it. It was only recently that the dream had started coming again. Since we had moved into Littleton Lodge I had hoped the hand had lifted.

Thomas was cold to me, but for the first time ever Lola and I were basking in each other. I could feel us, warming my arms like the afternoon sun. Being me, I had to tone it down, rein myself in a bit; rather than buy the four tops and the good winter skirt she would need, I bought her just one stupid-price thing from the vintage market she would love: a Sixties swing coat, cherry red. She took it, frowned, then her cheeks turned the same colour.

'Thank you,' she said.

Though she hurried away, that same night she recorded an old film she thought her dad had mentioned – sometime during their long and serious talk in his study – that I might like, *To Kill a Mockingbird*. I was certain she had not watched or read it, but I hardly dared speak to thank her, let alone find out.

I had a job to do, I was to get Lola through this – whatever she found that this might be – and to live up to my insistence that 'everything will be all right'; a pretty clear if open-ended brief.

Jus be careful. Nuh badda wid any obeah, gyal.

No, I had no intention of dabbling in any voodoo – as if I would know how to make a spell with a chicken's foot. Instead, Lola stayed home from college and as soon as Thomas had gone to work I took her straight to the chemist. We walked in silence up the aisle until I spotted the sign 'Family Planning'.

'Here we go. Did you have one in mind?'

'I don't … no.' She looked every bit as grey and drained as she had on her bathroom floor.

'So,' I said, eyeing the shelves as if they held a line-up of lovers. I picked up each one with a slowness that made her wince:

'This is a pretty reliable brand. Oh, but this one is the easiest to use. And this one …'

'Just … you choose. Please,' she whispered. 'Quickly.'

'OK.'

'Oh God. Julia.' It could have been Joanna or Janey or Juliet; her voice was barely audible.

'Who, where?'

Two girls of about her age were examining the mid-range moisturisers with all the intensity that nuclear physicists might apply to unsplittable atoms.

'I'll wait outside.' Lola dashed off, head down.

I picked up the test I wanted, walked past the future

Nobel Laureates (great skin!) out of some perverse and pointless curiosity, then paid and left the shop.

We entered her en suite in silence. More than any other time I had spent with Lola, these minutes mattered.

The light that streamed in through the high side window was dappled with dancing green, the sun shining through an empty absinthe-coloured stem vase – another of Tess's chic and tragic geegaws.

I explained to her that she had to pass urine straight on to the test stick.

'What?'

'Wee on this.'

I left her to complete the test, moving through to the bedroom where my eyes drifted to the drawers, the wardrobe. No, that dolphin book would not be surfacing anytime soon. Rather than risk getting caught searching for it, I perched on the bed, the packaging and instructions clutched in my hands.

A minute trickled away. Two.

I rose, knocked on the bathroom door and entered, took the stick and sat on the edge of the bath as she quivered on the loo seat. We did not speak.

I checked the phone display; another minute or so to go. But within a few more seconds the dye had given a clear answer and I knew what I had to tell her:

'Oh, Lola,' I said. 'I'm so sorry.'

She sort of fell forward, but I was there to catch her.

'You won't be alone in this, Lola,' I said, rubbing her hair, knowing this time she would not advert-flick it away. 'I'll be there at every step. And of course, I'm afraid we'll need to contact Will's parents ...'

'God, no, please ...'

'Shh, hush now,' I heard my voice ringing rich and wise over hers. 'Everything will be all right.'

Trust can be amazing when it's real.

The next day, I leaned closer to my husband as I cleared away breakfast things, and tried to explain what I meant. 'I know. I do understand now.'

'Do you though?'

I understood. Lola had been a different girl since our kitchen talk and now seemed utterly transformed after our bathroom lock-in. She did not answer me back any longer, did not snipe. It was peculiar and pleasing. I wondered whether our shared discovery might even have brought her some bright speck of relief.

'More than you could imagine, Thomas. Look, to be honest, there is actually something that you don't know.'

'So, you're ready to talk to me. The real deal? Because any more lies and ...'

'I know. Listen, have you heard of sorrel?'

Red Flowers

Sorrel is a drink enjoyed in Jamaica and all over the Caribbean. It's a dark red-pink holiday drink, you know: a good times, celebratory drink. It's made from sepals of the roselle, or sorrel flower, or Hibiscus sabdariffa, *which always sounded to me just like 'Hibiscus sadandrealfear'. I didn't know how it was made when I was a child, only that my parents said if you did it right the ice gasped and the glass turned red, misted up and turned cold. I can only remember having it on some Saturday mornings, whenever Uncle Malcolm came to visit.*

This was when it was just three of us, before my little sister, Jade, was born. I'm sorry, I know, I should have said. Yes, I know. But we're not really sisters now any more, so …

Anyway. I knew even then that Uncle Malcolm was not my real uncle; he was white for a start, and a neighbour, a fat, spectacled, freckly neighbour. A big man, someone of some standing, a councillor 'they' said, or soon to be one. Also big because he had this vast round head that loomed above his shoulders and always put me in mind of a moon. He'd tried sorrel at ours one Christmas, and he insisted on coming back for more.

'Good stuff,' he used to say. 'Good colour, ain't it?'

We had not long moved from Basingstoke to Elm Forest, a few miles away. Dad had gone from being a junior someone in Planning to the step above; not senior, but a someone. We were going places, but in this smaller town, we needed friends more than ever.

So we only gave sorrel, then, to this particular neighbour. He would thank us with a pocketful of fruit from his garden, fruit that was always too old or too young: sour plums, powdery apples, granite peaches, rotting cherries. We said nothing, thanked him, gave him more sorrel. My parents were so pleased to have impressed this man on the up with a drink from Home that they made fresh batches of this festive drink whenever they knew he was coming, be it March or May, never mind if a little Christmas magic was murdered: Malcolm was pleased.

Uncle Malcolm used to want to teach me things. I was about five. Four. He would make me go into this room, a cupboard really, that led off of the kitchen, and he would … No, it's OK, I'm fine, I have to tell you now or I won't be able … My parents were in the habit of going to town on Saturday mornings, whatever else might be going on. When Uncle Malcolm popped his huge head around the door my hard-pressed parents would jump at his offer of sitting with me.

They always said they would get twice as much done and so they left me in his care. Within minutes of them disappearing up the drive, he would say:

'Come and speak with your old uncle.'

We would sit at the kitchen table and he would ask me about my life, my friends, the games we played, my favourite things to do at nursery. I'd go:

'We wet the sand with water and put it into buckets …'

Then at some point, always the same thing would happen.

'Hmm …' he would begin. 'You're not really from round here are you, you funny lot?'

Then he would ask me a question:

'So, what is the name of that big town ten miles away? They tell you that already?'

'No, Uncle.'

'What? Right, let me teach you a thing or two.'

Now this normally calm man, who walked as if he had weights in his shoes, would fly into a fussing sort of rage and he would take me by the hand and lead me into the wide dark cupboard at the back of the kitchen, which I later learned was a form of pantry. It smelled musty and had a sort of milking stool or farmer's seat inside. Uncle Malcolm would sit his powerful arse on this stool – break, I would pray, right under his bottom. Please do, crack in two! But it never did break, Thomas, and he was ready as ever to reap whatever he reckoned I had sown. Shaking with some peculiar rage, he would, he would – no, it's OK, I can do this – pull me across his lap

265

and spank my bare bottom until my wailing grew loud enough to rattle the tins on the shelves.

Afterwards, he would go back to our kitchen, into our fridge and give me a catch-your-death cold glass of sorrel.

'Be quiet now,' he would say. 'There's a good little thing. Here, have some of this, see? Better? Your favourite.'

I would drink down that sweet red juice as quickly as I could, to get to the point when he said:

'Now. I won't tell your Mummy you were so naughty, so you can stop crying. I won't tell. Now go and play.'

Every visit he did this, for as long as I could remember, up until this one time … He wanted to … No, I'm fine … He wanted to show me what a kiss was. It was not a kiss and I fainted and … but I don't want to trouble you with all that right now. You get the picture, anyway. No, I'm all right, promise.

So. I did not tell my mum because I was convinced she would smack me twice as hard for cheeking our neighbour, this esteemed friend, the councillor. And anyway, what would 'they' say? Not everyone got to be friends with Malcolm Fletcher and many of those who did, council workers with their sights set high like my dad, would consider life far sweeter for it.

But I was forced to tell my mum what Uncle Malcolm had done years after, once knowledge slithered into my garden, aged thirteen or so; certainly when Dad was no longer with us.

I think the first thing she said was 'Hush your mout', but it was fast and quiet. Yes, really. She certainly told me 'they' said he was just a likkle bit of a pervert *and that 'they' knew not to mind him. But she then squeezed me hard and I think I remember that her eyes were wet and wide. I hushed my mout'.*

So that's it. That's what happened. That's also the reason I might serve you goat or plantain, but never bloody sorrel. So then a few weeks ago with Lola ... I know you know. Thank you for being so generous.

Thank you, but I really am sorry.

Yes, that's right. Uncle Malcolm is that same BNB bloke from the telly, Malcolm Fletcher. I tried to take him to court, when I was older, but they stopped me. I let their knives and punches stop me, but I shouldn't have, I should have fought on.

No, hear me out. It's OK now, really. Calm yourself, my croaking raven ... What? Oh nothing. Just saying all's well that ends well, my darling.

Don't worry about me, and thank you. So. Anyway. New subject: there's this party we've been invited to. My friend, Carla Moore ...'

Lola

DONE LIST 8

I have to get rid of it. This pregnancy is making me fat, already; it feels unbearable to me. I am so glad I haven't had any 'morning' sickness since, though, that just hurt <u>so</u> much. But I can't lie – I could probably do with losing a bit more food in a †Technicolor yodel. I am getting huge.

I was right to tell Darling. She is taking care of <u>everything</u> and helping us to get a plan together.

For a while, to be honest, I suspected that Darling was simply trying to fatten me up. All those hours spent in the kitchen preparing food for us. The endless piles of her traditional Caribbean chicken and whatnot, the constant offers of snacks, refreshments and so on. Stupidly, I thought she was jealous of my dancer's figure, trying to ruin me because she was <u>green</u>. Then I realised: she really was just trying to be nice.

That said, I can still hang on to a few of my doubts, if I want – they're mine, after all. Although I've mentioned them to Dad, obviously. He gave me a bit of a talking to when she told him about the BNB stuff, but he got that it wasn't really anything to do with me, that I was just wary of her. I do still worry. Most of all, I worry that she doesn't love him that much. I can't help it. I told him a while back that she might still be in love with Stevie's dad, that he had to watch out for himself.

Maybe I do want to grow up to be a proper bitch, after all.

Or maybe that's just my hormones talking.

They say that you are scarred by the traumas in your early life. No wonder my life is such a car crash.

It was the most terrible accident Blewthorpe had ever seen, they said.

We were in the high street, very near to where we used to live. I wanted sweets, badly, but Mum had said no, not now, later blahblah. I was so angry, stupid, and was running across the road to the newsagents before she knew it and she ran after me. I got to the other side, I'm fast. But she ran straight after me, slower, right in front of a speeding lorry. Like AT always says, there are no such things as accidents, but I hate it when she says that – I take it personally. Does that mean I wanted Mum to die? That I was in fact angry with her and did not actually want the sherbert lollies or whatever sugary shit it was that really does not matter now?

Maybe AT thinks that, maybe not. Maybe I wanted it, maybe not. But however you dress it up, I do believe that I killed my own mother.

Something terrible: I envy Stevie. He can never get pregnant, for a start, and his crazy sad little life is on 4D fast-forward. Every moment counts, I hear them saying, and it's true, there is good reason to cram all that stuff in. I talked about this with him when we were watching TV. I said something like:

'You're a pretty busy kid, Stevie, aren't you?'

He shrugged. 'I think so.'

'What's your doctor like, is he nice? Or is it a her?'

'I don't know.'

'What do you mean? You practically live there, silly.'

'But you don't go in, you silly-silly. You wait and Mum goes in and out, then you get ice cream.'

'What, you wait outside?'

'Yes, in the car. Until it's time for ice cream.'

'Oh right,' I said. 'Of course.'

What he did not realise, of course, cannot realise, is that Darling must have been sparing him all those horrible medical conversations. He has no idea that he will die young. If he were my boy, I think I would just give him the ice cream too.

Lola Waite – you'll have it all one day; all the love and all the ice cream. Lola Waite. Lola waiting.

Will called me, out of the blue! I honestly thought we would never speak again, but we did. It wasn't great. He didn't ask about me and he sounded a bit fucked up, slurry. He just said:

'Hi, babes. Can I have your postcode?'

'What, Will?'

'I need your postcode and I've forgotten the house number.'

So I told him our address. He hung up really soon afterwards, which was a bit weird. I've been wondering if it means he wants to send me something, maybe an apology. No flowers or card or anything have arrived as yet. But even though I want to keep hating him, I can't help hoping.

Achievements

1. Spent more hours in my room than anyone <u>ever</u> (other than every spotty Dovington perve with working WiFi). Trying to google my way out of this baby hell already.
2. All googled out. No choice but to totally trust Darling. My achievement? I have stopped myself from asking her what happens now ten times a day. We did talk for a bit earlier – she is still coming up with something. I've stayed in my room for the rest of the night. #actualnetflixactualchill

3. Also, finally asked Darling about Stevie's dad. We never see the guy! Think she told me everything, hard to be sure. She didn't sound that in love, to be fair. She swore he was all right, but I told her he sounded like a dick.
4. Actually wrote the word 'Blewthorpe' without throwing up. Kudos, AT, missing you already! Maybe there is something to this looking back lark, after all.
5. Tried all this evening to work out what this feeling is that I'm feeling right now and it's not easy because my body's fucked and my mind keeps skipping all over the place and nothing feels settled at all but I think I've worked it out. I feel scared.

Darling

THURSDAY, 17 NOVEMBER

It was a rare treat to see the man I loved regain his bloom. I had at last told him about Malcolm Fletcher and, later still, about the knife held to my throat by his right-hand hardman Darren Hodson, described it all down to the stench of those bins. Far from shrinking in horror, Thomas had once more become expansive; his relief at feeling he now knew the woman he had married showed in his skin, his gait, his brightened eyes.

Moreover, he was making an extra effort with me.

'We could go to the cinema, this weekend, if there's something you fancy ...'

'Why don't we think about going to that party after all, your friend ... Carla?'

Then, as I moved into the kitchen, trying not to disturb him as he read, he looked up and gave me a look so unequivocal in its affection that I did not want to move another step. After a moment's hesitation, he rose up, came over to where I stood and wrapped both arms around my shoulders. I leaned into him as if slowly shouldering open a heavy door, my jaws widened in a gasp although I did not dare breathe. This was the first time he had touched me in any meaningful sense since I had said the things I had said about him and Lola. And now I could not move, could not hope, could not take a breath, in case he thought any part of me might be moving away from him.

I need not have worried, he stepped back first.

But his kindness was a form of salvation. We would be OK.

A windfall of kindness, in fact, that morning. Stevie's Wonders had emailed me with a link to their fundraising page to see the latest totals. When you clicked on their video the girls bounced around, boinging off the pavement like buxom black-pink-white marionettes.

Their marathon walk for my son had raised £8,426.82 in the end, quite staggering.

The kindness of strangers; it could be a blessing beyond belief. It simply burned bright when you were all out of matches. There's nothing that can prepare you for that kind of kindness.

But it was my husband's kindness that moved me most. When I went upstairs to grab my slippers from my room, I found that they – and my dressing gown, my hypo-allergenic pillow, my Shakespeare, everything – had been moved back into the master bedroom without a word.

Every few minutes, I thought about what to do for Lola. What would be the best thing for her, now? What could be done that might, in the end, make her happier? There was no clear answer; the ground had been laid. We passed each other in hallways or on the landing and her eyes shot me secret messages which I read as: 'Tell me what to do' and 'Never tell Dad'.

Could I take Lola away somewhere with me, buy time to think?

When I had first fallen pregnant, I had considered upping sticks for Jamaica. I had once thought of our island as the answer to all my problems. Later, after my parents died, it became more symbol than country, never Home, but still a waiting sanctuary. I imagined it: an island of searing warmth, wet in a good way. An island of long, winding and interwoven experiences that wrapped itself around you, a bandage destination, good for cut fingers, vertigo, fevers, skin complaints.

But no, the present held us too much here.

In the minutes between thinking about the Lola question, I thought mostly of Jade. She could call at any moment, although she had not rung back since. With any spare seconds I thought of Stevie and then of Thomas.

I thought of them all, hard and in order until every thought muddled and merged so that it seemed they were all one and the same problem.

And then there was the bigger picture. We had received

more Bright New Britain leaflets through our door, two that fortnight alone, and each time I went online to see what Malcolm Fletcher might be doing.

He was retiring at last, as it turned out, due to age and, the puff-piece implied, a massive stroke he'd suffered at the end of his long and distinguished career in local government. A volcano had finally erupted in his big moonhead. This man had fathered a local group that had become a key branch of a national movement, as well as two children, now grown: Scott and Abigail. But he was no longer bright or new and my Britain was all the better for it.

I copied the article, and kept it close.

On Saturday morning, there was a knock at the door. Loud.

'Thomas!'

I had just got out of the shower. I could hear music coming from Lola's room.

'Thomas?'

I was hurrying to dry myself and pull on a clean dress so I could get the door. Rushing downstairs at last I pulled the door open.

'Hello?'

I cast a look around the driveway. No one. The mist bathed everything in grey, I couldn't see much. There was something else, though, something out there that had changed, that I was missing.

My car.

I grabbed the keys from the hall table and walked towards Mercy, stopped short. Stared. Long weaving marks ran from the bonnet to the boot. Scratched, keyed. Someone had been at her.

I walked closer; definitely keyed, on the side that I could see. The passenger side was hard up against the wall. Without stopping to think, I grabbed the driver's handle – unlocked, why was it already unlocked? – and slid behind the wheel and turned the key. I would move nearer to the door, call Thomas and give her a proper looking over.

I drove over the gravel knowing that something was amiss; Mercy felt lumpen and my gut groaned. I got out, walked around it. Such ugly scratches.

'Everything OK?'

Thomas had come to see what was going on.

'She's been keyed.'

'Oh, hell no. Really?'

'I know who did this …'

'Let me just …'

He stalked around the car, prowling for clues.

'They haven't gone too deep … but, God, what's *wrong* with people? Hold on …'

Now he walked up to the car, squatted down on his haunches.

'Oh, Darling, they've done your tyre as well.'

He hoiked himself upright, did a more thorough inspection.

'Three tyres. Three bloody tyres. Bastards.'

'I can't believe they had the nerve to come to our house.'

'You know who did it?'

'It's those Bright New Britain people. Darren Hodson or someone, I know it.'

Thomas shook his head and we eyed the scarred metal beside us.

'The police will sort this,' he said.

'Of course,' I cleared my throat. 'We do have to call them, I suppose.'

Thomas nodded, quite fast.

'Yes, enough, come on,' he said. 'We're getting this reported.'

We moved back inside. Thomas put an arm around me, again:

'You know what? Leave it to me. This is awful enough for you. Go and relax while I sort out the police and insurance.'

'Really, are you—'

'Go.'

As I turned, a glimpse of white peeked at me from the windscreen.

'Thomas, look.'

There was a thin strip of paper just visible under one wiper. I pulled it out, read it, passed it to Thomas.

It read:

SEE YOU SOON.

The police called to say they would be with us in a couple of hours.

It was time. I had to piece together what I suspected so that it did not play out in front of my husband as madness, paranoia, or – worse – step-parental spite. Lola might no longer hate me, but this had all come about through her.

I had to check that they were all still there, just clicks away, those bald glarers, those badtime boys. I played link-to-link on Facebook again, this time without hacking Lola's account, and somewhere I must have taken a new, terrible turn. I closed my eyes against it.

Waah wrong? Why yuh rinch up yuh face, Darling?

I looked again. Some blog, from a link on the BNB site.

It was called 'Shame'. Not so much a blog, in fact, as a populist rant, which made ugly jokes about celebrities and political figures, particularly those of colour and/or a liberal mindset. It included a few shabby paragraphs slating them for their crimes against society and a huge parade of photos, a mish-mash of people, famous and otherwise, some captioned, others not, who appeared to have nothing in common except the 'shame' of not being white. There was no witty reportage about them: whoever had cobbled the site together left their members to provide most of the abuse in their comments; one gay black actor and a woman who had taken the government to court had over seventy comments between them dating back months. *Go fuck yourself naggot* and *Back off our Brexit bitch*. It was a whole underworld party for trolls. I scrolled down the endless page of photos, amazed at how many people they wanted to feel ashamed. Then I spotted a splash of yellow and went cold:

Darling White, 37, cocoslut

The first three comments:

Next time wash your hands after love

Me is one nasty minging bitch!!!!!

Kill urself

The horror was too great to absorb at once, but it came to me in pieces. Me. Yellow dress. Chocolate stains that looked like shit. Stevie's birthday, the corner of his blue party hat bottom left. Lola's photo … Lola.

Lola gave these people the photo of me at our family party, when I thought we were all at our happiest.

I scanned more comments that hung below my image. No. Not this, not these worst words and the psychotic hatred and the filth and the threats. Not this. I was plunged into shadow, that enormous hand above us was descending, the dream no dream at all. Of course, the police would know what to do and this could all stop here, today, but could she really have done this?

I knew though, before I had finished asking myself the question. Lola. Lola had not just been 'going' to the BNB ball. She had sold us down the river: that torrid river of blood 'they' had always wanted to spring into being. This was it then. We were coming to the very end.

'So, Mrs Waite,' the police officer said, 'your husband said that you feel the damage to your car may be part of a wider—'

'There's a photo of me on a website. We have to stop them, we—'

'It's OK, Darling. Take it slowly.' Thomas, with me on the sofa, touched my arm.

I told the police about all of it – the online photo, the note on the car, my history with Darren Hodson, the men who pushed in alleyways, the car again.

'We have noticed a spike in these sorts of crimes in the last little bit. We can instruct the organisation to take down this image or face prosecution.'

'Thank you, that would be a start,' said Thomas.

I said, 'It's too late. Where else might that photo be now?'

'We'll be looking into that,' he said, 'which will take a little time. We'll also hang on to this note. But I wouldn't worry too much, Mrs Waite. If this person wanted to get to you so much, he would have hung around, ignored the car. They just want to scare you.'

'They're succeeding!' said Thomas 'We've been worried about my wife even leaving the house.'

'Just take the usual precautions, Mrs Waite, and you too, sir. Keep your phone charged, tell each other when you're going out. We'll be checking the CCTV on the main road here, leave it with us. As for the photo online, you seem to think that came from a family source.'

'Yes,' I said. 'Unbelievably.'

PC Arnold looked at me. I looked at Thomas.

'This photo was only on my step-daughter's phone. She has shown interest in these … this "group" before.'

Thomas started up, 'But as we've said, that doesn't mean, I can't imagine that—'

'Where is your step-daughter now, Mrs Waite?'

'Oh, she's here,' I said, an acidic note in my voice. 'She's upstairs. Probably online.'

'Darling—'

'Do you think we could have a word with your daughter, Mr Waite?'

A beat. 'OK, sure. I think she's out of the shower now.'

Lola came down. Hair damp, she had pulled on the dress she wore to our wedding. In the eyes of the young officer she would look beautiful. He smiled at her:

'Miss Waite. We've been talking about the photo your parents found online on an offensive website—'

'I know, they told me. I can't believe it.'

'Yes. Well, it seems possible that the image originally came from your phone. Do you have anything to say about that?'

'Mm, I've been thinking about that. It's really likely. I put the photo on Facebook.' She looked straight at me, then back to him. 'So any of my friends would have had access to it.'

'Friends like Will?' I butted in. 'Or your other so-called friends?'

'Who's Will?'

'Will Benton, goes to Dovington,' I said. 'I reckon that that smarmy git—'

'Mrs Waite—'

'Darling—' said Thomas.

'OK. Oh, I know it's not her fault, exactly. She has been mixing with some of the BNB lot though, haven't you, Lola? Getting in with the wrong crowd a bit?'

'Darling!' said Lola. 'But you know I would never. We've talked …'

I couldn't look at her; stared down at my feet.

'That lot were never proper friends of mine,' she said, her voice dull.

'Are you both referring to the right-wing group, Bright New Britain?'

'Yes,' said Thomas. 'That MP got in up north and they've been starting to flex their muscles around here more lately, but that doesn't mean—'

'Do you know any of their members?' PC Arnold asked Lola.

'No, not really,' she said.

'Yes, you do,' I said. They all looked at me. 'What about that Daz? You know Darren Hodson.'

'Oh yes, there's him,' said Lola. 'But he's not a friend of mine, Will knows him.'

I couldn't resist: 'Like I said.'

Lola looked at me with something approaching disappointment, but I was too angry to care.

'Can I go now?' she said, her voice flat. 'I've got an essay to do.'

'Yes,' said Thomas.

'I think that's all for now, Miss Waite.'

We watched her turn and go upstairs without another word.

Thomas sat forward:

'She's going through a tough enough time already. I don't really want her to get tied up in all this.'

'What if she already is?' I asked.

We looked at each other.

The police officer coughed.

'I see. Well, I think we've got enough to go on for now.' He rose. 'We'll be in touch.'

There, as if it were finished and satisfactory, the rest of us all but forgotten, wiped clean from PC Arnold's mind by the scent of Lola's skin cream.

I rose and went straight to the dishwasher, clattered a few bowls into cupboards so that everyone knew to stay away. I managed to chip one, but just stacked it at the bottom, like a child's secret.

Was I being unfair to Lola? Possibly. But fairness would not guarantee my safety, my son's safety. I wanted to believe it was a thoughtless share by a teenage girl, the theft of my likeness by a stranger. But so much doubt had swirled around us, for so long. And who puts on peach to speak to the police, anyway?

Forgiven, forgotten? Either would have done for my husband, whose eyes now shone with naked relief every time I went within a foot of his daughter. The truth was that I had simply made an accommodation with myself whereby I would give Lola not my full trust, but my energy. No one else could help her. I was putting some serious effort into devising a workable plan for Lola and the time was coming when it should all pay off. Holed up in her en suite once again, all talk of stolen photos shelved – she had apologised twice more for putting me, smeared, on Facebook – we counted the days that had elapsed since Will day on our fingers together. I told her that she might be fewer than six weeks pregnant and that we had time to do the right thing, that all she had to do was trust me.

Was there anything else she wanted to tell me?

I stood and wound up her forgotten blind, looking away, giving her time. Lola explained, twiddling hair, eyes down, in fits and starts that, as I had come to suspect after reading her two DONE LISTS, Will day had not actually been the first time but a second time, and that it had all started a while back at some festival.

'Mungyjacks?'

'Yes, Mungojaxx.'

'I thought there was a whole group of you …'

'We sneaked into this tent together. No one knew.'

I smiled. 'Ah, the old tent-share ploy. Smooth.'

'Not really.' A scared peep up at me through her hair. 'He nearly kicked it over!'

'Ha! That's what too much stolen vodka will do for you.'

A hollow laugh – an inevitable, guilty-as-charged echo of a laugh – and just there, that was it. The exposure of teenage transgression disguised as good humour, of course, but so much more: our one moment of flawless connection.

That it should come *now*. Still, I had to move on.

'When was Mungojaxx again?'

'Twenty-third of July.'

I looked up to the ceiling, as if the days were unspooling in my mind. But she talked into my counting, wispy stunted words, trying to make sense of it all:

'You know, I've just found out he's even told all the boys I was bad at it.'

'Oh. Horrible.'

'Yes. Can't *believe* I made videos for him, as well as the Facetiming; I gave him actual proof. Someone said that he has even put a video of us online, but I can't find it and now I'm—'

'OK, stay calm. I have to think about this one. Maybe it's not too late to … sort something out. Leave it with me.'

Just a courtesy call, Mrs Waite.

The police had not hung about, they took these matters very seriously. They had spoken to Darren Hodson about his possible connection to scratched cars, anonymous notes and breathed phone calls; about a historic assault on a fifteen-year-old girl. He had alibis for some, denials for others, blank outrage for the whole fucking-bang-out-of-order lot. A misunderstanding; an innocent, if sweary, man. A man free to walk the streets.

No need to worry, Mrs Waite. We'll continue with our enquiries.

But I did worry. I checked the front door was double-locked and quizzed Thomas once again about the precision of the intruder alarm. I left on a spare room light, locked Stevie in, and kept my shoes close to my bed, in case I needed to run.

I worried.

The next night, the end began.

It started with a thank you. A heartfelt embrace from my husband to thank me once again for having opened myself to him so completely, for explaining why I had reacted to those abandoned knickers in the way I had. Once again, he pulled me to him.

'God, thank you; you were so brave to tell me, about the … sorrel. Thank you for giving us a chance.'

I said nothing, breathed him in.

'And your sister? Has she called you again?'

'She may well have tried, she withholds her number now.'

'Maybe you should—'

'No! You can't trust a word that woman says! Anyway, she won't bother us again, not now she's spoken to you …'

I was trying to convince myself as much as him. I drew back:

'Come on, please, Thomas, forget her. You've been hinting that I had to be bored only seeing you all the time, wanting us to do "something fun" together. Should we give this party a shot?'

That evening it was the drinks party of Carla Moore, a woman who was still grateful for the drawn-out medical advice I once gave her about caring for her mum; she still called me her angel, 'no word of a lie'. So, sort of a friend, you could say. I thought that drinking her warm cocktails as I mingled with people to whom I was not married might be doing both the hostess and my husband a favour.

First though, I made another quick check, to confirm the answer I had sought out since breakfast: yes, my photo was no longer online. There was nothing: no me, no dirtied yellow dress, not even one pixel of Stevie, nothing at all. The whole site had been shut down. I eased, just a touch. Not too much. I was still smarting with the shock of having seen us and all those other strangers, the many random dark faces: the man, forty-seven, the woman, sixty-eight, the man, age unknown, face after face, and the horror did not switch off altogether; it went on standby.

Now though, we were to have a break from it all, have a drink, maybe a dance. If we could find the right sitter. Ange the childminder did the odd evening when asked. But Ange, who was *always* available, was on voicemail, over and over, and then I tried her eldest niece, her back-up; no joy there either. I went through my contacts, trying to remember if the nervy girl who had once covered for me with Stevie while I hauled ass to the wards on short notice was Sarah L or Sara R. I had started to look through old emails to find out whether I was in fact about to leave my son with a long-dropped babysitter or our one-time female plumber, when Thomas finally staged an intervention:

'Stop harassing yourself. Lola's in, she can do it.'

'Is she?' I lied. 'Oh I know, but it's not fair to—'

'She can just—'

'We don't have to—'

'Stop,' he said. 'We can't live like prisoners. Lola has it. He'll be fine.'

I folded into his hug, wondering how cross he would get if I now started to feign a headache. Then the heat and musk of his arms began to seep through and I stopped peering into that grotesque hall of shame and thought: *sixteen*.

I changed into my red dress.

'Maybe just for an hour or two.'

What could go wrong in an hour or two?

At the party, we started out as a tight little pair of observers, watching the same people walk through the door and sharing the same silent thoughts under all the music. It seemed right; Thomas was behaving like a man who had never felt closer to his wife. At one point someone else from the architectural world came over and his partner made a beeline for me and we were no longer standing together. Soon we were ten people apart, the woman still chattering at me about some course she was doing.

'Sorry, I'll be back in a tick.' I held up my empty glass.

I should have gone to Thomas, but I went straight to the drinks table, stayed there, topping myself up too fast. Sign of a successful couple – wasn't it? – to be too relaxed and confident to monopolise each other at parties. I would stay away for a little bit, leave him to hold court. But at heart I was worried. Worried that I should not, after all, have burdened Thomas with my tales of sorrel, and worried that just in being there I had been seduced by stupidity's comforting embrace. Lola and Stevie home alone, together; people knowing where we lived. That had to be a mistake.

I was on edge, and because I was on edge I over-enthused to those who tried to make conversation, got into a dangerous rhythm with the rum and whatevers, lost track of time and of myself. Thomas was still too busy chatting about the Stephen Lawrence Prize shortlist to his new friend to notice. I wended my way back to him, but by around 9 p.m. I had fallen off the edge and was starting to mistake my own fizzing, fuzzy mind for 'having fun'. I started to dance, a light bounce, at Thomas's side.

'It is actually good to be out, isn't it?'

'Yes, Darling, and it's high time. But just this last one, I'm afraid, then we had better get back.'

'Yes,' I stopped bouncing, let sobering thoughts in once more. 'I had been thinking that, too. I agree.'

The cold air slapped a little sense into me, but only a little. Not enough to get a sense of whether the danger I could smell was real. The late evening did not buzz, it hummed with end-of-the-weekend purpose, its street lights throwing out an orange glow into the black, creating the uncertain gloom that passed for night around these parts. High Desford was not a city that never slept, more a town that could not rest. We hopped on a passing bus back to the Old Town, something Thomas had not done for years, so already it felt a bit daring, an oldie transgression.

As we neared the right stop, we passed a shifting crowd on the high street. Girls laughing and shivering in too few clothes, eking out the last of their fun, men smoking under street heaters, pints in hand; a knot of big men, hard domes of head catching the light and in the middle of them all, him. Face on, unmistakably him.

'Darling, what is it?'

'I think I saw ...' But we had passed the pubs and cafés and were turning in to a quieter road. 'Let's just get home.'

The key turned in the lock. And then it happened.

As soon as we went in, she started talking.

'You came back just in time,' Lola said to Thomas and me. No, there hadn't been any problems, she had a special show for us both, she said. She explained, as if I did not already know, that she had been hanging out a lot with Stevie. She had been trying very hard to do the right thing, for Stevie. Here my skin began to prickle, the blur struggled to sharpen, focus.

'He's really quite a bright kid, entertaining, you know?' she said. 'We've been practising a show for the parents. You're going to love it.'

She strode to our side of the room.

Some cute skit, that would be all, some corny cuddly punchline, then time for bed. But with my mouth drugged too slow, frozen in its gasp, I watched as my Wonderboy pulled off the half undone KAFOs.

'Mummy look!' he said.

'Walk to me, Stevie,' she said.

'What? Lola no! He can't—' I began at last, but it was already happening.

Stevie was walking towards her across the room, with no callipers. A bit faltering, but with no lurch, no falling. My breath held, but it was no more than he did at bedtimes.

'Now skip and jump and kick, like I showed you, Ninja!'

'No!' I cried. 'She could snap his bloody bones!'

Dancing? Was she making my boy *perform*?

'Take *that*, Lolly!'

'Don't, Lola! Stevie!' shouted Thomas.

Too late. Stevie the martial artist was jumping and spinning and flicking out his legs at his step-sister and crouching low then pounding into the air with each foot, with sick-making vigour, just missing a vase. All the dangerous, unmistakable vigour of a healthy child.

'Darling?' said Thomas.

The air had been kicked out of my chest. Lola's metal eyes turned on me with nothing soft and light in them. They were all steel.

'I'm—'

'Darling? What is this?'

I had already grabbed Stevie.

'I'm—'

'Darling?'

I was strapping him back into his KAFOs.

'Sorry, I can't, I'm not up to this, sorry.'

I did not stop to pack anything this time, I simply threw Stevie over my shoulder. But Thomas stood in the doorway:

'No, you can't simply try to run off whenever—'

'Out of my way!'

'Mummy?'

'Darling, please, stay here, she was only trying to help. What is this?'

Stevie was wriggling, trying to get down and the blur in my mind felt raw and the fuzz was clearing and getting tight and all I could see ahead was Thomas wanting answers.

'No! Please.'

Thomas and Lola both took a step away from the door and my son went slack in my arms. I held Stevie closer so that he did not fall and hurtled out of that heavy door into the ever-orange night.

Lola

DONE LIST 9

I have done something terrible. I encouraged Stevie to dance, as if he could walk properly, when apparently I 'could have done him serious damage'. It was pretty dumb, but I thought I was helping. I went online and was trying to help him but I must have got it all wrong. Another major not-joking fuck-up – like me sharing some stupid photo of Darling on Facebook ages ago (I'd honestly forgotten) when we were just taking the piss out of her, which actually ended up in the <u>police</u> coming round our house. Then I asked Stevie to dance and now Darling's finally stormed out and Dad is pretty confused. She'll be back though. She has to come back. Everyone is just making too big a deal of this.

The more I read and find online, the more not-joking this looks. I should have just asked Dad, or dealt with it some other way rather than making Stevie dance. But that visit really threw me. Not the police guy. Get this – as soon as they set off for that party, literally a few minutes after, the doorbell went. I shouldn't have answered it, but it was still light and I thought it might be Ellie, because she was in town. It wasn't Ellie, it was this woman. This other black woman.

She asked me if Darling was in. I said no. Then she asked if she could see Stevie and I said, 'Sorry, who are you?' I was getting a bit worried. Then she started gabbling, quite fast and looking over her shoulder, said that it was OK, she was a teacher and she was a relative, Stevie's auntie, Auntie Jade, and that if she could see him for five minutes, then she would leave us in peace.

I said I could phone Darling and Dad, just to check it was OK and then she started getting all jumpy, saying that would be a waste of time and not to bother. Really weird. She looked like she might cry and said she was going, muttered a lot of crazy stuff, like she was going to drop to her knees right there. But the last bit I remember, she said:

'Forget it, you can't help, but thank you. I've got to go. Please give Darling this and ask her to call me as soon as she is back.'

I took an envelope from her and went to shut the door.

But then she said 'wait' and handed me a piece of paper too. She said: 'This one's for you.'

It was this leaflet. I haven't stopped reading it:

Munchausen syndrome by proxy (MSBP) is a mental health condition in which a caregiver makes up or causes an illness or injury in a person under their care, such as an elderly person, someone who has a disability, or a child …

I've gone over and over it, I've even checked it out online. It does make some sick sort of sense, but how could I have been certain without testing it out? That's when I knew I had to see if Stevie could jump and kick.

I did make too big a show of it, I guess. I needed to see if she would react. But then again, I wasn't bloody wrong.

I've got even bigger problems than this Darling stuff. It's all over social media – in two Ben Wischer retweets alone – Will Benton thinks I'm 'munt'. But of course he does and of course it's online, why would it not be? Come join the shit-kicking party, Wishy and gang, make yourself at home! Why the hell did I ever believe for a moment that Will ever really <u>saw</u> who I was?

Perhaps because he told me he did.

Fuck.

Bad: still no sign of Darling. Whichever way this is going to go I will need her like never before. For starters, questions I can never, ever ask Dad:

Dad, what happens if I drank alcohol when I didn't know? Before?

Dad, how do I stop labour hurting?

Dad, how exactly do you change a nappy?

Dad, is breast <u>really</u> best?

Oh God. Is this happening? (That was a real question.)

Holy goddamn cannoli, what's wrong with me? No one was on my side more than Darling and then I had to go and upset her. Why didn't I just ignore the stupid leaflet? #serialfuckups

I'm sure she'll come back. She knows I need her. She's a nurse and they're angels, right? How can she not come back?

OK, I actually am a total melt. I had the answer all along: my iPhone, Family Sharing. She's in some house only about twenty minutes away. Her sister's? Dad said to leave her to cool down, but it's already been a whole day. I'll walk. If I could just find that stupid envelope that I swear was right

there and leave now, we could all talk it out and I'd have her back before dinner time.

Wish me luck, kids. Oh, just realised. That's really not funny any more.

Achievements

1. Tried to talk to Dad about what Darling's sister said, but he said that we should not believe a stranger and that Darling would have an explanation. Probably made it sound like I didn't trust her – bad move. Whether I trust her or not, she's all I've got.
2. Threw her sister's letter down somewhere while I got my head around this stuff (should I steam it?) but have somehow managed to make it disappear, WTF?
3. Used the app to find Darling. Thank you, God.
4. No more achievements, ~~everything's just gone really~~ it's too hard.
5. Maybe one achievement after all. Got Ellie to invite me over asap. Because we really need to talk.

Darling

TUESDAY, 22 NOVEMBER

One night in this online-booked flat and I was ready to crack.

I sat wondering whether to email Thomas or phone him. If I were to phone, the words needed to be right. An email might get missed, miss the mark. Too much to say for a text. A phone call might be too live, too raw, or it could be the shout-out that would save the day.

I searched for answers. Literally, online. Theories. But nothing would come, nothing that I could say to Thomas without imagining him giving me the look that would stop all my fussing and striving for good.

What would Thomas be thinking of me?

I rang. I rang and rang. The first call failed. And the next – what did this mean? I moved to the window to get another bar of signal. Nothing. The next few calls went straight to voicemail and by the seventh or eighth attempt I felt I was nearing some critical mass that might tip me permanently into the realm of the blocked. I stopped, saw a look of growing appetite on my boy's face. An early dinner might do as a distraction. I had stocked up that morning thinking we might stay for a week, and Pattie's best oxtail had already been lime-washed, trimmed, tossed in Jamaican herbs and spices, and then left to marinate. (If you couldn't feed your family in a crisis, then you couldn't feed your family.)

Time to cook. I fried the meat, consoling myself that when he turned on his phone, if he turned on his phone, Thomas would at least see the moderate but meaningful chain of missed calls, a trail of communication crumbs leading back to his lost wife.

As I chucked water, carrot and onion on top of the oxtail and left it to simmer, it occurred to me that, depending on what he had gathered from that shameful kicking-Ninja scene, he may well wish me to stay lost.

To take the edge off that thought, I had bought a bottle of aged Appleton to watch over me while I watched the pot.

I needed to move. An hour of rum in me and as I stared at the news on TV I could feel the amber glow of both screen and glass turning my spirits darker. High Desford station had been cordoned off and armed police drafted in as they carried out a controlled explosion of what could be an abandoned suicide vest. Maybe real and a dud, or a fake; either way, an ineffaceable evil. What did these people hope for? To win a future where all lived as they commanded or else had been obliterated in a shower of their flesh, blood and bone. And what other pulse of horror would have to run through even the most murderous mind in order to make one's own being a lethal weapon? These days, that was the question.

My son, I would see to my son. I could not just sit there, I had to help him, to *protect*. He was playing, legs out in the usual V before him, at my feet on the sitting-room floor.

'Stevie! Come here.' I shifted off my seat into a squat and hugged him until he squirmed. 'Do you feel a bit tense in your legs, darling?'

'No, Mummy, I'm OK,' he said, looking at me with wide calm eyes. I could see now: he wore his bravery as some children wore glasses.

'You do, don't you?' I could always tell. 'Don't you worry, we'll take care of it. Mummy'll do it for you.'

Mass out, chile, keep cool.

I took off the KAFOS and gave him a great physio session. I flexed his joints and gave him weight to bear, but not too much. I did everything for him that he needed. Of course I did, that's what I do: I'm his mummy and more. I am a nurse.

He had certainly become a bit more 'kicky' since Lola messed with him. He felt unbalanced, unsettled, and I could sense it in each joint. But the physio seemed to tire him, irritate him even, and so I urged him into our new shared bed, with the promise of a favourite cartoon on his tablet and also one of the new pills I had bought that morning to calm him and make him feel better.

I shut the door on him. The rum was weighing on me and somewhere out there I could feel my sister watching, waiting. But that was nothing, compared to the inevitability of *him*.

A knock.

God. Surely it wasn't—

But Lola was at the door, shivering in trainers and that velvet blazer, which was far too worn for this weather, and not waterproof.

'Hi, how did you find me?' I asked, knowing full well.

'Oh, I …'

'Doesn't matter,' I said. Where was her red coat? 'Come in.'

In a cute flourish, she brought out some bright tulips from behind her thigh:

'Here. I stopped on the way, I know you like them.'

She had bypassed the petrol station buckets of carnations and turned off her route to buy them from the gift boutique on Fields Avenue. I recognised the hand-tied raffia. Maybe she did not yet think I was a monster.

Yuh si? Like mi always sey: one, one coco full basket.

'Come on,' I said, laying the flowers by the simmering beef. 'Through here, let's talk.'

'I'm so sorry, Darling.'

She was still standing.

'I didn't know what I was doing, making him dance like that.'

I choked a touch, breathed out a cough.

'You … no.'

'I got it wrong.'

'Yes! Thank you.'

'I'm sorry.'

'I forgive you, Lola,' I said. 'It's all OK, sit down.'

Once seated, she looked uncertain, and said nothing for a moment.

'Dad would love you to come back home, you know?'

'Would he? That's good.'

If this were true, then he had not fully understood, but he would, one day.

'Better than this place, right? Not that it's …' She peered up for a second. 'Also, I need you back. We were going to find a plan. Weren't we?'

'Yes.' Too weary to think, I reached for my rum.

'Are you worried about Stevie? I'm pretty sure he hasn't hurt himself.'

'No,' I said. The alcohol had ceased to either burn or soothe my throat an hour before. 'Stevie's just fine. He's watching something in our room. He's fine.'

'Good. Because I know your illness makes you worry too much about that stuff. I get it now. Jade said—'

I rocketed upright. 'You've spoken to Jade?'

'Yes, I wanted to tell you. She came to the house last night and wanted to see Stevie. That's what made me think I should—'

'You believed her? When she said I was ill?'

Now Lola sat straighter in her chair, looked about the strange flat.

'I'm not sure,' she lied.

On and on she talked, about syndromes and mistakes and understanding and why I must not worry. She talked on. This rum was starting to taste too sweet, too much of cinnamon and cloves. I pressed my hands into the arms of the chair. Rose up slowly.

'Don't you worry about me, poppet,' I could hear my slowed, unsteady tongue. 'It's you we need to think about. Wait here.'

I went to my rented bedroom. Stevie was sitting with earphones in, staring at his tablet. It would have been so easy to shout 'Lolly's here!' but so unfair, on us all. I had to stay focused. She had now spoken to Jade.

The room offered a few shelves with fewer books. No plays or sonnets. But there was an odds and ends box I had examined earlier, with reels of cotton, a ruler, a pencil sharpener, needles, pins, scissors, the back page of a guide to Spanish grammar and, amongst the dross, a tape measure, the type you used for sewing.

I retrieved what I needed and went back to her. She stayed for another half an hour, and then she was gone.

The oxtail was sure to be ready soon. I could smell it, hoped it hadn't caught on the hob. When I went back to the kitchen, I saw that some of the tulip petals – just the very edges – were in the blue flame, charring and smouldering. Lola's gift, ruined. I turned everything off and poured another rum, feeling only the dullest surprise that the smoke had not set off the alarm.

Then I threw the flowers, all of them, in the bin.

Lola

DONE LIST 10

I had to come back and pack a bag, and to write this ~~in case som~~ but I can't stay now.

I can't believe it. I really can't believe it.

I'm going to be a mum. It's too late for anything else. Darling told me last night.

But before even that, how the hell can I cope with the pregnancy, let alone the kid? Surely no better torture could have been created for me.

I realise now that my only hope of getting through this is to let Darling take care of us all. I've just come back from this flat she's in – shit, it was all so weird. But ill or not, she's a nurse, she knows what she is doing. We will need her more than ever now. Now that I have ruined everyone's lives … Still couldn't find that bloody letter so I didn't mention it in case it pissed her off. But his parents will be getting a letter too soon, Darling said we had to.

No, it's too much, I can't do this.

I think maybe I am losing my mind. What's wrong with me? I no longer feel in control.

Only I have brought us to this point. If I had taken more care, paid more attention, then nothing would be the way it is now. None of it. I've done this. I wish I could work out how to fix it but my brain feels like I do – bloated jelly, a beached whale. I can't think. I can't remember why I agreed to do what I did with Will. Can't believe I lost my virginity to a boy who thinks it is OK to steal almost £300 from his mother and then gets the cleaner sacked for it (she's got two kids and, now, a bad reputation). The sex was stupid enough but ~~to have helped him to go after Darling was~~ I should have kept him away from the family. And all that nasty stuff online, God. I think he only wanted to impress his BNB friends, so he used me. I feel totally used.

Found it. The letter was stuck inside my magazine, right at the top of the drawer I'd looked in ten times #blindbloodybitch.

I read it.

Fuck them all, Dad and Darling and her son and her 'sister', fuck Will, and most of my friends and all of my failures. I think I have lost it already and now I have this thing growing inside me. But that is not even the worst thing of all. I have ruined everything and ~~I just want to~~

OK, calm. It <u>will</u> be OK. It all has to be OK, but I can't do it like this any more. I'm going to go to Ellie's right now, she's being really solid (at the moment). Actually, thinking about it, my only real problem is that I always seem to need people who let me down. Happens to the best of us, right?

Whatfuckingever. Enough.

Achievements

1. Done my DONE Lists and now I'm DONE.

Darling

An alien light, green. I was not where I was supposed to be. Ah, here then. The clock was shining its news at me: 3.14 a.m. Even before I tasted the old rum in my gorge, I knew I might vomit. The hand above me was now pressing down on my crown, on all of us. The blear of fear before my eyes was bright as day, but I knew it was night. Time to act, not sleep.

At this time though, the middle of the night, all I could do was lie and stare into the dark. What had I done?

By 5.59 a.m., I had decided. Now sober enough, with enough dawn to justify me, I carried Stevie into the car and drove back to Littleton Lodge. I sat in the drive, engine idling, wondering whether I could knock at 6.15 a.m. In the event, Thomas came to the front door.

'Darling, what on earth?'

'Is Lola upstairs?'

A flash of confusion as memory fought sleep.

'Lola? No, she's fine, she stayed at Ellie's last night.'

'Ah, sorry,' I said. 'Good.'

'Are you coming in, or …'

'I'm sorry, I shouldn't have come so early, no we'll go back—'

'OK, fine, whatever,' he said, sounding tired as death.

But it was not fine and I was not going back. I had to find Lola. I had to put her straight.

I drove to Ellie's house.

All the lights were off and it was only 6.47 a.m. I would wait until either one came on or it hit 7.30 a.m., then ring the bell.

'You all right, Stevie?'

'Yes.' In my rear-view mirror, he was rubbing his eyes.

'We won't be too long here, sweetie.' In my healed car, looking up through the half-light to strange windows, I tried to imagine which curtains Lola might be behind, or whether she was sleeping. If I acted fast, all this could be put straight.

I would never again be petty or short with her. I would understand better, listen more. I would not be jealous or unkind. I would make amends. I would chill the fuck out. I would love her, if I could just get to speak to her now.

A light came on, top right.

I knocked. A knock ought to be less of a shock than a ring. It was so early. Thudding on stairs, a shadow that became a crease-faced man:

'Can I help you?'

'I'm very sorry to call so early. I'm here for Lola.'

'Oh, of course. I doubt they're up but – hang on.'

Then he pushed the door to a touch, either to keep out draughts or me, and went back upstairs. I could hear voices.

He returned, shaking his head.

'She's not here?'

'Really? My husband said—'

'She was, but she left first thing—'

'OK. Sorry to disturb you.'

Now fear was rising in my chest. Where was she?

I called Thomas:

'Is Lola back with you yet?'

'No. Listen, Darling, should I be worried?'

'She might be on her way. I don't know … Look, I'll speak to you later.'

I could not bear to hear his voice, could not bear that he did not know a single thing that mattered, could not yet bear to explain.

I dialled again:

'Ange? Hi, it's me. Listen, could you take Stevie for the day, call it emergency rates? Thank you, thank you, life-saver …'

I swung by Ange's and Stevie hurried to the door, ever pleased to see her and her young son, Joe. I waved, drove around the corner and parked up in the first free space.

313

Find My iPhone, tracking Lola. I could know where she was in seconds. I launched the app. A grey dot still hovered over Ellie's house. Her phone had to be off. Her phone was never off.

I had nothing, nowhere.

I drove to Littleton Lodge. This time I used the key.

'Darling?' Thomas was hunched over a coffee. 'What's going on?'

'I know you must hate me.'

'What, why? Lola was saying some stuff, but I can't believe this strange long-lost sister, or whatever, would know better—'

'No, of course you can't. Silly of me to storm out like that. I just felt so angry but … OK, this is not important right now, forget Jade. We need to find Lola.'

'Yes, why don't we know where she is? We have to talk this through, together. I'm calling her, right now—'

'Don't, I—'

My heart nearly pounded its way out of my chest as I realised that, if Lola picked up, there would be no way back for us, ever. I could hear three rings, four …

He looked up. 'Gone to voicemail.'

In those seconds I had seen the answer, the only way. My hands started to shake.

'Listen, look. You've got to leave for work in a bit. I'll make you breakfast and then wait here for her. I remember her saying something about popping to a few friends, now

I think of it. Let's just let her get on with it and try her in a little while, yeah?'

'OK, that's probably best, it's not even eight o'clock.'

'Good. Go. Try to relax. I'll make you breakfast.'

We ate, then I left him to dress, with another glance at my watch. Lola, Lola. I would tidy the kitchen cupboard – it had got quite out of control.

Spices, herbs. With rustles and banging, I took out all the well-used jars. I wiped around with a cloth soaked in detergent and breathed in the acrid lemon. Then I set about putting everything back inside in alphabetical order. Allspice, bay leaves, bouquet garni, cardamom pods, cayenne pepper, celery salt, cinnamon sticks ...

'Darling! God—'

... cloves, ground coriander, cumin ...

'Darling!'

I raced upstairs to find him shaking in the doorway of our en suite in shirt, soaked tie and boxers. He was white and although eyes should not flicker and sweat, his did.

'God, I'm—'

I loosened his tie, his worst, a dark red-pink one. I took it off, began to unbutton his shirt.

'I'm ... sorry,' he said. 'I feel ...'

We wondered, between building heaves, how this terrible food poisoning had happened. He confessed that he and a few colleagues had celebrated a minor win with some paper-swaddled fried efforts from the Dalton Road fish and chip van the previous lunchtime. Bad cod, we said.

Then he about-turned, slamming the door behind his slumping back.

He was vomiting with an alarming frequency – every five minutes – and I could not stop him for long enough to get him in the car to the hospital.

My head fell forward. So much sickness. This had to be the worst. How it turned me inside out, turned us all inside out, that there should be so much sickness when my every fibre lived to heal, to nourish. When did I get so tired, so *old*? Maybe, like in the sonnet, that old spark – my youth – had in the end been 'consum'd with that which it was nour- ish'd by.' Now I could not see past that closed door through to what needed to happen next. What if I lost him too, what if it was all already too late? Every tendon and ligament and muscle was in that moment exercised, stretched taut – hard and thin as my mind. I was on a rack and knew that my husband was sick, very sick and that he would have to stay home all day.

The heaves grew more violent, and I felt that I would have to scream out for it to stop, all of it. But then his sickness subsided and he dragged himself from the bathroom to bed.

'I'm sorry, Darling, I need to—'

'I know, don't worry. Nurse, remember?' I said, my heart beginning to slow at last. 'You need to lie still for a while. I'll leave you to sleep now. I'll shout if there's anything. She'll probably wander back home later.'

I shut the door on my husband. Just me then. Just me alone with the things that I had done, and the things that I needed to do.

8.11 a.m. Her phone was off.

8.14 a.m. Her phone was off.

8.21 a.m. Off, off.

I stood at the sink in the kitchen, washing the frying pan and blender cup as Thomas dozed, wondering at how fast life could change. There was still time. I would tell my husband – one day soon, if he remained my husband – about Cara and perhaps even the day of the St Foillan's lift; at least the parts he would understand. I would tell him about the baby girl I had given birth to long before I met Demarcus, when I was much younger, twenty-seven, and that the father (some stocky Kos wanker, it didn't matter) still did not know to this day. I would tell him how she was a sickly baby, how I helped her, nursed her, was everything to her despite whatever my little sister might try to say. That she died, but not because of my care, or the treatments that only I knew how to give; she just gave up the ghost and left me. That I had nourished the thought of her, that ghost of her, for an age, nourished it like hope. That when later I had Stevie, my Wonderboy, I knew I had to do things differently, better. And now he was six.

8.29 a.m. Her phone was off.

Thomas was in a deep sleep now, I could sense it.

My mind roamed from past to phone, future to phone, tumbling as if I were still swilling rum, or spinning tales in my mind.

Lola was gone.

Some kisses stayed with you.

Jade had come.

I had to find her.

Uncle Malcolm tried to visit us again, after the last of my childhood was blasted away behind the pantry door, but I would not stay in the house: even the smallest gardens had crouching exits and a sky to escape into. Then he faded off for many months and I started to write my stories, but they all warped and split until uncontainable visions of him ended up pouring right into the quietest part of my head, every time. I stopped writing; of course I did.

After Uncle Malcolm had shown me what he meant by a kiss, nothing mattered for a long time. I made sure that nothing mattered by fucking up everything that might have come close in garish, spectacular fashion: my exams, my sanity, my sense of myself. I read, yes, always, but I also dabbled in, had a go at, went over the top of, and wilfully tried on all the naughty. All the wrong parties; the wrong choices; boys true, false and don't know; a long powdery line; a wayward join-the-dots leading from an Elm Forest terrace all the way to the glaring Greek sunshine. There was no one to mind, after such a kiss, no one to look after or care for, certainly not myself at least. Only Jade, then nine months after Kos, Cara. But then there was no Cara. And then later only Stevie. Thomas did come along and try to cherish me, but that was not the most important thing of all. There always had to be Stevie.

Yuh draw bad caad, but yuh cya get tru …

My mother had watched it all. Watched me skid from doubt to despair via disaster and back and onwards again until I too knew to live out my natural-born nursing. She died a few months after I enrolled at college. She watched it all, she knew.

Yuh draw bad caad, but yuh cya get tru …

9.05 a.m. Her phone was off.

Lola had broken me. Even now, she was not thinking about any baby, she could only be plotting to fill my life with torture or ache. Who was she with, Will and his lot? Was this some ploy, a last-ditch play? Did she believe in me now, or hate me? After everything, did she still want my *destruction*?

But then, she had said sorry, brought me flowers …

The night before, she had spoken those words to me as if she might care, as if *she* was the nurse telling me what was wrong. Of course I knew about all that Munchausen's syndrome by proxy stuff, but it simply did not *apply*. I was kind, not cruel, and rarely cruel to be kind. Her being so damn smart, chatting on about the terrible consequences of early trauma – she and I both, then! Childish, I knew, but she did go on and on, about how severe stresses could arise in traumatised parents, flaring up like crackpot birthday candles when their own children reached that same devastating age. All that, as if she were a shrink; as if she, the shrunk one and all of sixteen, were teaching me a thing or two!

I did not react as I should have. I should not have done what I did. But I did, I suppose, stay calm. Unflapped. Professional, as only born carers can be.

9.11 a.m. On. Her phone was on.

I launched the app, a green dot shone. She was in London. Harrow-on-the-Hill.

I drove to the station. When I got on the train, my carriage was almost empty. A few seats ahead a couple of girls were laughing and whispering; there were two or three business types jabbing at their phones, one standing cyclist, a man in a bomber jacket with his back to me.

We pulled out and I lost the WiFi. 'Cannot Connect'. I would have to wait for some 4G and pray that Lola didn't get on another train, or bus, or even plane before I reached her. Nothing I could do, for now, except hope hard.

I picked up the local paper from the seat opposite. An unknown celeb and some depressing political scandal on the front page. I got as far as page 2. It was him. The man in the photos was Darren Hodson, the guy from the supermarket, the one who had hurt me all those years ago. The wing-tips of his tattoo were showing. The headline read:

BOUNCER IN PUB RACE ATTACK

I read fast:

> Darren Hodson, forty-two, has been charged with an assault on a man, twenty-seven, of Eritrean origin, outside the Rose and Crown where Hodson works as a bouncer. The victim is being treated in hospital. He is an asylum seeker and reliable witness accounts lead police to believe the attack was racially motivated. There may be further drug-related charges. Hodson is being held in custody.

By the third reading, all I could think about was the custody-holding and the reliable witnesses. It was not a conviction yet but, again, I would hope hard. And, for today at least, his eagle tattoo would not be swooping through our streets.

The train to Harrow-on-the-Hill took forty-seven minutes. The dot was still just there, where it had been for more than an hour, right opposite the station we pulled into, at the

Lemon Grove Café. I waited for the traffic to part, rushed across the road. At last, I pushed into an airy room, what Thomas would call 'the sort of place we used to call hip'. A young crowd, music; I scanned fast. Almost empty, no Lola. Puffed out, I slumped into the nearest hard chair. If one of the ponytails bounced over I would order a cappuccino; she had to be in the loo. Sitting at a corner table I watched three or four Tuesday-night-clubbing patrons prod suspiciously at fry-ups, testing the quality of the sausage with their knife and seeking out the advertised black pudding under their duck eggs and home-sauced haricot beans. Post-come-down fry-ups, far from a bed that cared.

Where *was* she?

I refreshed the app. The same green dot: here, it said she was right here.

I waved over a young waitress.

'I'm sorry, is there another room here, maybe? A back room, or upstairs lounge?'

She shook her ponytail in pretty denial.

'Just here, just us! Can I get you anything?'

'Give me a moment, please.'

I lifted the menu, ignoring the flat whites in sizes Live it Large, Spoiler and Basic Ration. I passed over the croissants with rooftop-churned butter and manuka honey, the dense, rare-breed, orange-yolked poached eggs. I was hungry for nothing, no one but Lola, Lolly, Lolapaloo.

Where are you, Lo?

My mind was churning with ideas for her, explanations, what I would and would not say; cunning ways to pull parental rank should matters take a turn for the worse. My mind was bright, full of clean white light, dazzling with intention. I let it turn and turn.

I had to try harder.

I played with my phone, waiting for some sign. Then I saw it, an 'i' in the bottom right of the screen. I selected 'Satellite'. There, no doubt it was this road. Refresh. Zoom. I tapped until the image grew. She was definitely here, the green dot insisted. My mind gone grey, I tapped once more.

'Shit!'

I had dropped the phone on the ground, shattering the screen. From the floor, I picked up my device with all its integral power, the secrets it contained. No, hopeless; the unprotected screen was impossibly fragmented, beyond the reach of my touch.

I had to move fast now, she was here. I knew she was here. Where was she?

The ponytail was approaching again. I took out my purse.

'Hi, listen,' I said, pulling out a tenner. 'I'm so sorry, I'm not going to order anything, but do you mind if I have a quick look around?'

'Go ahead.'

'Thank you.' I left the note so that a large corner peeked out from under the menu, then rose. 'Are the Ladies upstairs?'

She nodded.

The stairs to the first floor were narrow and bent back on themselves. The landing had three doors. I went into the first, the Ladies. Just three cubicles, one occupied.

'Lola?'

No answer.

I waited by the sinks. After a moment, I bent to see the feet: trainers. I was going to call out again, but then, there, a flush. My heart skittered faster as – *chuk* – the lock went and …

A young woman of about twenty, Korean maybe, slipped past me to wash her hands.

I looked again. All three cubicles empty; a check around the corner, no one. I left.

Had to hurry. Two more chances on the landing: the Gents and a Staff Only door. I went for the latter: a push, a peek, a few coats, a kettle, a young girl in an apron, texting. Not Lola.

Gents, then.

I barged in. A lone man, fifty-odd, standing at the urinals with business in hand. His face contorted in nascent outrage and then – incalculably worse – he smiled.

'Sorry! Wrong door.'

I wheeled about. Thanked all that was holy that I could see from where I stood that all the cubicles were empty; I did not have the balls to go in. Downside: no Lola anywhere.

Back on the landing, I trailed my hands along the wall, the windowsill, looked out. Nothing but a small concrete yard, some large bins. Beyond the fence, ranks of head-stones, sheltered by trees and woven through with swept paths. A flash of red caught my eye.

A red coat. Lola.

She was walking away from the fence towards the far end of the cemetery.

I rapped, with some force, on the glass. She didn't turn.

I hurried down the stairs and out of the door, turning hard left and left again, trying to get to what I had seen from the window; no, it was all fenced off. I turned back and broke into a jog, keeping going, now run-running on rocky pavement, following my nose. I cranked myself up to the max, until my teeth juddered and the daylight shook and a low moan started up in my lungs. I dodged swinging arms, bending backs, banging builders and straining dogs as I slapped my fast ugly feet over two, four, seven pavements to find her. At last, I stuttered through the gates of the cemetery.

Red, red, where was she?

'No. Not you, not here.'

I looked left. On a bench against a wall was Lola. Hunched over, something scrunched in her hand that looked like cellophane. She got up, came over.

'Lola, I'm so—'

'Did you know, it was her birthday, yesterday? Mum's. Dad forgot; first time ever. Everyone forgot. I just woke up and thought: 'We're forgetting ...'

'Lola, I'd like to—'

'I don't care!'

She walked past me, binned the flower wrappings and started to jog; then she was running, running away, running flat out.

I had no choice. I ran again, anchoring my gaze to her back as she darted up the high street. The sight of a young man shouting as she caught his shoulder, already too far away for me to hear. She kept going. Then, right under the station sign, she slowed and nipped up the steps.

I ran on, rasping my breath, until I reached the station entrance. The steps. I threw everything into bounding up and up until – there, I was inside. I rushed on, looking around. She was nowhere. I ran through to the main ticket hall, still no sign, then on to the concourse.

There. She was there, in her red coat, next to one of those tapioca-ball juice concessions, looking lost. Utterly lost.

'Lola, hang on!' I called.

'Oh God,' she said, walking away fast towards the platform gates.

'You need to come home, sweetie.'

'No! I don't want to live anywhere near you! You've ruined my life!'

'Don't be silly,' I said. 'I'll look after you ...'

'Fuck no! You lied.'

'Lola!'

'I know you lied. Pregnant? I know I'm not, now.'

'I know that, I came to tell—'

'Ellie and I did another test. And another one, just to be sure. I'm definitely not pregnant, you lied.'

She was almost running again now.

'Was just going to … we're—'

'We nothing! And even if I had been pregnant, it wouldn't have been "too late".'

I was panting hard. 'I needed. To take control. Of situation.'

'Control of me?'

'To help. You were—'

'I know! A fuckup. I *know*, I … *God*.'

'You need to be taken care of, Lola. But now you think that I'm a monster?'

'You know about your own illness, don't pretend you don't! What do you reckon?'

'Well then.' So, me too now, that betrayal of fake cheer. 'We still need to work together, don't we? At least to stop that Will from his antics. Can't let him off the hook, can we?'

'It's total bollocks.' She was pacing across my path. 'Even your own sister thinks you're—'

'I don't care what she thinks!'

We were at a set of barriers. Lola had her ticket ready and was through and on a platform to God-knows-where before I had moved. She turned and we looked at each other, divided by the metal wall. She lifted her chin as she said, too loud:

'Jade gave me a letter for you and I've read it. She was right. About everything.'

She went to turn away and in a second my feet were all motion, nipping behind an Asian woman to go through on her ticket.

Lola walked faster, right along the platform, to where the roof ended and we were exposed again. Hurt as strong as rage propelled me onwards as she threw words over her shoulder:

'Jade knew if she grassed you up then Stevie would end up being taken into care. She doesn't want you locked up, she just wants to look after him, she won't tell anyone about your … She promised she'll take care of him from now on. Why don't you—'

'He's mine!' Only powering strides could keep pace with her, she was *pumped*.

'She knows you've been through a lot. She just wants to help.'

'You listened to that woman?'

We were on the platform, dark suits weaving around us. A train would be in soon but she could not – *could not* – get on it.

'I had to, Darling! Jade spelled it all out in her letter – your illness, the first baby, the things you've put your own son through. Probably shouldn't have read it, I know, but I have to show this to Dad.'

And end our world.

'You can't do that. It doesn't belong to you.'

'I have to.'

She was turning, pacing in helter-skelter steps as I neared her on the platform, off her nut.

'Please, Lola. Give me that letter and we'll go home together.'

'Dad needs to know.' She turned, took another step.

'You're not yourself, Lola. Let me help you.'

'Dad needs to know that you're ill and that you lied. I'm not pregnant.'

There, a detonation behind that metal stare. I could not look into those eyes.

'Here, just give me that.' I reached slowly, slow, for Jade's letter. The train was coming.

'No!'

It was not stopping here.

'Please, Lola.'

She pulled the letter away, lurched back. Her foot went back, far back, her toe pointed in some complicated dance step.

'Lola!'

'No!'

My hand flew out as she snatched the papers back, yanked back far too far until she balanced on the platform's edge. Her body waving, wavering. My palm flexed and I reached out again. I had to reach out.

'Please, Lola, come!'

The look she gave me, everything stripped away. My fingers strained further.

Far too far, she was leaning back, a weird half-smile on her face. I reached out hard towards her, but then I held only paper and she was flailing with horrific grace, arcing back as she fell, a curling red lip, as the train came at her.

What's Done is Done

She is dead. Now only I am left to love him and it's all my fault.

Yesterday, Thomas asked me why I seem to be taking it even harder than him and I told him: I missed it. She needed me more than anything, and I missed it. My job is to tend to needs that people may not even know they have.

The post-mortem had shown that Lola was definitely not pregnant.

'She and Ellie must have got themselves in a state about nothing! Why didn't she just do a test?' Thomas did not understand. 'Surely she could simply have peed on a stick or whatever.'

I tried to explain to him that she was a sick girl. Such girls got things wrong, exaggerated to their drama-queen friends.

I can't now give every reason, or justify each word, except to say that I knew at the time it was what she needed. To hand herself over completely to my care. To allow herself to be totally taken care of. I lied not to hurt but to heal.

We are devastated, you understand. My husband, Thomas, did not need to know that I had done a test for his daughter, or that I had declared the positive result. That I slithered a tape measure around his daughter's waist in that strange rented flat and declared her to be 'too far gone'. Or about any other tests, for that matter; or even to understand the full ferocity, the tenacity of the bulimic urge. We did not need to discuss any of it.

Not, that is, until the pathologist's report found, on top of recent cocaine use, evidence of the use of emetics in Lola's system. So I suggested another, longer, harder look around her room and there we found the sick-making syrup, ipecac, that bulimic's best friend (if these ever-longing girls – food in! Food out! Release! Thinner! – didn't mind about the potential damage to heart muscle). It was the sort of thing you can easily get in the shadiest corners of the internet for less than the earth. There it was, wedged behind the corner of her bed. Yes, I had agreed with Thomas, most strange that it had been missed before.

Do you know about ipecac syrup? It can set you off vomiting within twenty to thirty minutes, which would make it the sort of thing you might want to wash down alone. Perhaps in a pissed-off glass of Pineapple Punch, blended and brought up to your room on the night of some toxic racist knees-up. Mistakes – mad, regretted, repeated mistakes – can still taste sweet at the time if you have been starved for long enough.

Anyway, Lola's state of mind is now clear to us – little wonder she ran so wildly that she fell. But if some violent fear had propelled her too far, we are now certain that it was not that of morning sickness; her unhappiness could not have solely been down to some lie of a pregnancy – so please pipe the hell down, Ellie Motte-Ryder!

Yes, she did feel lost. She did feel guilt, or some other needless self-hatred, shame perhaps at all that racist foolishness (she had been *Going*, she had *leaflets*), or maybe that acute self-loathing that we only feel when we realise we have been duped. I know she blamed herself for believing all the pretty – and the ugliest – lies of that boy. Terrible, the lovers we think we're worth, the torments we think up for ourselves. But in the end, she fell.

Why, though, could she not simply take my hand? I did reach out, but to hold her; Thomas knows this. Why did she *smile* as I called out her name? I knew, I *know*, that I was trying to save her. I wanted that piece of paper too, of course, to shred those words to pieces. But that was not all. I needed to save her.

I never poisoned her. Poisoning is designed to kill.

Only the syrup, just a very few times, the largest dose to stop her going to that warped dance with him. Once also in her father's breakfast, just so I would be free to find her. I only ever wanted to look after her.

To *protect* her.

Now though, I must continue to try to understand. I have failed. I could not protect her from the pressures in life that were making us all sick. Lola could not have known, when she flew into that train, that she would become my greatest failure. She is destroyed and I can never, now, cherish her.

One morning before Christmas, when the clouds were falling too low upon us and the town was more gripped by the mad weather – the energetic to-ings and fro-ings and blowings of Storm Barbara – than by the coming of Christ himself, I made a decision. I told Thomas about the dramatic improvement the doctors had flagged with Stevie, that we now fully suspected a misdiagnosis. Stevie's legs were a touch wasted from the KAFOs, but any deterioration had now halted. A mother knows, and Thomas is not a medical man. Stevie will live to be old. We wept, a golden reprieve. We were too happy to sue; the mistake had been caught soon enough. Stevie's Wonders were ecstatic, when I rang them, that our prayers had been not only answered but yodelled back across the void with a resounding, 'Yes!' All the money raised will go straight to the official Duchenne charities as planned; nothing to reconcile there. All OK. I have done a good job with Stevie, though that is something no one may ever understand. I worked to help him regain the strength in his legs, although I did worry that some of the shine might have been rubbed off his wonder. He was just a little bit quieter than before and needed his mummy more than ever.

Until the New Year. They came, in the end: Demarcus, as I knew he would, asking for his boy, and Jade. They arrived within minutes of Thomas leaving for work, always bloody watching and waiting for their moment, Jade running out from the car after Dem, crying too, which was a bit unnecessary.

'Give him to us, now, or do we need to come in?' His voice scuffed harder than gravel.

All three of us knew the answer. Still, I tried to catch her eye, begged her with a smile, but she was crying too much to say anything. But even as I stood shocked by them, by her tears, I knew what had to come. So I rushed to pack my son's rucksack and a bag in five minutes flat and told him we had a great surprise.

Dem loves my boy, and Stevie is enjoying the longest ever Daddy-holiday, at least until I can figure out where to go from here. Even Thomas thought it made sense, when he came home and I told him what had happened. He said it would be best for our boy to get away from the sadness that was hanging thick in the air despite us, along with Lola's faded scent and the unending cellar dust.

No choice. As I folded Stevie's clothes I dared not stop to think how hard I had tried, or to wonder whether he had enough of his favourite things; whether there would be anything he might miss.

I will get my son back one day, I know. Have no doubt about that.

I even sorted out my shattered phone, so we can text and call each other. There was one photo on there that I had never seen, the last one on the roll. No idea when they took it. Lola and Stevie messing about in a selfie: bare-faced, unwatched, laughing.

And Thomas? I love him, just as I have always loved him. Just as I loved him when I first saw him.

He didn't remember me.

We were both going down. The lift in St Foillan's went up and down, like all lifts. But only *hospital* lifts going down can echo your own private plummeting. This lift was never empty, but that day it was, except for the two of us. Three, in fact, as Lola was there: a white-haired wisp with questioning eyes.

Floor 7. I got in, without Cara. She was gone, and all I had to show for her were some pastel cotton clothes in a plastic bag, clothes she would not need now; so tiny, as if they could go unnoticed. A knitted jumper – it was mid-December – smaller than a handkerchief. My mouth was tight, working itself into a silent fury at its useless words. Harder words still jingling around my cane-rowed head from Jade, who had gone on at me about the ward-borrowed medicines she had found in my bathroom.

I know what's right for my baby, I had said.

Jade was not a mother, she could not possibly have known.

My likkle Jade, she too faas yunno! But she's a gud gyal.

She saw the light, in the end, or at least faded her chatter out. Twenty-three months and my baby girl had been so sick. She had needed me, she still needed me and I could not, cannot, bear to think of some lonesome, over-crowded heaven where she must wait, alone or with sharp-toothed ghosts from the past, *needing* me. No, she was just gone.

Floor 6. In they came. The dark-haired man and the little girl. Afternoon, he said. Tonsils, he said, as if proud. She'll need rest, I said, pulling the bag closer to my chest. I should know, I'm a nurse.

I love nurses, he said.

Then he, this man, this well-crafted man with his sharp cuffs and planed vowels and soldering gaze, spoke of a pressurised service and angels and long hours and an ageing population and how lucky we all were – he didn't know, about Cara, how could he? – and I just looked at him. *La.*

I love nurses, he had said. We had both known what he meant but then it was the ground floor and he was gone, and the dead weight in my heart would have to wait.

Years later, to get away for a while, I would go to a little café up the road called Andante. The man from the hospital lift would sometimes be sitting there, with one coffee and no newspaper. Just waiting, waiting. I knew straight off it was him. Turned out even his surname was meant for me; for all of us.

I ran to the supermarket, the morning after the Brexit vote. Not just for cigarettes, but for him. I saw him, far off, and I ran. I ran towards my one chance to be *reborn*.

He didn't remember me, but I already knew those cuffs, that hair; I knew he loved me. And I was right, wasn't I?

We met and we met; we married, and we lost Lola. But we are still here.

As is Will Benton. The police did call him soon after pulling in our tattooed friend. But the boy has a silver-plated tongue: a friendly chat, a form filled in, and then he was right back on his smooth road to a smooth future. They say he wants to backpack around the Far East before Durham.

We still plan to construct our stuperbous new home. We will build Lola into the bricks day by day; paint her in, day by day. Little memories that might otherwise fade, thoughtful words that will not be denied, laughs we must still share. We've gone for a redevelopment of an existing home, a wrecked mansion only twenty minutes away. In my mind I am already at work. Before the diggers go in, before the scaffolding can come, in my head I re-lay the foundations. I repoint the walls and lay on hardy bricks where the old ones have crumbled away. No fake holes will sit in our tiles, enough real voids out there without creating an artwork of imagined ones; they will be all new-fired clay. The landings will speak up and the doors will protect and the walls will be silent and strong. A skylight room up top, L-shaped, where we can misname the stars.

And then, of course, we must not overlook those other important opportunities to make life better. Maybe a holiday, a chance to wrap myself in searing warmth. Maybe nursing, which I might now go back to part-time; I've been looking for just the right thing. The longing to heal never leaves you.

Love always wins.

Herald

Elm Forest

19th January 2017

HOME CARE NURSE WANTED

A local family is looking for a highly motivated registered nurse to provide day-to-day care for an elderly gentleman in his own home. We are urgently seeking someone experienced for this client, a well-known former councillor recovering from a stroke, living in the Elm Forest area. You will take responsibility for assessing all his physical, mental and social needs for the duration of your employment. All qualified applicants welcome, experience of geriatric care a plus. £Excellent + neg + holiday.

For further details, please contact the COLBY CARE AGENCY and quote ref: AFletcher190117. This is a fantastic position for the right person. We are an equal opportunities employer.

Acknowledgements

Thank you to my agent, Joanna Swainson, for her sound judgement, smartness and flair, her kind guidance and her confidence in me.

To my editor, Anna Kelly, without whose exceptional instincts, discernment, patience and enthusiasm *Darling* simply would not be; my most sincere thanks. Also, many thanks to Michelle Kane and Katie Fulford; to Heike Schüssler for the remarkable cover; to Anne O'Brien for copy-editing and Amber Burlinson for proofreading; to Tara Al Azzawi, Fran Fabriczki and the whole team at 4th Estate, HarperCollins.

To Mrs Kaminik, wherever you may be: you turned the light of learning up brighter than I had ever hoped. To King's College London for cementing in me such a love of literature that I dared not write for years and, later, could only rest when I did dare to write. To my one-time Arts Council 'prize', Catherine Johnson: mentor, role model and the first writer I ever met. To my first editor, Rowan Pelling, for the joyful break into publishing short fiction which changed my life.

A special thank you to my dear friend, Anna Christofis, for being the first person to tell me, long ago, that I ought to be a writer. Then, soon after, to insist – quite emphatically – that I already was. And so, I wrote: heaven. Most recently, for having read *Darling* several times, and for feeding back each time with generous and galvanising praise.

To Robert Peett for his advice, encouragement, adroit criticism, wit and friendship over the years. They have all helped to shape me as a writer.

To Alister Veitch and Susie Little for their gracious early readings of the novel. To Emily Reay for her final-draft reading (and for a youthful exuberance to equal that of her mother, Fiona).

Thanks again to Susie, and to Tamandra Christmas-Baxter, for above-and-beyond friendships, ones that have helped keep this particular show on the road for more years than I care to mention. Tamandra, for the writing retreat at LPF that saved me, I can never thank you enough; to Jane Lloyd-Evans for embracing every last thing about *Darling* (and for that epic Antipodean brunch); to the 'Queenbees' Miranda Glover, Lucy Cavendish, Jennie Walmsley and Anne Tuite-Dalton for years of creativity-firing, inspiring friendship; to Nicky Macdonald and Jeannie McGeehin for their long-standing encouragement of my desire to write; to every last one of my friends for all their support.

A sincere thank you to Muscular Dystrophy UK for providing information that assisted with my research.

Finally, to family. To Mum, Patricia, with whom it all started: for the love, sacrifice and fathomless care. Thank you for a lifetime of extraordinary nurturing (and for answering endless questions about matters Jamaican). *Soon come.*

To my late father, Dr. Okon Tom Nkere-Uwem, I will forever be grateful for your erudition and your belief that education was paramount. I only now understand how brave you were.

To Emma and Charlie, thank you for forgiving this bizarre business of mine that is writing. The many hours in my Writing Room and other, stranger, locations; the half-burnt dinners and half-baked eccentricities … Thank you for your faith and for allowing me, your stepmum, to love you.

To my husband, Peter, who has always said 'follow your dream' and backed it up with every kind of support imaginable. None of this would have been possible without you; all my love and heartfelt thanks. We did it: Happy Days.